Dedication

Dangerous is dedicated to my mum, dad, brother Johnnie and sister Shirley, who sadly are not with us anymore. Not a day goes by that I don't think about them, I miss them all so much. My mum and dad were two very special people who gave their love to us all unconditionally. Johnnie and Shirley were real people, real characters whose happy memories will always be with me.

Even though they're not here to read it – or to see what comes next – I know that all of them are looking down, champagne in hand, saying, "Well done, girl. We knew you could do it! Happy days."

For

I've been blessed with my four children: Jemma, Jade, Mark and Reece who have brought me so much happiness. My three grandchildren Jaime, Johnnie and Darcey who are the sunshine of my life.

And also Pat, Marg and Chris, sisters we would all love to have.

I am so lucky and blessed to have such a wonderful family.

Debbie Ellis, Julie Bailey and Lisa Wright - it's a privilege to have you as my friends. Who needs a psychiatrist when you've got great mates. Onwards and upwards girlies. Mwah

And of course I can't forget my two adorable dogs, Dylan and Jet who have tolerated my writing between their walks.

From the bottom of my heart, thank you to you all for the love you have given me through my life.

My thanks to everyone who reads Dangerous, I hope you all enjoy it.

HAPPY DAYS

Our life is made by the death of others

Leonardo Da Vinci

Prologue

5th November 1971

Bobby Taylor is dead.

Bobby Taylor is dead.

Bobby fucking Taylor is dead ...

Mickey rolled his shoulders, sank deeper into the bath water. His body felt stiff and tense, his nerves tightly wound in anticipation of the day that lay ahead. A nice soak would do the trick, get him relaxed, give him time to think, prepare himself. This was a big fucking day, the biggest of his life, and he had to get it right. One misstep and he could lose it all – one fuck up and he could wind up dead.

But much as he wanted to focus on himself, Mickey couldn't stop his thoughts drifting back to Bobby. He tried to imagine what might have been going through Bobby's head, tried to reconstruct his final moments. They had found his body in the driver's seat of his car with a bullet through his right temple, his brains splattered all over the inside of his beautiful E-Type.

Mickey grinned. Bobby loved that car – he would have had a shit fit if he'd seen the state of it! Served the cunt right! He was a vicious, wicked bastard who had fought and fucked and raped and killed his way through the past thirty years of his life, and finally it had all caught up with him. But how? How could Bobby Taylor, the king of Dagenham's underworld, wind up with a bullet in his brain?

Suicide the police called it, but then they were all in his pocket, had been for years. The last thing they would want was the strife of investigating Bobby's death. Easier to say it was suicide, and hold out their hands for a nice pay off from the family. Scum bags.

Mickey slid down under the water, felt it rush up around his head, swirl in his ears, cover his eyes and nose. As a kid he'd spent hours in the bath, seeing how long he could hold his breath and stay under the water. One, two, three …

So which was it? Suicide or murder? Murder or suicide? It would be easy to believe that he'd shot himself, just move on, but Mickey knew in his heart that Bobby was the last person in the world to shoot himself. He was such an arrogant fucker that there was no way he would have topped himself – it had to be murder. So if Bobby didn't kill himself, then who did? Fifteen, sixteen, seventeen …

The gun was in Bobby's hand when he was found, so there was nothing to point to anyone else being involved. No additional fingerprints in the car, that's what the police said, and the position of his body and head wound were consistent with a self-inflicted act.

Twenty-eight, twenty-nine, thirty... Mickey could feel his chest tightening.

Bobby was left-handed, so why was the gun in his right hand? Mickey burst up out of the water, wiped his eyes, pretended to point a gun at his own temple – first the left hand, then the right hand. Like Bobby, Mickey was left-handed. If I was going to top myself, he thought, I would definitely use the left, that way I'd be more certain to do the job. Either that or stick the gun in my mouth. What I wouldn't do was hold the gun in my wrong hand ...

Mickey stood up, let the water run down his muscular body. In the cool of the early morning it was cold in the bathroom, and the steam curled around him – he grabbed a towel, began to vigorously dry himself. There was something he was missing, something he had overlooked. Mickey would get the truth, he had to ...

~ ~ ~

It was unbelievable, he thought, how everything could change in just a few weeks. Just a few weeks ago Mickey had been walking home from the pub, stone cold sober, top of his game, ready to tear the face off the world and piss in its eye sockets. Then, bam! Out of nowhere, he was knocked down, a hit and run. The doctors told him he was lucky to be alive. Mickey didn't feel lucky – his left arm had been smashed to smithereens. The scarring on his elbow looked horrible, although they said it would fade in time. They'd put a metal pin in his left elbow, a plate in his arm, it hurt like a fucker, was giving him some real jip, so he was taking Demerol to take the edge off it, but they didn't seem to make any difference. Mickey paused, stared at the scarring, still fresh and pink. Would he ever get used to the look of it?

Mickey had only been out of hospital for four days, had been aimlessly walking the streets, just thinking, trying to come to terms with his life. The fact that he would never box again. Trying to accept that his chance to be middleweight champion of the world was gone, forever. Mickey was gutted. He had just strolled in the Merry Fiddlers and ordered a pint when the phone call came. It was Georgie, his older brother.

'Mickey? It's dad. He's been shot ...' He knew by the way Georgie spoke that he didn't mean wounded.

Silence.

'He's dead Mickey,' added Georgie. 'Mum's freaking. Just get home quick.'

Finally Mickey spoke. 'I'm on me way, Georgie.'

Mickey put down the receiver. He could hear his heart beating furiously in his chest. He felt a bit light-headed, couldn't breathe properly. It must have been the shock. He couldn't take it all in, he felt completely numb as memories of his dad flooded his mind. It all seemed so unbelievable, so unreal.

The ultimate hard man who was feared, hated, respected, adored and ridiculed was dead. No more Mr Bobby Taylor. The icon of icons was brown bread, wiped out in a moment. Finished, done.

Life was a funny thing, Mickey thought. None of us know what's waiting round the corner, what life is waiting to throw at us, even the king of the hill. Even Bobby Taylor didn't see that one coming, thought Mickey.

Some people said Mickey was a lucky fucker; he'd been left a legacy. He'd inherited his dad's business. Inherited his desk, his chair, his businesses, his gun, his debts, his whores, his reputation, his friends and his enemies. Especially his enemies. Trying to fill his dad's shoes was going to be fucking dangerous, and Mickey knew he'd probably end up dead. Already Mickey could sense the danger coming. He could taste it, feel it oozing from every pore of his body. But he didn't give a fuck. Bring it on – he was scared of no man. He was ready and waiting for whatever happened next. He was going to stamp his authority on the manor, and any fucker who got in his way would pay.

Until it happened, Mickey hadn't thought about the consequences of Bobby dying, what would happen, how dangerous it was going to be. But now in an instant he had switched gears, his mind was buzzing with what he had to do next. Starting with the funeral arrangements and the endless list of phone calls he had to make.

Mickey couldn't remember the walk home after that phone call. Everything was a blur; his mind was somewhere else. The next thing he remembered was walking into the house, it was like a fucking ants' nest had been kicked over, people everywhere – his brothers and sisters all freaking out, his mum totally out of it, Old Bill sniffing around, neighbours, friends, everyone had emerged from out of the woodwork and under the skirting boards.

They had found dad's body in his car, that's what they told him, he'd died from a single gunshot through the head. Fuck! Fuck!

~ ~ ~

Mickey had to go to the morgue and identify the body. He would never in his life forget that night; it would always be etched on his mind. Seeing him lying there stone cold and dead. It didn't even look like him, one side of his head gone, just a big hole. He knew it was Bobby, but he couldn't take it all in. Georgie had wanted to come with him but this was something Mickey had to do alone – he was stepping up, had to step up, and this was the place to start.

He walked into the cold, silent room. Two thin fluorescent lights struggled to light the corners of the dim room, leaving pockets of shadow, places for ghosts and bad memories to hide. But Mickey found the atmosphere strangely peaceful, especially after the mayhem back at the house. No noise, no one asking him a million stupid fucking questions, just peace and quite. Not something you usually got around Bobby.

Bobby was there straight in front of him, laid out on a hard stainless steel table, naked apart from a sheet covering him up to the waist and a bandage draped over his head. Mickey stared at him for a long time, watching, waiting. Waiting for what he didn't know. It was all so surreal. He was there unmoving, quiet and still. His stillness absolute. No pulse, no circulation, no heartbeat, no more thoughts or feelings. Unable to hurt anyone again, no more beatings, no more abuse. Just silence.

Mickey touched his hand – it was freezing cold. His nails were spotlessly clean as always – he was meticulous when it came to his appearance. Bobby still looked good for his age, didn't have a grey hair in sight. Every one said that Mickey was the spitting image of his Dad, but he couldn't see it himself. He thought their faces were so different. Mickey always thought Georgie was more like him in appearance; but Mickey was like his dad in other ways.

~ ~ ~

Mickey stood with Bobby for ages in that cold, sterile room. Long into the silent, diminishing hours, just thinking, reflecting. The morgue assistant came in, tried to hurry him out, but Mickey turned his cold eyes on him, gave him a look that sent chills down his spine. "Get out of here right now, before I tear your fucking eyes out!" Mickey didn't even look to see if the man left – he knew he would go and not return. That was what Mickey did to people.

Mickey gazed at his ole man, felt the cold of the morgue seeping into his bones. Even though he had hated the cunt with every atom of his being, they were still flesh and blood, still family, and no one, no one fucked with the Taylors. When they killed Bobby, they declared war on Mickey, and that was a war that Mickey was going to win.

He would find whoever was responsible for trying to destroy him and his family, and he would kill them. He took a deep breath. Something about his dad's death wasn't right. It was all going seriously wrong and Mickey had to find out why. Even Jesus had a Judas. Mickey didn't care that he was dead, but he wanted the answers. He would do anything, anything it took to get answers. He would stop at nothing to protect them all, whatever the cost.

Mickey looked at him for the last time, his dad, the stranger. He wondered what he really thought about him? What they could have been together. Thinking how they were together as father and son.

Mickey stepped closer to the body, lifted up the bandage to look at the gunshot wound. You miserable fucker. Did you see it coming? Was it someone you had raped? Someone you had beaten and humiliated?

Mickey's jaw worked as he gazed at his dad. Finally he let loose a big gobbet of spit, right across the old man's face. How'd you like that, eh? Another one you didn't see coming! He grinned as he dropped the sheet across Bobby's face. The only tie they had ever had was blood, and that tie had been broken a long time ago. It couldn't be tied together again, once it was gone, it was gone. As Mickey turned on his heel, he thought of him as he really was – one fucking nasty bully.

Mickey's footsteps echoed across the cold floor of the morgue. He would get on with his life, and if he ever thought about that night it would not be with sorrow –no tears, no regret, no pity, no pain. He didn't feel anything; he was just glad that Bobby was dead. Mickey walked out of the morgue that night ready to live up to his reputation, as dangerous as everybody said he was.

~ ~ ~

He dropped the towel, picked up his neatly folded clothes from the bathroom floor, began to dress. From now on, everything was strictly business. Mickey was going to find out who killed Bobby, and waste them. Whoever was responsible for trying to destroy him and his family, for trying to muscle in on their turf, was going down. His face masked his anger. His body was motionless apart from his sharp jaw slowly moving up and down. His mad, murderous eyes were dark against his pale, taunt face. His mood was a homicidal climate of cold, calculated revenge.

He smiled to himself; he was ready to confront whatever happened next. There was a time for tears and a time for laughter, a time for mourning, a time for dancing, a time for loving, a time for hating, a time for war and a time for peace. He knew there would be plenty of time for grieving after tonight. He had scores to settle and he'd been saving his grievances for a rainy day.

It was time to go to war. Bobby Taylor was dead, and Mickey Taylor was no more. From now on he was simply, Dangerous.

Lizzie

It was cold, so cold in the icy room. Lizzie Taylor could hear the rain hammering viciously on the windows; a storm was brewing. She shivered as she dragged the blankets closer to her haggard body, wishing the day was over before it had even begun; she felt as if she were on her way to the gallows. All she wanted was for things to return to normal. But Lizzie had forgotten what normal was. She was angry. She was lonely and tired, and she was trapped in the darkness of her despair. Her feelings lay buried deep inside, patiently waiting to erupt. Could she ever rebuild the shattered remnants of her life?

She lay in bed trembling, couldn't stop herself from quivering and shaking, not knowing if it was from the cold or her memories. She shivered convulsively; she should feel safe, but she was still petrified, a nervous wreck, all jittery, jumping at the slightest noise or movement, expecting him to come through the door at any moment. But she didn't have to be scared anymore.

She snuggled closer to Martin, her youngest son, and watched as he lay sound asleep next to her. Just looking at Martin brought a smile to Lizzie's sad face, but she couldn't disguise the pain in her vivid blue eyes. Martin was curled into a ball, his heavy snoring echoing around the otherwise silent room. The jigsaw scars on his young face were like those of a man who'd fought and lost many hard battles, not what you'd expect to find on a cocky ten-year-old. As Lizzie wrapped her arms around him, she promised herself that no one would ever hurt any of her children again. She gazed at Martin as he lay in slumber, flinched in revulsion as the hot tears welled in her eyes.

Martin's angelic face was a total mess. His mournful eyes were firmly glued together with congealed pus and blood, courtesy of the last beating Bobby had laid on him, his cute button nose splattered across his bruised and swollen cheeks. He looked like he had been in the boxing ring with Mohammed Ali. Martin was never an angel, far from it. He was a little fucker, a brave little fucker who played outside the rules, but how could he be any different? He had tasted revenge. He had smelled fear, seen retribution, touched hate. Life had already torn away his innocence.

How could she have let this happen? She hated herself so much; she should have protected him, should have protected all of her children. There was no one else to blame, it was all her fault. She had let them down, how could they ever forgive her?

Lizzie lay quiet and still next to Martin; she didn't want to wake him yet. She closed her eyes and sank back against the pillow. Her hands clasped her blue rosary. Trembling, she began to whisper the Lord's Prayer and the Hail Mary, over and over again, begging God for His forgiveness and mercy for all the sins she had committed. She was too scared to live but too frightened to die.

Today, she would have to face herself, as well as what had happened to her children – Georgie, Mickey, Sharon, Terri and Martin. They all had to live out the life sentence Bobby had imposed on them. How could they ever forgive her? There was no one else to blame or punish. She had let it all happen to them. They were all paying the price because of her. A sob caught in her throat. She owed them all so much. How could she have let it go this far? She was as sick in the head as Bobby had been for letting it happen.

Did they love or hate her? Lizzie wasn't sure of anything any more; everything had gone so wrong. This wasn't what she had expected or could ever have imagined her life would be.

Lizzie opened her eyes. She had wanted it all to be a bad dream and go away, but she knew it wouldn't. She had to get up and face the day ahead – everyone would be arriving soon. She slipped slowly from her bed and wandered aimlessly around her bedroom, finally stopped in front of her two large wardrobes, threw the doors open wide. She had so many dresses and suits in there, alongside the boxes of shoes stacked high inside the wardrobe, a bag to match each pair. Bobby had gotten her all these lovely expensive clothes – he would bring them home and torment her, make her parade around the bedroom in her new clothes, being whatever he wanted her to be at that moment. But she could only wear them when he said she could, when she had his permission; they were for his eyes only.

She had secretly tried them all on when Bobby wasn't home, and now she was doing it again – she had tried on four dresses and five suits already this morning and she still couldn't make her mind up. It was hard to accept she had a choice. She was free at last of his presence, his dominance and control, but she was paranoid, kept looking over her shoulder expecting him to come through the door and rip the suit off her back, fuck her, give her a good hiding. He was dead at last but she was still filled with fear and doubts. She shook her head, angry with herself for not even being able to make a simple decision.

~ ~ ~

The storm got louder and louder, furiously banging and crashing on the windows. She wished she could stop thinking; all she wanted was some peace and quiet. Her head was thumping, she felt like it was going to explode. She wished all the noise would stop, rubbed her temples trying to ease the pain. Lizzie felt sick inside; her stomach twisted and turned in a huge knot. It was going to be another gloomy, bitter, miserable day.

Thunder crashed and a flash of lightning illuminated her as she stood gazing at the mirror, a dress held against her thin body. The events of her life showed with awful clarity on her face. Lizzie was still pretty, but she looked ten years older than her thirty-eight years. Years of being married to Bobby Taylor, years of chain-smoking, years of benzos for breakfast, lunch and tea to get her through another awful day. But how would she get through this day, she wondered?

This was all one horrible nightmare. Not a day went by when Lizzie didn't feel guilty for putting her children through such misery; it would stay with her until the day she died. She had destroyed their innocence. She deserved to be punished and be in this pain and despair.

Lizzie had to get herself together, calm herself and gain control. Today was no dress rehearsal, it was her final performance. She had already faked many smiles and worn a thousand different faces; she didn't know who she was any more, but one thing she did know was that she had to face today and be strong. She had travelled stormy waters before, but today she needed an elixir of strength. She reached for her bottles of pills, her hand shaking violently as she shovelled tablets into her mouth.

She listened to the raging wind howl down the chimney as she tiptoed slowly across the cold linoleum floor and peered out through the nicotine stained net curtain onto the Heathway. It was quiet outside; the grey dawn light and eerie silence enveloped the street. Lizzie watched trickles of condensation roll down the inside of the window as the cold rain splattered against the glass.

Flowers had already started to arrive. Placed in the centre of the garden stood a pillar of red rosebuds with a placard displaying the inscription, 'From Big Frankie.' Lizzie slowly shook her head. Would the past ever leave her? She wanted to scream, run far away and hide forever.

Even Bobby's death was made into an exhibition, used to show his status. A grand audience would surround her today; the circus was definitely coming to Dagenham. That thought made Lizzie laugh nervously with fear. The news of Bobby Taylor's death and how it had happened hadn't taken long to circulate through the manor; it was the sole topic of conversation on street corners and in every pub in the East End of London. Bobby Taylor was dead. Dead by his own hand. The news of his suicide had whispered through the streets, house to house, pub to pub, street corner to street corner.

She could hear the sound of it now, shrill in her ears.

'Fucking hell, terrible news.'

'How awful. What a way to go.'

'How could he?'

'He must have seen it coming or he wouldn't have done what he did.'

'I never knew, we never thought…'

'The coward's way out!'

~ ~ ~

The news had travelled further and further, gathering spice as it went along. Bobby Taylor's suicide soon became murder.

'Whose fault was it?'
'Gutted!'
'Rotten bastard deserved it.'
'What comes around goes around.'
'Who was with him last?'
'Sickening, he was a decent bloke.'

~ ~ ~

The good and bad would arrive soon, along with those who were too scared – or just too fucking stupid – to stay away from this glorified pageant. They were just a load of nosey bastards wanting to feel important by being at Bobby Taylor's funeral. They all respected her, not for being Lizzie, but for being Mrs Bobby Taylor. Lizzie could deal with that. What choice did she have? Her self respect had disappeared years ago.

She heard the front door slam shut downstairs and glanced down onto the street. It was Terri, Lizzie's youngest daughter, on her way to the church. She had been going to church every day since Bobby's death to light a candle for his soul. For a fifteen year old, Terri had an old head on young shoulders. She was as good as gold and never brought any bother to her door. Terri had always been quiet and reserved, silent but always listening and seeing. At school, she was doing well and working hard. She always had her head in a book.

Lizzie remembered how she would sit and read to Terri for hours by the blazing fire on the rare days that they were on their own together. Lizzie was so proud of her, was sure that Terri would make something of her life and better herself. Terri was always pleasing and cheery, with a warm loving nature, but she didn't have many friends. Not that she wasn't well liked – she was; there was always someone knocking on the door for her, but she always made excuses. Terri preferred her own company.

Unlike Sharon, her eldest daughter. The cocky, self-confident, loud and rebellious one. She was sixteen going on twenty-five, a right feisty little cow. Just like Bobby in strength of character and phenomenal temper. She was a force to be reckoned with. If the school board knocked on the door, it was always about Sharon; she couldn't stay out of trouble for long and was always up to mischief. Sharon's voice was always the first to be heard, mouth almighty, that was her.

Being Bobby's favourite, Sharon had always gotten her own way. She knew it and definitely tore the arse out of it. He would smile down at her and lift her into his big strong arms when she was a child. He was a powerful man. His brilliant dark brown eyes, that their sons Georgie and Mickey had inherited, would look down at Sharon when she was little, full of love.

All the kids were dark except for Sharon, with her white blonde curls and huge green eyes. Everywhere they went people looked at her, stared at her and talked about how lovely she was; a little angel. Bobby was in heaven with that child. Sharon would throw a tantrum if she didn't get what she wanted. She was a stroppy little mare and she always had to have the best, just like Bobby. Despite Sharon's faults, Lizzie loved her dearly, as she did all of her children.

Terri and Sharon were close, but still like chalk and cheese. Lizzie had had her fair share of trouble with the pair of them – they were so different, just constantly arguing and fighting like a pair of banshees. They would hurt one another, slag each other off, but nobody else could do it to them, they always looked after each other. If either of them was in trouble, the other one would always be there, standing at their side. After all, family was family.

The bed creaked as Martin turned over, stretching and yawning as he kicked his skinny legs out of the blankets. Lizzie turned slowly, and walked softly towards him, covered his bruised body with the blankets and tucked them around him, threw her new fur coat on top to keep him nice and warm. She wiped her forehead with her sweaty palms. At that moment the armoured fortress she had built around Martin got stronger.

Lizzie stared remorsefully at the family photos propped up on the dressing table among the overflowing ashtrays, pill bottles and a statue of Jesus. Everyone had a smile on their face. Their eyes had laughter in them. She could remember when they were a family, when they talked, laughed, cried, cuddled and joked together. That didn't happen any more.

Lizzie gazed at the photo of her sister Sadie. She sat on the edge of her narrow framed bed, chewing the tips of her nails, lost in thought. Sadie had been so good to her; she had cared for her, protected her and shielded her. She had always been the strongest of the four sisters; a kind loving woman, who was quietly self-confident and not easily swayed by loose words and promises.

Sadie had been so attractive, with her dark raven hair and sparkling blue eyes. She was tall and slim with a great figure even after having the kids, and had always had a way of making Lizzie feel happy and at ease, always there with a shoulder to cry on. Her love for Sadie would always be special. She'd been gentle and joyful with her love; it was strong and given when it needed to be. Lizzie took a long deep breath and closed her eyes, willing the tears not to fall. She shook her head; it had been over sixteen years since Sadie's horrific death. She shuddered, only God knew what Sadie had done that was so bad that her husband, Alfie, who adored her, had felt compelled to murder her.

An icy chill ran through Lizzie's slender body as she thought how her life had changed in that moment. She opened her eyes, powerless to stop the tears rolling down her cheeks. If only Sadie were here now to help carry this burden. The family had never been the same since she died, was never complete without her. Lizzie missed her so much. There had been so many funerals in her life. She considered all the people who had gone – her mum and dad, Sadie and now Bobby. This made her children more precious and important. Lizzie had to keep going for them all, there was no time left for regrets.

She sighed inwardly and picked up her wedding photo, recalling how she had felt when she became Bobby's wife nineteen years ago, carrying his baby at the time. Lizzie gave a half smile. She would always remember those times with happiness. She fell into a deep brooding silence, full of bitter-sweet memories. She was transported back over the years to when Bobby was a good man – Georgie was born out of love, not out of lust, anger or hate. She had brought him into this world with such joy, such high hopes and dreams.

Georgie had always been a good boy and Lizzie had always felt lucky. He was very clever and did well at school, he even passed his eleven-plus, but there was still enough mischief in him to reassure her he was normal. He always tried to look after her, tried to be the man that Bobby wasn't. Georgie was loyal and loving with a great sense of responsibility.

Mickey, on the other hand, took life as it came. He was a risk taker, a go-getter, always wanting something bigger and better, and he wouldn't give up until he got what he wanted. He would always be a winner, never a loser – from an early age Mickey knew the name of the game was survival. Situation and circumstance made his life what it was.

Mickey was born awkward and had been awkward ever since. He always left mess and chaos behind him. When he was a kid he was sweet, tender and quiet but somewhere after the age of ten he toughened up, became a right little bruiser, his knees and knuckles always grazed, a look of menace in his eyes. A cheeky bugger with a smile so sweet and innocent you couldn't be angry with him for long, but he was definitely not one to mess with.

Georgie got a high on solitude, where Mickey got a high on danger. Lizzie often prayed to God, asking Him not to give Mickey any more of the Taylor traits. He had paid enough penance in his young life already.

Mickey had his mum's good looks, but the rest, to Lizzie's everlasting regret, came from his dad. He was definitely a chip off the old block, and just like his ole man, he was capable of anything. She had noticed how Mickey was now treated as the head of the family – he had stepped straight into Bobby's shoes. Lizzie didn't have to worry about Mickey; he could handle himself. Mickey had learned as a kid how to defend himself with his fists. He had a reputation as a fighter – not as a bully but as a protector. Mickey would kill any man who tried to take a liberty with him or his family, he looked after them all, even Georgie. He was young, smart and tough. Everyone wanted to be Mickey's mate.

Now that Bobby was dead and Mickey had stepped in, Lizzie should have felt safe. But the demons murmuring secretly in her head threatened to surface and tear her family apart. These reflections from the past were dangerous, very fucking dangerous. She had to bury them away, put them in the ground with Bobby.

The last nineteen years of Lizzie's life had been a dreadful haze of pain, surrounded by fear. She had faced it daily, knew its sounds, its smell, even its taste. Life's unpredictability scared her. How would she survive without Bobby? They did have some good times together but she could never forget every sad, horrible thought, every unhappy moment. Bobby may be dead, but he would always be close by, watching and listening, tormenting and haunting her. She would never be free.

Lizzie didn't know the truth from the lies. She had lived in a fairytale world of her own, so blinded by her love for Bobby she couldn't see the evil monster she had married, unaware of the gossip that went on around her. She hadn't wanted to listen, hadn't wanted to hear the truth. Lizzie had blindly believed that she was lucky to be Bobby's wife and that he had needed her, wanted her, and loved her. She could care for him, look after him. She was so desperate for his love and attention that there was nothing she wouldn't have done for him. Always satisfying his bitter demands, she was the only person who ever truly forgave him.

She could never quite believe how she had attracted Bobby, he was so charismatic. She had felt so lucky that this perfect gentleman had swept her off her feet, totally overwhelmed by the intensity of his emotions, just so happy that he was hers. Lizzie had danced and swirled in the clouds, oblivious to the real Bobby, and had fallen helplessly in love with him. Lizzie knew her life would change when she got married, but she could never ever have imagined the consequences and circumstances of marrying Bobby Taylor. The reality of her marriage was something she was only just beginning to confront.

Lizzie stood still and silent. Her fingers gently stroked the image of his mysterious face. Bobby was so handsome and alluring, with perfect high cheekbones that gave him a stunning look of sophistication and power. His head was cocked to one side; his liquid brown eyes promised you his time and respect, things that he never gave to Lizzie.

Tears welled as she smiled. She was still captivated by Bobby's magnetic charm. Love flashed in her eyes for a brief moment as she remembered how wonderful things had been in the beginning – for just a short time, she had been touched by the beauty of love. She had to relive those memories, cling to them, hold them, and cherish them because they were all she had left. Bobby had filled the hollow emptiness inside her, and now he was gone.

~ ~ ~

She remembered how she had thought she would show her sisters and anyone else who interfered that he was a decent bloke – nobody knew Bobby like she did. They were only jealous because she had Bobby and would have everything she had ever dreamed of. The perfect husband, the perfect kids, the perfect home and the perfect life. Why hadn't she listened to them all? How could she have been so blind and stupid and not seen what he really was?

~ ~ ~

Lizzie was born and bred in Poplar, East London, part of a close-knit community, where everyone knew everyone else, knew their business. It was a rough old place, but full of good, down-to-earth people. The street door could be left open day or night and you knew you were safe. Everybody looked after each other, a bit of ducking and diving and a few misdemeanours, but you had to turn a shilling somehow. They were all in the same boat, just struggling to get by. Lizzie never forgot her roots and where she came from.

Lizzie was respectful, from a good family raised with a strict Catholic upbringing and traditional church values. She had principles and morals different to those of the girls Bobby was used to. They say opposites attract, and no two people could have been more different. Lizzie was beautiful, and could have had her choice of men, but no one dared to confront a man like Bobby.

Lizzie and her three sisters, Sadie, Sheila and Rosie, had survived the war years, though their parents and two younger brothers were killed during the blitz. They did have one bit of luck: a great uncle, whom they had never heard of, left them three acres of land on Carpenters Road, Stratford, where Bobby and his brothers-in-law started up a haulage firm. One acre of the land they used for their business, the other two acres were fenced off and separate, rented out to Irish Mick, a gypsy friend of the boys. It was earning a nice rental income. Irish Mick had two vicious Dobermans on patrol twenty four hours a day on his land. No-one dared go in there uninvited.

Soon after the war the council began rehousing, Lizzie was lucky to get a three bedroom house with a garden in Dagenham. After the war years, she had been excited at the prospect of a new beginning and a fresh start.

At first, Bobby had been everything Lizzie had ever wanted in a man, her fantasy become reality – good-looking, kind, caring and generous, and he loved her. It was just so perfect, he would give her the love and happiness she needed, and she would never be afraid or alone again. Lizzie knew she would always be safe with Bobby by her side.

Bobby was a lovable rogue, with direct and self-reliant qualities she liked. He had wild ways but would tighten his belt when they were married. He liked a good drink, like most of the men around her area – Bobby was no different. He was a 'tea leaf' but he never took anything from his own, and he would give you his last two bob if you needed it. If you were in any trouble, you went to Bobby Taylor and he would sort it. Everyone knew Bobby and the laws of the streets – if the Old Bill knocked on the door, you knew nothing, loyalty was the bedrock of the community.

Lizzie's body tingled as she remembered that first night when she gave herself to Bobby. She was in ecstasy. His strong warm hands pulled her gently towards him, and he kissed her softly on the cheek. His protective arms wrapped around her, engulfing her in his undying love and affection. His dark eyes gazed deep into hers as he smiled like a man besotted.

'Lizzie, I love you.'

His voice was sweet and soothing as he touched her flawless body, whispering to her how much he loved, needed and wanted her. Lizzie put her gentle hands to his cheeks and pulled his warm lips to hers. He stroked her face with the tenderness of a man in love.

'You're lucky to have me Lizzie.' Giving her a cocky wink. 'You know that, don't you?'

Lizzie stood still in front of him, slowly nodding her head up and down.

'Yes. Yes, Bobby. I'm so lucky to have you. I love you so much,' she said with a voice filled with thanks, happiness and joy.

'Tell me again Lizzie,' he murmured, his dark eyes twinkling in the dimness of the night.

Lizzie looked into his shining brown eyes, his hair short, black and sleek. The face of an angel. She couldn't believe that Bobby Taylor not only wanted her, but that he loved her.   'I'm so lucky to have you, Bobby,' she said, her voice slow and very, very sexy as she spoke.

He placed one hand gently on her chin and pulled her closer to his firm, hard body.

'Say it again Lizzie,' he replied with a satisfied smile on his face.

'I'm so lucky to have you,' she repeated, her eyes shining full of gratitude.

He laughed softly, cupping Lizzie's cheek, and then kissing her gently, whispered, 'Don't ever forget that Lizzie.'

Their eyes locked and Lizzie knew she would always be his and his alone. She wanted and needed Bobby more than anything in the world. She was hungry for the pleasure he could give her; the texture of his huge hands touching the smooth curves of her breasts; the ecstasy of his long slim fingers stroking her perfect body, so gentle, so soft, tenderly exploring new and exciting paths to pleasure.

Her breasts tingled as he pressed his body to her hard firm nipples, waiting for his smooth mouth to kiss, stroke and suck them. She felt the shiver of her skin exploding in a savage impulse. He began softly stroking her soft flesh beneath her clothes. She hesitated for a moment, but he made her want him, made her want things she had never had. She was desperate to touch him and feel touched. Bobby Taylor made her happy, made her smile and he loved her.

He drew her closer to his soft body and his strong hard thighs moved up against her. She trembled, smiling as his fingers travelled down her spine. She had never felt like this before, it was beautiful, amazing. Kissing her gently all over, he whispered softly, 'Lizzie, you will always be mine, always.'

Bobby walked slowly over to the window and closed the curtains, plunging them into darkness. Slowly, one piece at a time, their clothes fell to the floor and lay scattered around their bare feet. He pushed her onto the bed with one hand, cradling her back with the other. He slowly examined her body, stroking her nipples, breathing in the smell of her perfume. She lay on her back watching his handsome face devour her body. She could feel his soft face against her thighs, his tongue searching, seeking. Her hips moved in rhythm, wanting him, needing him. The spasms ran through her body. She gave herself to him completely.

~ ~ ~

Another loud crash of thunder made Lizzie jump; she was back in the real world. Her heart missed a beat. Those days of love and happiness were long gone. They had been wonderful – why couldn't each time be like the first? Why did everything have to change? Lizzie never wanted much, just his kiss, just his hand holding hers, a gentle touch, a sweet smile, just to hear him whisper those three words once in a while. That would have been enough. She was always reminding herself of the vows she had made. She kept telling herself that she was expecting too much.

Lizzie admitted sadly that her fantasy was exactly that, a fantasy, one that she had created for herself. If it had been reality she wouldn't have been treated like a slave, a whore, and wouldn't have felt so useless, unwanted, humiliated, demeaned and disgraced. How could she still love him? Love, honour and obey? For richer, for poorer, for better, for worse? 'Till death us do part? Well now death had finally done its job.

She held the wedding photo in front of her and looked into his eyes. Why hadn't she listened to her sisters and friends? Why, when they had all been right about him, could Lizzie not accept the truth of what he really was? She had blocked it all out, pushed it out of her head, buried it all very, very deep, hoping it would all disappear and go away forever. She threw their photo across the room – the frame smashed against the wall, scattering tiny shards of glass across the floor. She hated Bobby, but hated herself even more. Lizzie's knees gave way, and her frail body collapsed on the floor among the shattered glass.

'I thought I knew you Bobby,' she moaned, 'I thought you loved us, I thought you loved me.' She lay there crumpled and utterly exhausted. Her head was buried deep in her hands as she whispered, 'Why? Why? Why? What did I do wrong?'

In the eerie silence, Lizzie felt a gentle tap on her weary shoulders. She looked up into Martin's haunted face, clouds of cold mist appearing as he spoke in a whisper. 'Mum, you ain't gotta cry anymore, he's gone now. I love ya and I'll always look after ya.'

She pulled Martin into her dull and aching arms with all the strength of her love and he sank into their comfort. Lizzie cuddled him close to her. They sat together, lost and lonely, their arms tightly wrapped around one another, sobbing. Their shoulders rose and fell as the scent of despair seeped from them both, the sad odour filling the cold, dark, damp room. As Lizzie's sobs diminished she began rocking; gently stroking Martin's head with her soft fingers she spoke to him with a tone of such confidence, he felt safe. 'Don't you worry, everything will be all right, no one will ever hurt you again. I promise.'

Terri

The new day crept in slowly. Terri stirred in the early morning darkness, lost in the dead quietness of the house. A whimpering sound echoed in her throat as she tossed and turned in her sleep. She was huddled deep under the blankets, sobbing, her slender body trembling as she tried to end the horrible dream, make her voyage of darkness and terror come to an end. She hated going to sleep; the nightmares always came to torment her. Her tears fell rapidly, rushing out in a torrential storm, falling on her flushed cheeks.

Shivering on the damp sheets as the sweat dripped from her soaking wet body, Terri was locked in that dark, gloomy cavernous room again, fear flooding her trembling heart. She had to get out of here, get away. Her frightened eyes frantically roamed the shabby, stinking place. Giant cockroaches crawled the walls, floor and ceiling. Their long antennae cracked like whips; they were going to get her, crush her, rip her apart bit by bit and eat her alive.

Slowly, she turned and stepped on a cockroach. She heard its hard armoured shell crack and crunch under her feet; frozen with fear she was scarcely able to breathe. As Terri looked up, her face turned ashen with fear. He was there, hanging by his neck from a rafter on the ceiling, swinging to and fro, his eyes bulging from their sockets, his face red and bloated, his tongue drooping down the side of his mouth – but he wasn't dead. He was mocking her, that evil high-pitched, hysterical laughter echoing around the room. She could hear his snide cynical voice hollering and shouting at her, demanding that she got him down, freed him from the ropes. She had been a naughty girl again, what else did she expect? This was her punishment.

Terri stood trembling in despair, she had to get out, escape. She looked behind her – the door was closing and disappearing into the darkness, the room getting smaller and smaller. She was trapped. If he didn't get her, the cockroaches would. She couldn't breathe. She took a tired, heavy step, turned and looked up at his handsome face. She knew those intense chocolate brown eyes, knew who he was, but didn't know his name. He didn't have a name. She felt sick, she had to get away. He was getting down, and he was going to get her, hurt her, torture her, rape her, kill her, just like every time before. She could see it all in his chilling smile.

She tried running but her feet were stuck to the floor. She couldn't move, was helpless and alone, going nowhere, her blood frozen in her veins. He was getting closer, much closer – she could smell the stale whiskey on him, feel his stinking vulgar breath on her, hear his intimidating and mad voice screaming at her. He was next to her, she felt him against her. Her time was up. She knew she was going to die, this was the end.

She woke with a cry, filled with horror, just as he was about to get her. It was always the same nasty dream, the same man, the same room. It was all so real, so horribly real. Would he ever leave her alone? He had made every day of her life a misery while he was alive and he still tormented her when she slept. The nightmares had become part of her life, just like the hatred she felt for him had become part of her life. Her breathing was hard and fast as she tried to calm herself, bring herself back to her senses. She grabbed the corner of the sheet and wiped the beads of sweat from her face.

Terri got up from the bed, still shivering from head to toe though the sweat was rippling down her forehead and back. She stood still, trying to regain her composure. Her slim fingers gripped the end of the bed, her hands clammy with fear. Her face gave nothing away as her vacant eyes strayed around the room. She looked at Sharon's bed and saw that she hadn't been home all night – out clubbing and on the piss again. She knew Lizzie worried about her, but Sharon didn't give a fuck about anyone, only herself. Terri had to get moving and get to church. She knew that it wouldn't be locked. She hurriedly got herself bathed and dressed, ready to face the day ahead.

She didn't want to think about the past or the future, she just wanted today over and done. Terri placed all her bits and pieces in her handbag, liquid and powder foundation plus the rest of her make up, key ring, tissues, purse and bracelets. Then she rummaged through it, double-checking that she hadn't forgotten anything, before finally closing it. She reached for her black coat, draped over the end of the bed, pulled the dark garment around her in a grand gesture and swung towards the door, her magnificent hair swinging defiantly, moving with great dignity for someone so young and so hurt.

She was extra careful as she passed Lizzie's room, trying not to make any noise – her mum had been robbed of enough sleep in her lifetime – then slowly headed down the stairs, carefully avoiding the creaky floorboards. She could hear her Auntie Rosie pottering around in the kitchen making a cup of tea. She had been a great help to them all this week, especially to her mum – Terri didn't know how they would have got along without her.

Halfway down Terri stopped. She could see the light shining from the living room and could hear an awful noise. She walked over towards the gap in the door and, peering through, saw Georgie, her eldest brother. She stood still, terrified to move, it was such a horrible sight – Terri had never seen or heard a grown man cry.

Georgie was sitting at the table, his arms folded in front of him. His handsome face was streaked with tears, his eyes were red and heavy, and there was an empty bottle of scotch next to him. Terri had noticed over the past few months that Georgie hadn't been himself. He slept little and drank a lot, and the harder he drank the more depressed he became, withdrawing further into himself. Something was bothering him – she had asked him many times what was wrong, but Georgie would just look her in the eyes, put his firm hands on her shoulders and smile his lovely smile. 'Terri I'm alright, there's nothing wrong with me,' he would tell her. 'I'm OK.' But she knew better.

She stood there, watching him in silence, not moving. She knew he couldn't see or hear her; he was staring past her into some sad, lost place. Terri felt her eyes fill with tears in sorrow for Georgie. She loved him so much; he had always been her best friend, he was always a source of comfort for her, always forgiving and never critical. His strong, sturdy shoulders were always there for her to cry on. She hated seeing him in this horrible mess – it was so out of character for him, she wanted the old Georgie she knew. There was something very serious bothering him – she had an idea what it might be, but quickly brushed the thought away. It couldn't be what she was thinking.

Quickly, before she lost the courage to go, she moved towards the front door and walked quietly out. The raw breeze howled through the hallway as Terri pulled the string with the key on through the letterbox. She was trying not to make a sound but the sharp wind blew the door shut with a loud slam as she stepped out into the porch.

'Shit.' Terri just wanted to be alone to savour the moment of being totally safe. To not have to talk to anyone or answer their stupid questions. *How are you Terri? How are you feeling?* Well! How the fuck did everyone think she felt?

Terri took a few short breaths as she stepped outside into the cold miserable morning, skulking out into the new day in the midst of her own darkness. It was bitterly cold and raining as she stood still and looked back at her house. Home is definitely where the heartache is she thought as she shivered, the damp air gusting around her. She glanced at the front garden adorned with flowers, saw the beautiful wreath dedicated to "Our beloved dad" in yellow and white roses. It was stunning. A stunning lie.

She blinked back the hot tears stinging her eyes. She wanted to scream and shout, wanted to find the courage and the dignity to stand up and tell them about the real Bobby Taylor. The man he really was. She never knew the words "dad" or "daddy" and he never heard any of them. They were words he never understood. He'd been a man with no morals, no conscience and no heart. It didn't matter that he was gone, things wouldn't be any different. He hadn't cared about her, he didn't care that she loved him, that she needed him. She had wanted a daddy, so why had he hurt her so much? What had she done to make him hate her so much? Her father was dead, but Terri was just as she'd been before – lonely, with no purpose in life, alone without a daddy.

The rain fell heavily from the black clouds, running down her pale face. She put her head down, her hands deep in her pockets, and set off towards the church, trudging along through the puddles. A man passed her walking his dog. 'Good morning,' he said with a nod. Terri nodded and grunted at him, burying her head deeper into her coat. What was so fucking good about this morning, this day, this life? As she walked in a dreadful haze of pain, her eyes watched her world, a world that she would never forget or understand.

~ ~ ~

Terri faced the wind and walked slowly along the Heathway, a long, busy depressing road lined with identical red-bricked houses, rows and rows of them, street after street. The rain was falling in thick sheets to the pavement. It was so quiet at this time of day.

This was Dagenham, the over-populated massive council estate, at its best – everyone asleep in their beds. In this town of machinery and cars all the families were just the same, just like hers – never going anywhere, trapped in a spiral of poverty, debt and desperation.

Some of the houses looked quite nice, with well looked after front gardens, tubs and baskets and decorative fences, pretty net curtains, a vain effort to add colour to their lives. But when you looked closer, Dagenham offered nothing to soothe the eye or the soul. Terri's footsteps were getting heavier and heavier. She was deaf to the early morning traffic racing by, the bright headlights of the cars cutting through the darkness.

Her thick dark hair tumbled to her waist, becoming curlier as the pouring rain fell on it. She walked slowly, dragging her pain along with her. It was several minutes before she realised that it wasn't the rain making her cheeks wet, but her own tears.

Terri was alone as she entered the church. This was where she spent most Sunday mornings. Her family attended regularly – they had all been baptised, made their first Holy Communion and been confirmed here. Terri had always thought that she would love to get married in this church, to marry a man who loved and respected her, but now she was no longer sure that such a thing was possible, that such a person actually existed.

She had seen Lizzie crawl on her hands and knees like a dog, begging Bobby to stop shouting, screaming, abusing, intimidating, tormenting, insulting and punching her while her frightened children huddled in the corner, watching. Terri swallowed deeply, feeling sick inside. She didn't love or pity her father, her love had congealed and turned to hatred. Repulsed by his behaviour, she lied to her friends and teachers about him, never wanted to invite anyone to her house. The shame of them finding out what he was really like would have been embarrassing, shameful. Because if they found out about Bobby, they would find out what she really was. She hated herself for being what he wanted her to be, what he had turned her into.

She had never fitted in anywhere; she had always been different, unwanted. Even the girls in class thought she was strange and different. No one could believe that she cared about her schoolwork; that she didn't go out with boys or talk about sex. What difference did it make, who cared? She did. She was used to being different and having the piss taken out of her – her dad had done it all the time – but Terri still had her dreams and was determined that no one could take them away from her, not even Bobby.

She wanted a career, a nice place to live, a proper and exciting job, to travel the world and eventually find a husband whom she loved and respected. There must be more to life than Dagenham. Terri never told anyone about her fantasies, they would just think she was going off her head and ship her off to the funny farm. She certainly couldn't imagine a life like her mum's – trapped in a marriage to a man who paid no attention to her at all except for the unwanted kind, never listened to her and never cared what she was thinking. Lizzie wasn't allowed to think for herself, not allowed to make any decisions, have any choices, even have an opinion. She was treated like an animal. Bobby didn't give two fucks for anyone but himself. Terri wanted so much more.

She looked up, peering ahead towards the statue of the Virgin Mary, another suffering mother who stood with her arms outspread. Terri's light footsteps echoed on the cold marble as she walked slowly around the church reading the Stations of the Cross, whispering softly to herself.

'Jesus is condemned to die.' She looked at Jesus and his crown of thorns. Each movement driving the thorns deeper into his head, fresh blood dripping down his face. Broken.

'Jesus carries his cross.' Her voice was heavy as she gazed into his eyes, seeing the anguish, the freedom and surrender. A huge crushing weight lay upon his shoulders as he walked the path of misery and suffering.

'Jesus falls for the first time.' She stared at the exhaustion in his frail body, the fatigue, the burden. Terri shivered; it was so cold inside the church, so cold inside her heart.

'Jesus meets his sorrowful mother.' She studied them carefully. She could see the sorrow in his mother's eyes, her unutterable suffering – it was a look she recognized from her own mother. How pained Mary must have been to see his tears.

'Simon helps Jesus carry his cross.' Terri peered into his face seeing the weakness and struggle. Conquered by the pain of the cross, such a heavy burden.

'Veronica wipes the face of Jesus.' She looked deeply into his eyes seeing pain as he suffered his vile and abusive treatment. She wished someone would wipe her own pain away, but nobody knew or cared.

'Jesus falls for the second time.' She gazed at him. He was hot, tired and sweating, on his knees bearing the weight of the cross. The agony was taking its toll on his torn and bleeding body.

'Jesus meets the women of Jerusalem.' Terri wanted to comfort them. Their eyes were full of love and gratitude, loss and fear. She could feel their grief.

'Jesus falls for the third time.' She watched him, collapsed under the weight of the cross, paying the price. There had been times in her life that she had fallen and she would fall and fall again. Confronted by the same things again and again. But she vowed that she would always get back up.

'Jesus is stripped.' No shield, no security. Such nakedness. Fresh humiliation drenched with gall. She recognized that.

'Jesus is nailed to the cross.' She made herself look at the cruel nails driven through his flesh. Hammered into his hands and his feet, hanging in agony. She wished she could make the hurting stop.

'Jesus dies on the cross.' She watched him. His head bowed forward as he surrendered his last breath.

'Jesus is taken down from the cross.' She stood still, shivering from the cold and shame, trembling with fear. She beheld the scene at the foot of the cross. A lifeless body in his mother's arms. Would someone come for her? Be there for her when she needed it?

'Jesus is laid in the tomb.' A deep sigh echoed through the empty church. Her heart throbbed painfully in her chest, the familiar panic rising.

Terri walked further along the aisle, her head bowed, keeping her fragile eyes fixed firmly to the ground, tortured by the memory of all her yesterdays. She felt just as she did then, on the day of her first Holy Communion, all those years ago. She should have felt like the rest of the girls and boys, happy and joyous about receiving the body and blood of Christ for the first time. It was the holiest moment of her life and she should have been filled with joy. Instead she was filthy, dirty and ugly. She didn't feel special or grateful because there was nothing in her life to feel special or grateful for. There were no reasons to laugh or smile. Terri only hoped that it would make her a good, clean girl again. God knew she was a bad girl because God knew everything, knew the disgusting and humiliating things she had done.

Everyone was there – aunts and uncles, friends and neighbours. Everyone smiled at her as she walked down the aisle of the church to kneel in front of the priest to receive communion. All a big charade, another one of Bobby's shows. Always an event that people remembered, talked about, loads of booze and food, a great big party, just another excuse for a piss-up, just another way to make himself look like something he wasn't.

They had all said how lovely she looked in her beautiful crepe satin dress, a picture of purity. Lizzie had got yards and yards of knocked off material and spent weeks and many lonely hours deep into the night, hand sewing the opalescent sequins and sumptuous diamantes on the white fabric. She had finished it off with a pretty organza ribbon attached to the slim, fitted waist.

It should have made her feel special, pure, sweet, innocent and untouched. But Terri felt soiled and unclean. Not like her sister Sharon, the perfect one who was always right and could never do anything wrong. Sharon always got the part of Mary in the school nativity play, Terri was always in the background singing in the choir. He never came to see her in the school play; it was just to see his precious Sharon. In Daddy's eyes, she was perfect. His little princess. Terri was always trying to please him. Whatever she said or did didn't make any difference; he always turned his back on her. She never existed in his eyes. He never gave her what she wanted: love. She was invisible to him, unless he wanted something.

Terri looked at her mum that day, and saw the tears glistening in her eyes. Those eyes that looked at Bobby filled with love and fear. She still didn't know whether they were tears of pride and pleasure or tears of sadness and pain for her daughter. Lizzie gave her love to all of her children and tried to protect them from their father's cruelty whenever she could. But she couldn't really protect any of them from his vindictive spite. They were always subject to his torment. Lizzie had fought all her married life for her kids though the truth was she never stood a chance. But she tried the best way she could. Terri couldn't understand how Lizzie kept her hatred from welling up in her heart.

Terri heard her praying every night for her sinning husband, for His deliverance and forgiveness for Bobby. Then getting into bed, sobbing into the pillow, crying herself to sleep. Lizzie would have no memories of happy times, no laughing times. Bobby had manufactured misery and left death, darkness and corruption behind him.

Bobby had always displayed anger and annoyance at their presence; he thought kids should be seen but not heard. They never knew what to expect from him, sunshine or showers. One minute he would be as right as rain, then something would happen and they would have to endure his evil torture.

Lizzie didn't dare defy him because it would only make things worse. She tried to protect them, she was a loving, kind, caring woman, but Bobby represented an unquestioned and absolute authority, non-negotiable, a coldness that froze their emotions. Lizzie gave what she had out of love, whereas Bobby gave to buy your silence and ease his conscience. What happened with her dad was something she couldn't talk about to anybody. She never dared tell her mum or anyone because no one would believe her anyway. They'd just say she was a liar. She knew if Mickey ever found out he would kill Bobby. At least since Georgie and Mickey had gotten older, things had gotten easier and it didn't happen anymore, thank God.

Terri looked up, peering ahead towards the statue of Jesus nailed to the cross. She was as still as the statue looking upon her. Terri, wide-eyed and tremulous, stood frowning as she thought about the money collected for the church poor box. The fruits of sex, violence, drugs, gambling and robberies. The priests of the parish gladly accepted money from Bobby and the rest of his disciples, all of them trying to buy redemption and a place in heaven. She shivered; goose bumps covered her slender body. Her throat felt so dry, she licked her top lip with her tongue and could taste vomit.

She remained still, afraid to take another step forward. She was relieved that Bobby was dead, but was once again consumed with guilt and shame. She rubbed her clammy hands together, willing herself not to cry. She had wasted so many tears and wished her daddy could have given her what she cried for. She never knew and could never understand him.

Terri recalled looking down into his face for the last time at the chapel of rest last night, in a massive oak and bronze casket. Bobby Taylor always had to have the best and always got what he wanted, whatever the consequences. Ritual humiliation, intimidation and the infliction of punishment were the way of his world. You were Bobby's friend or foe. Either way, you had to obey him. He knew nothing of guilt, ruined relationships or wrecked lives.

At forty-one, the years of drink and debauchery hadn't removed his good looks – his sins hadn't touched his handsome face. Bobby worked hard on keeping a youthful appearance, always wanted to be younger, look younger. He liked proving he was young and virile with any little slapper or anything in a skirt that came along. The conflicts that lay within weren't evident upon his smooth face. As he lay in the coffin he looked sad, not peaceful, small and shrunken in this huge coffin finely padded with soft blue silk. His hands were clasped together in prayer, crimson rosary beads entwined in his fingers.

Terri shivered as she said her last goodbyes to her daddy. He was dressed in his best silver grey Armani suit, a crisp white shirt, gold cufflinks, black leather shoes, black silk socks and a red Armani tie. On his left wrist was a square Rolex watch. Glistening from his middle finger shone his gold initial ring RGT – Robert George Taylor. He was dead and empty, just as she felt. Taking a long deep breath, she placed a single yellow carnation in the coffin.

There was nothing subdued about Bobby's appearance and demeanour in real life. He was always well-groomed and immaculately dressed in his tailored suits, white shirts and carefully selected ties. He was good-looking, but his immaculate exterior belied the fact that he was the epitome of evil. He was always so self-confident with an infectious charisma that suggested the perfect man, the perfect husband, the perfect dad, but there was a darker force lurking just beneath the clean-cut image. To the outside world, Bobby was the very image of respectability, but on the inside, he was a cold, clever, evil, manipulating man, and nothing and no one meant anything to him. Bobby was empty of any warmth or love, he could never love anyone. For Bobby it was simple. Me, myself and I. That was it.

Terri continued walking slowly along the long, narrow aisle. Her heart thumped in painful bursts, pounded loudly through her thin body, the aching pain inside her feeling as if it would last forever. Her love for him was shattered because she had let things get out of control.

Terri shuddered; she could smell his aftershave, the whiskey, beer and fags as he pressed himself against her. She wanted to throw up, could feel the vomit rising in her stomach at the memory of her defilement. She swallowed deeply, trying to keep the sickness inside. She closed her eyes tightly, trying to stem the tears as she prayed to the Virgin Mary for forgiveness. She stood with quiet dignity in front of the altar.

How did he have such a hard heart when he could see how much she loved him? He always turned away. Bobby died detached from everything. Silent. He had lived and died in fear, truly known by no one.

The nuns from the convent would be here today – they revered Bobby because he treated them with respect and because he was generous and helpful with their causes. They had been telling her that they didn't believe what the newspapers said about him, said she should be proud of him, he was a good man. Terri shook her head slowly from side to side. What a load of old bollocks. Bobby wasn't a man who lived his life with reverence for the church and God, but for himself. He had wilfully broken all the Ten Commandments and made his own Eleventh Commandment, the only one that had any meaning in his life – *Thou Shalt Not Grass.*

Just like her mother, Lizzie had a beautiful smile, and also like her mother, she rarely found a reason to use it. She was sweet, but unpredictable – her mood could change in an instant. At fifteen, she was blessed – or cursed – with full and firm breasts, a tiny waist, and slender hips. She was an acutely attractive young woman, with probing, extraordinary blue eyes, yet the heavy shadows of darkness were evident upon her pale face. Her stooping shoulders lay heavily upon her tall, trim figure.

Terri listened to the rain pouring down outside, getting heavier as it fell on the intricate pre-Raphaelite stained glass windows. She hoped the weather would keep some of the mourners away today. Everything about this funeral was grotesque – it would be packed with people standing around Bobby Taylor's coffin, and then the show would begin, the handshaking rituals, the sad nod of the head, the sorrowful peck on the cheek, the hugs and the awkward pat on the back, the mumbling of words of respect.

Everyone would be looking as if they'd just had a slap in the bollocks. They would be wandering around, chit-chatting about his death, muttering the usual platitudes – about how sorry they all were, how tragic it was, so shocking, whoever was responsible would pay for this, wasn't the weather poxy and the rest of the bullshit that would come out of their mouths. She wished they would all piss off and leave her and her family alone.

No one really cared about the pain felt by her family. The sympathy cards would be stuffed with money and given to Lizzie, all meant to salve the pain. She rolled her eyes. The filth would be here too, sniffing around to view the faces of the criminal underworld.

Her solitary figure stood in the centre of the church. Her eyes travelled around it as if seeing it for the first time, so peaceful and calm. She read aloud the Latin verse painted beautifully in gold leaf around the church.

'Domus mea domus orationis vocabitur.'

My house shall be called a house of prayer.

'...tu es Petrus et super hanc petram aedificabo Ecclesiam meam et portae inferni non praevaluebunt adversus eam.'

You are Peter and on this rock I will build my church and the gates of hell will not prevail against it.

Terri didn't think she would ever feel she was on the sea of serenity. She was shutting her horror up deep inside, drowning in her sorrow and despair, with no one to catch her tears. Could she ever break free? He was always there, reverberating around her mind, wanting to be heard, appearing in her thoughts, in her dreams, screaming and shouting at her. An icy chill ran through her. Bobby Taylor had violated all of the Ten Commandments, the rules of the Church and of God. But inside the church he was flawless – he would kneel and pray, reciting the Our Father, the Creed and Latin verses while outside he lied, cheated murdered.

Terri shuddered; she was shit scared and was afraid to face the implications of the day, passionately wishing it were over. She walked slowly backwards, her fragile eyes never leaving the huge crucifix on the altar in front of her. She had to pay penance.

Panic was apparent in her eyes as she fumbled around in her handbag, but then a satisfied smile appeared on her perfectly sculptured face as she pulled out her key ring with the small sharp penknife attached to it.

She gripped it tightly, slowly twisting and turning the sharp blade from side to side, her restless eyes were alive and gleaming as the silver steel glistened on the raw razor edges. So many times she had tried to stop, she really had tried, but she just couldn't. It made her feel better, soothed her. She needed to do it. The pain was a strange relief, it calmed her mind and thoughts and she didn't feel so bad. Terri remembered a quote from the film Lawrence of Arabia that Georgie had told her – 'The trick is not to mind that it hurts.' It was a trick well worth learning in this bloody family, she thought, and it had served her well.

She took off her coat and put it on the pew, genuflected, and stepped into the deserted confessional box. She pulled the sleeve of her jumper up as far as she could, her pain, confusion and chaos reaching a climax as she raised the small blade then plunged it down into the top of her left arm, ripping her delicate skin apart, praying for mercy.

'Hail Mary full of grace.'

Carving.

'The Lord is with thee.'

Dragging.

'Blessed art thou amongst women.'

Tearing.

'And blessed is the fruit of thy womb, Jesus.'

Slicing.

'Holy Mary, mother of God.'

Digging.

'Pray for us sinners.'

Twisting.

'Now and at the hour of our death, Amen.'

Smiling.

She could smell the sickly sweetness as the blood seeped from her deep cuts. The deeper the better she thought as she smiled serenely to herself, watching red-hot tears flow freely, splash onto the icy white marble.

Terri sighed with contentment as she ran her fingers down the sharp wet blade, the voices now quiet in her head. Peace at last. Her soul felt soothed.

She leaned back against the hard wood of the confessional, allowed herself a gentle smile. This was just the start of the blood that would spill on the pavements of Dagenham today …

Martin

Martin smiled as he watched Mickey getting ready, tarting himself up in front of the mirror. Mickey loved a mirror, always checking his appearance, making sure he was just perfect. He looked the bollocks standing there in his designer labels, his shiny Italian leather shoes, expensive cashmere coat, over black trousers.

Martin thought the world of Mickey, looked up to him, wanted to be just like him. Everyone knew who Mickey was, so they all knew Martin, Mickey commanded respect, Martin got respect. People looked at Mickey differently; they knew he was a somebody. Martin wanted to be just like him – a somebody. Mickey had everything, he was a good looking bloke, always had loads of money, drove a pukka car. He had loads of mates and was always out and about with them, enjoying himself and having a great time. All the birds were after him, knocking on the door, phoning him up. Putting bits of paper through the letterbox, their names and addresses scribbled on, some who were lucky enough to have a phone indoors left their number. Anyone would think he was a pop star or something.

Martin would sit at the bottom of the stairs when Mickey and his mates were in the front room discussing business. They didn't know he was there listening. He would sit quietly still, in the dark just listening and watching. The secrecy that pervaded his childhood, his time spent watching, waiting, hidden. He would hide underneath the coats that were hanging at the bottom of the stairs. He had heard all the stories of what Mickey and his mates got up to. His mum would have a fucking fit if she knew what went on.

He would watch them through the gap in the door where it was slightly ajar, as they talked shop over their beer and fags.They would all sit around the big oval table that was in the bay window looking straight out onto the main road, ready and waiting for whoever walked up to the gate. Mickey could see who was coming and going. When the evening came, the big heavy curtains were drawn. But you knew when the front gate was opened or shut as it squeaked loudly.

He would hear all about the jobs they had done, what was going down. He heard who was a decent bloke, who you couldn't trust, who was a waste of space. All their stories of the punch- ups they had, who was a good shag, what girls were decent and who weren't. Fucking hell, Martin could tell you a few stories that would make your hair curl. Martin had learnt a lot during those nights, sitting on the stairs, but all these dark deeds stayed secret.

The deals and the amount of money that had passed hands in that house were astronomical, a king's ransom. Mickey made most of his money from arms deals and extortion, with a string of pubs and night clubs in his prostitution racket. Mickey didn't get any hassle from the police and the authorities, he'd learned it was good to have friends in high and powerful places. Have them on the payroll. Look after them and vice versa. What went on within them walls was nobody's business. Some of the scenes in that house could have been out of a film. They were all villains, but they were good people and they trusted each other. Everyone knew each other, helped each other out and stuck together. Everyone's door was always open for friends to come and go, and nothing got pinched. They had morals and standards.

Martin had even seen the Kray twins around his house a few times. Despite what Martin had heard about them, they seemed decent enough geezers; they treated his mum with respect, that was good enough for him... Because no one was ever going to hurt his mum again, not while he was about.

Martin had heard the same stories over and over again, they loved recounting among themselves the parties, weddings, deaths, births, funerals, but he hadn't once heard them discuss his dad's death. Martin was devoid of any emotion where his dad was concerned, he didn't give a fuck he was dead, he hated him. Mickey, like his dad was a man with many sides, known and feared. Unlike his dad, Mickey always looked after his family and mates, they were important to him. Mickey was his role model, his provider, his protector. Mickey would never let him down. They lived in a dog eat dog world, and Mickey was a hard, but reliable man – if anyone asked Mickey for anything he was always there if he could help you out. Mickey cracked him up, he was scared of nothing. Mickey's rise was brutal; he definitely lived up to his name. He'd even seen him kill a man with his bare hands.

That night they were all sitting playing cards around the table, smoke hung above their heads, a statch of money was in the centre of the table, the winnings. It was like looking in the public bar of the pub. Martin had been sitting there this night for about an hour. He knew Mickey wasn't right, something was pissing him off. Martin always knew when Mickey wasn't very happy, he could tell by the look on his face. He looked just like his dad did, fucking scary. The tense line of muscle around his jaw, his eyes twinkling; watching him that night he looked fucking dangerous, and someone sitting around that table had upset him big time. Anyone who betrayed Mickey's trust had the worst fate reserved just for them.

Dangerous, as Mickey was called certainly lived up to his name. The look in Mickey's eyes could slice you into pieces

Mickey had many reasons to be happy and just one making him very angry, and he was looking at him right now – Lenny Harper. It turned out he had been mugging Mickey off for a while. Mickey had put his trust in Lenny, given him a good job looking after one of his clubs and he had been skimming a fair wedge of his earnings. Martin saw Lenny, his glazed eyes, his lips constantly at work, he was definitely on something, he was high as a kite. That was obviously what he'd been spending Mickey's money on, dirty thieving bastard. You never took off your own.

The conversation was getting heated, Mickey was not a happy man.

His eyes stared straight ahead, and he gave a brief, somber smile. He got up from his chair, his eyes dark and twinkling. Mickey walked behind Lenny; he slid his arm around his head and the other around his neck. He jerked his strong arms violently. Lenny Harper slumped onto the table with a broken neck.

Mickey looked at the others, none of them could, would meet his eyes.

Their faces around the table ranged from passive, to intrigued, to horrified.

Martin would never forget it. He saw nothing wrong with what Mickey had done, The arsehole should never have done what he did and Mickey always said don't take his kindness as a weakness. Serve the prick right, he shouldn't have done what he did.

After that night, not another penny went missing from his tills.

Martin sat and visualized how, when and where, he was going to start doing his stuff, and be just like

Mickey, the pictures would flicker through his mind; he could replay them whenever he wanted. His thoughts unreadable and unknowable above the surface. Martin used to get worried about this feeling, but now he wanted it, he understood it. Martin couldn't go anywhere else with this except deeper into it. It was his vocation.

Mickey

Mickey Taylor examined himself in the full-length mirror in the small hallway, standing tall, proud and fearless. He tucked his gold belcher chain inside his shirt, did his top button up, then pulled his tie from his pocket and took a step closer to the mirror as he tied then straightened it. He hated wearing a tie. It felt tight and restricting.

Pulling the cuffs of his crisp white shirtsleeves down, he shook one trouser leg then the other. His gold MRT initial ring reflected off the mirror as he fiddled about with his cufflinks. He swallowed hard – they were Bobby's. He sighed deeply, combing his fingers through his thick raven hair, knowing this was one of his dad's gestures too.

Mickey stepped backwards, smart, handsome, self-assured, surveyed the reflection before him. He turned to his left, then to his right, taking a deep breath and holding his stomach muscles tight, carefully appraising himself. He had to look the business.

He grabbed his Crombie from the banister, put it on over his black Armani suit, then glanced at himself in the mirror once again. He leaned forward, cocked his head to one side, gazed into his own eyes. 'You're a good looking fucker,' he said aloud, smiling at his reflection.

Satisfied with his appearance, he walked over to the front room and poked his head round the door. Georgie was sitting down with his elbows resting on the dining table, lost in another world. A pang of sadness went through Mickey as he met Georgie's red rimmed eyes. Unlike Mickey, Georgie had wept openly, not afraid to show his sorrow.

'Georgie, I'm just popping out to find Sharon. I shouldn't be too long so meet me in the office in about an hour. We've got loads to do before the funeral this afternoon.'

Georgie turned his head, pulled back to reality. 'I can't get there Mickey, I gotta go somewhere. It's important.'

Mickey narrowed his eyes, the sense of foreboding that had plagued him since his dad's death growing inside. He had swallowed his irritation all week as Georgie's attitude had gone from bad to worse. He accepted his brother was grieving, but he was well out of order today and Mickey's patience was growing thin. What the fuck was on his mind? Was there something he wasn't telling him about his ole man's death?

Mickey stepped towards him. 'Fucking important? There's nothing more important than your fucking family, so whatever it is, Georgie, that's so important to you, it can fucking wait!'

'It can't,' Georgie muttered, shaking his head helplessly.

Mickey stared hard into his eyes. 'I'll only say it once. Make sure you're at the office Georgie. Family is your priority.' Mickey wanted to smash him in the face, he turned and stormed out the room before he did something he might regret.. 'I'm going now. I'll see you there.'

'What choice do I have?' Georgie replied resentfully.

Mickey stared hard at him from the doorway. 'You've always got a choice.'

He turned to the kitchen and waved bye to his aunt. 'See you later, Rosie. Thanks for everything '

She turned to Mickey and smiled. 'No problem, Mickey, that's what families are for,' she said waving him goodbye. 'See ya when you get back.'

He was glad she was here. She had sorted Lizzie out earlier and managed to calm her down. Mickey was really worried about his mum, he wanted to help her but he didn't know how. She had been in a right two and eight since it all happened. His main concern was his family, he had to look after them, protect them, hold them together.

He was glad to get out of the house for a while; he was not very good around people crying. They were all in massive shock and denial, he understood that, but Mickey found displays of emotion embarrassing and awkward.

Mickey checked his trouser and jacket pockets, making sure he had everything he needed. He jangled his car keys and smiled to himself. His new motor, a white Triumph Stag, was parked outside. It was his pride and joy. Though, he grimaced, he shouldn't need to be chasing around after his sister Sharon. The cheeky bitch hadn't been home all night and now his mum was worrying. He couldn't believe that on the night before her father's funeral she hadn't come home. She was taking the piss, as if he didn't have enough running around to do without all this as well. He'd fucking kill her when he got hold of her.

He opened the front door and stepped outside into the porch they shared with their next-door neighbour Betty Young. She had lived there for donkey's years and knew the Taylor family inside out. Martin, his little brother, had always called her Nanny Bet; she loved him like he was one of her own and she spoiled him rotten, treated him like the son she'd never had. Her affection for Martin was near obsession – he spent more time in Betty's than he did indoors and knew that he could wrap her around his little finger and get what he wanted. She would never have a bad word said against him. Betty idolised him, thought the sun shone out of his arse.

Betty had helped Bobby through his front door when he was pissed many times over the years. She could tell you a few stories, but Betty knew a still tongue made a wise head. She saw a lot, heard a lot, but always kept schtum. Bent as a nine bob note, she would do anything to turn a shilling, but she had a big heart – if she couldn't do you a good turn, she wouldn't do you a bad one.

She had also hid Mickey from the Old Bill a few times. Love her or hate her, you took Betty as you found her – she never minced her words, she would call a spade a spade. Mickey liked her a lot and he had a lot of respect for the old girl, she was as good as gold.

Betty was a petite woman with greeny blue eyes and a great sense of humour, and despite her small frame, she had a wicked temper. She smoked like a trooper, always had a fag in her hand, lighting her next with the one she was just finishing. She always had a lot to say and when she started rabbiting she couldn't stop. No one else could get a word in edgeways; she could talk for England that woman.

He grinned; she was like mutton dressed as lamb, still thought she was twenty-one, not an old bird of nearly sixty. She cracked him up; she was dripping in gold, half a dozen chains around her quaint neck, her huge loop earrings dangling from her small ears, a ring on every finger plus her armful of bracelets wrapped around her slender wrists. She must have had more gold than Archie's pawnshop up the road.

Mickey shut the front door behind him, shivered. 'Fuck me, it's cold.' It was miserable outside, the rain had fallen in torrents last night, and though it had eased up a bit, thank fuck, it was still drizzling. He hoped it would stop. He had promised Martin he would do a bonfire and have fireworks in the garden tonight. He must nip over to Barking later, after the funeral, to pick the fireworks up from the shop his mate owned. He didn't want to let Martin down; the poor little fucker had been through enough as it was.

He pulled the collar of his coat up around his neck, plunged his hands deep into his pockets. His eyes roamed slowly across the front garden, overflowing with flowers and heartfelt tributes. Mickey smirked sadly at the "Up the Hammers" wreath in claret and blue chrysanthemums. It was from all the boys at the Boleyn pub in Upton Park. Bobby and Mickey had had a few good lock-ins in at that boozer.

Mickey dragged his feet around the garden stopping at each floral tribute, reading each handwritten card. He bent down, wringing his hands together.

R.I.P Bobby, I can't believe this has happened. You will be forever in our hearts. Paula and kids xxxx

He swallowed deeply, grief choking him.

Big man with a big heart. God bless and may you rest in peace. Andy Brooks.

He squeezed his eyes tight shut with a long deep sigh.

My thoughts are with Lizzie and her family. I'm sorry to hear this has happened. Keep strong. Much love. The Mahoney family.

He ran his big hands through his thick dark hair.

Goodbye Bobby, I will miss you. You always said hello and had time for a chat and would help anyone. God bless. Maisie Miller xx

Slowly moving his head side to side, blinking back the tears, his heart heavy.

R.I.P Bobby mate. You will be sadly missed. We had some funny times and some good laughs. I'm so sorry for your family xx Michael, Rita and family.

He shook his head softly.

You always had a smile to share, a laugh, and a joke. Your friend Freddie Matthews and all the boys at Dagenham Amateur Boxing Club xxx God Bless ya.

That one really hit him. Mickey had a lot of respect for Freddie. He was a good geezer who had helped him out many times over the years and done him a few favours. He was a huge bloke, built like a brick shithouse, sixteen stone of pure muscle with a jaw like granite. Mickey and his best mate Stephen Black had been going to Freddie's gym at the back of the Church Elm pub a couple of times a week since they were kids. They would sit there just watching, listening and learning, but Mickey had always been the one asking all the questions, wanting to know all the answers.

Freddie had noticed how keen Mickey was and immediately recognised his young talent and love for boxing. But most importantly, he saw Mickey's desire to win. He took him under his wing and gave him the confidence to believe that he was capable of anything when he came out of his corner in the ring. This suited Mickey; he hated losing and always wanted to be a winner, never a loser. He thrived on a challenge.

Mickey had knuckled down and worked hard for years under Freddie's fearsome and ferocious guidance. Freddie knew the boxing game inside out and had taught him so much. He made sure that Mickey was down his gym every day – sparring, hitting the punch bag, doing the weights, and then finishing off with a three mile run. If anyone else had told Mickey to get down on the floor and do some press-ups … bollocks. But with Freddie he didn't hesitate or question it.

Freddie knew what to tell him, how to do it, when to calm him down and get him to just shut the fuck up and listen. It was Freddie's way or no way. They had the utmost respect for each other's roles and together they formed a great partnership. Mickey had never worked so hard in his life; he took his training deadly serious. Freddie had pushed him and pushed him, always told him, 'Don't give up, boy.' At the end of the day Mickey would walk out of the gym feeling indestructible. Freddie was the man who had made him the fighter he was.

He would never forget winning his first junior ABA title. He was over the moon that night, on a high, a total buzz. It was amazing. He would always remember that awesome moment of being handed the trophy. His trophy. It was the start of a collection he wanted to continue to add to. He could see his family and loads of his mates at the ringside as he raised his hands above his head – they were going mental in the crowd, laughing, crying, screaming, cheering and shouting, jumping up and down, hugging each other and everyone around, sharing the joy he felt inside. Yes, yes, he was a winner, a champion! It was out of this world. He was elated and wanted that feeling again and again and again. Nothing and no one was going to stop him.

At fourteen, Mickey started entering the NABC tournaments. He was on a mission and looking forward to a career in professional boxing. The British title, the European title and then the World. Mickey definitely had the punch to do it; his dream was there waiting, ready for him to grab hold of with both hands. He was ready for bigger and better things.

Mickey knew Lizzie was proud of what he had achieved but she never came to see any of his fights. She couldn't stomach it, the thought of all that blood made her feel sick. She thought it was torture, like a lamb going to slaughter, she just couldn't do it. Instead, she would stay indoors with her rosary beads in her hands and just pray and pray. She made him laugh; it was the poor bloke who dared go into the ring and challenge him who needed her prayers, not Mickey!

Without fail, after every fight, his mum would run him a nice hot bath filled with loads of bubble bath, scented candles burning on the windowsill. She would warm the towels by the fire while he lay soaking in the hot tub. It was luxury. Then she would have his favourite dinner ready for him, rump steak and chips, always cooked to perfection – she knew just how he liked it, rare with blood still oozing from it. Lovely. Then, all fed and watered, he would go out with the boys for a beer, then go home and sleep like a baby.

The next day he would be back down the gym to start all over again. He was at his peak mentally and physically, and at eighteen had gone from being a promising junior to being rated as one of the best British fighters around. When Mickey walked into the ring there was always a smile on his face and a twinkle in his eye, a razor sharp focus on what he had to do. He would get in there and get the job done – there was no sympathy from Mickey.

He put his left hand on his smashed elbow and gave a long broken sigh, remembering vividly when the doctor told him that he would never fight again. He'd been gutted – he still was – and had struggled coming to terms with it all. He could have made it big time but that fucking car accident had put an end to his boxing career. He was finished. He had had a few knocks in his time but this was a sickener. It was the hardest punch he had ever taken and he didn't know how he was going to handle it. Mickey took a long, deep breath. Life was a lot easier in the ring than out of it.

All his life he had been a fighter, on the streets, in school, in the pubs, in clubs, but in the ring it was different. The first time he had got in the ring with his gloves on he was ready to go; this was what he wanted. It was right up his street. He had found out who he was. Boxing was his life; it was all he was good at, all he knew. It was who he was, a fighter.

Mickey walked out of the hospital that night and roamed the streets for hours in total shock. He couldn't believe what the quack had told him. He didn't know who he was or what he was going to do any more. He woke up every morning and went to bed every night just thinking about boxing. His next fight, his tactics, his training, his corner, his sparring pals. He was completely fucked. He had a horrible, horrible feeling inside of him. He was lost. He felt like a different person, a different man.

But that was before his dad died. That was before everything changed. Now he was the Big Man, the top dog. Now the manor was his – his to rule, his to fuck up. He'd better get it right …

He glanced back towards the house, saw the curtain twitch, the wave of a small, pale hand. Martin. Mickey grinned, gave Martin a quick nod. Mickey hadn't got the belt he had dreamed of, but he was determined to see his little brother get to the top. Martin was a naturally aggressive fighter and at ten years old he already had the boxing bug. He was young, strong and eager and had inherited his boxing prowess from his dad, like Mickey. He would get him down the gym, gloves on and onto the mat, train him hard and make sure that everyone knew who and what Martin Taylor was.

He had Martin's future mapped out for him, Mickey could see it all. Martin on the front page of the newspapers and boxing magazines, a boxing spectacular. The fans arriving in droves as he signed autographs. He would fight in some of the biggest venues in London and the world – the Royal Albert Hall, Madison Square Gardens, Caesar's Palace, all the top places. His name would be in lights and thousands would attend his fights, cheering and chanting. He would become a boxing legend alongside the best – Sugar Ray Robinson, Muhammad Ali, Howard Winston, Freddie Mills, Henry Cooper. It would take years of blood and sweat, but Mickey would make it worth his while. He would make sure Martin made it, no matter what. Mickey's obsession with seeing his little brother at the top was going to be the start of something that would take over and change their lives forever.

Mickey stood up, stretching his legs and rolling his shoulders backwards, trying to get rid of the tension he felt inside. He couldn't read any more of the cards, they were fucking with his mind. He must remember to tell Fat Jack to collect all the cards from the flowers to see who'd paid their respects and who hadn't.

'Mickey.'

He turned. Glancing over his broad shoulder he saw Dave Mitchell standing at the gate. He was an old friend of Bobby's, a decent bloke, a very quiet and intelligent man. Bobby and Dave had spent a couple of years together in the Scrubs where they'd spent many hours playing cards and chess together. Forgery and chequebooks were Dave's game, and he was on a nice little earner till it all went pear-shaped and he landed up doing a five year stretch. He lost a lot of money and ended up without a pot to piss in.

'Dave. Good to see ya mate.'

Mickey held out his strong hand and they shook. Dave didn't let go. He held on for a moment, his eyes closed, his face pale and quiet. All the memories of his mate came flooding back. He knew Bobby lived a dodgy life, took risks, took chances, pulled a few scams, but what had happened was sickening. He was remembering a couple of years ago, near to Christmas. Bobby knew he was going through a rough spot and was skint. He handed him an envelope with a good few quid in it, saying to him, 'You and the kids have a good Christmas. Happy New Year, Dave.'

Dave was gutted. He couldn't believe what had happened to Bobby. He would help anyone when they were in trouble; that showed a good mate.

'I'm so sorry. You know if there's ...' Dave mumbled.

'Cheers mate,' Mickey replied as he patted Dave's back awkwardly and then pulled away. If he heard anyone else say I'm sorry, he would punch 'em on the fucking nose.

At that moment Martin came strolling out of the house towards the gate where Mickey and Dave were chatting. 'Where ya going?' he demanded, tugging at the sleeves of Mickey's coat. Martin thought the world of Mickey, he was his idol, he looked up to him. Ever since Martin could remember he had wanted to be like Mickey, be part of his world. He was someone, something. Everywhere he went he knew everyone, and people looked at him with respect. 'You look like a real gangster, Mickey, all suited and booted,' chirped Martin. 'You really look the nuts today!'

Mickey looked down at Martin's large mournful brown eyes and knew he was going to be a dangerous fucker in the future. He was only a kid but he knew what he wanted and where he belonged, already he had the same arrogance and presence of his dad, of Mickey.

'Sorry Mart, not now. I want you to stay here, close to the phone box and Mum. I need you here to answer any calls and take my messages.' Mickey handed his brother a pound note. 'Put that in ya pocket. I've gotta go now. You go in and help mum and auntie Rosie – and don't forget to listen out for the phone.'

Martin grinned. He felt important, needed. 'Cheers Mickey, will do.' He turned to Dave. 'Me dad's dead, Dave,' he announced as they stood in the damp mist and drizzle. 'Do ya fink he done himself in or someone murdered him?'

Mickey felt the words slap him straight in the bollocks as Martin spoke them. Mickey and Dave both held their breath. Both lost for words, ignoring the question. Dave glanced at Martin; it was heartbreaking to see the Taylors going through this nightmare. 'Ah mate,' Dave said quietly. 'Your ole man was a diamond geezer.'

Mickey turned to Martin. 'Martin, do me a favour, take Davey boy indoors to see muvver and get him a drink.' He motioned Dave and Martin indoors. As they turned, they saw Betty standing in the porch, gesturing them toward her.

'Martin? Why don't you come indoors with me and bring Dave wiv ya?' Betty called out. 'We'll go in to see ya Mum in a little while. Give her a chance to get herself ready.'

Too choked for words, Mickey nodded to Dave as he strolled out the gate towards his car, his shoulders pulled back and his head held high. He was going to find that stupid bitch Sharon, and then he had places to go and people to see. The war was only just beginning.

Georgie

Georgie was terrified. He wasn't going to go to the office, he couldn't face it yet – he would tell Mickey later, after the burial. He paced the living room floor, running his fingers through his hair. Walking up and down. Stopping. Going round in circles, backwards and forwards, scratching his chin, trying to clear his head, trying to make some sense of it all. He hadn't been to bed all night, he felt completely and utterly fucked. He had to sober himself up a bit sharpish, people would be here soon paying their respects, he couldn't let anyone see him in this state.

Georgie sat down heavily at the front room table. His black suit made him look taller, thinner and much older than his nineteen years. A feeling of frustration came over him as his deep dark eyes travelled around the room. Everything looked the same, was the same, but everything was different. Nothing would ever be the same again, least of all Georgie himself. He sat solemnly, rubbing his strong hands up and down his handsome face, over his tired eyes.

A wife without a husband, sons and daughters without a dad, nephews without an uncle. He felt like a stranger, empty.

All the memories of his dad kept flooding back with a vengeance. He slumped and put his hands over his face as a wave of nausea swept over him. The images filtering through his mind made him feel like he couldn't breathe, his heart pounding ten to the dozen, a toxic mixture of emotions rising to the surface, riding along on a roller coaster. Dread, fear, panic, anger, relief and guilt consumed him.

He sat thinking how things were before. What it had been like, what Bobby was like, the things they'd done, things they didn't do, the things Georgie should have said and done. He wanted to know when he would stop thinking about him, when he'd stop seeing him every time he closed his eyes, expecting him to walk back through the door. The house was quieter now – most of the rowing had stopped. He wouldn't hear him walking up to the gate, coming up the path; there was no shout of hello, no whistling of a tune above the tapping of his black polished shoes as he came in the front door.

When would Lizzie stop going into their bedroom so she could feel his clothes, still hanging in the wardrobe? She'd fall asleep, sobbing his name into his pillow, clutching his silk shirt close to her, smelling his aftershave. When would Mickey's face stop looking like a slapped arse? When would Terri and Sharon stop crying? When would Martin have some kind of reaction? There were tears sliding down his cheeks ... Oh God ... Georgie buried his face in his hands while he cried. He didn't know how he was going to get through the day. He opened another bottle of scotch, his hands shaking so violently that he couldn't hold it properly. He dropped the bottle on the table and the whiskey poured onto the floor.

'Bollocks.'

He placed his hands on the table in front of him, trying to stop them shaking. Everything reminded him of Bobby. The chair he sat in, his baccy tin, his reading glasses, the cup he drank from, his leather belt. The leather belt.

Another wave of nausea swept over him as the bile rose deep from the pit of his stomach and he felt the dampness of sweat on his back. He sat still and stiff backed, taking long, slow deep breaths, trying to pull himself together, telling himself not to panic. That everything would be all right. Gradually his breathing eased. He tried moving his arm to get a cigarette but he couldn't move his hands, they were fixed firmly on the table. Georgie was paralysed with fear, just like the day years ago when he was a boy.

He was here sitting in this same chair, this same room. Bobby was standing upright directly opposite him, a wide gleaming smile on his face, his evil eyes twinkling as he pulled his belt slowly from his waistband. Georgie watched his dad standing still, holding the belt in his strong hands, examining it, and caressing the smooth hard leather. His dark eyes were twinkling as the high-pitched crack of the belt echoed in the room and filled Georgie's ears. He looked into

Bobby's eyes; they were filled with burning venom. He was always angry; Georgie didn't know what he'd done wrong to make him so mad, but there didn't have to be a reason, it was just the mood he was in. Bobby slowly brought his dark eyes to Georgie's terrified face. Georgie knew what was coming, he could smell the violent rage pulsing from inside Bobby, and could see the pure pleasure in his smile.

Georgie couldn't pull his hands away as the lashes came raining down. The pain was unbearable; it ripped throughout his small slim body. His tiny hands felt like they were on fire, crimson welts opening up, spewing his red raw blood onto the beige carpet. So, so hot, he felt he was in hell, burning. This was his punishment; he was a bad boy and he deserved it, every bit of it. As much as Georgie wanted to die, he was petrified of the punishment waiting for him in hell. He must go to confession. He was wicked and evil, he would have to pay penance for his sins.

Then Mickey came steaming through the door with a broom handle in his hand and began whacking Bobby. That might have stopped him from belting Georgie, but he continued with his sadistic pleasures, turning to Mickey, stripping the shirt from his back.

Georgie held his breath as he watched the bite of the belt rip Mickey's back apart. Georgie sat under the table, his legs and knees shaking, looked into Bobby's eyes, alight with anger. Sweat ran down Bobby's forehead but he kept on going, blow after blow. Mickey's wounds were torn, open, raw, but his eyes were dark, full of hatred.

Georgie was on his knees begging for mercy, begging him to stop as the lashes rained down onto Mickey. This was nothing compared to their eternal suffering in hell. Georgie's bloody hands were clasped over his mouth, his eyes wide with fear, his fresh blood curdling between his fingers. He sat and pissed himself as he watched the huge mauve, red and blue criss-cross welts open up on Mickey's back.

When Mickey came to bed that night he crept under the covers with Georgie. Two small bodies, bruised and battered, covered in blood.

'I'm sorry, it's all my fault,' Georgie cried. 'Sorry, Mickey.'

'For fuck sake will you stop saying sorry to me. It ain't your fault. It's that fucking prick.' Mickey looked deep into his brother's eyes, 'Believe me Georgie, I promise you, he ain't never gonna hurt none of us again.' Mickey wrapped his arms protectively around him, 'I'll kill the cunt first.'

They held each other close. Georgie knew he meant every word he said and he knew Mickey wouldn't go to sleep until he knew Bobby was asleep or out and that they were safe – only then would he close his eyes and exhaustedly give in.

Georgie loved him so much. Mickey always tried to look after him and protect, though it should have been the other way round. Georgie was two years older than Mickey, he should have been looking after Mickey instead of always letting him down.

Shaking from the memory, Georgie picked up the Bible, clasped it tightly to his chest. He stared at the ceiling, praying to the God he hoped was there. Guilt consumed him. He sat still, taking long, slow deep breaths trying to pull himself together. He shook his head and sighed. God, what had he done? Georgie had been waiting years for this day to come. He wanted a peaceful life, devoid of all the horrors that lay behind him, but what scared him most was what lay in front of him.

He had risked acute danger in his life in this savage environment. He could smell the fear seeping from his skin. He would have to be honest and truthful, his life was built on lies, one lie on top of another, but now he had to tell them all the truth. Georgie had promised himself this ordeal for years, it had kept him going, his strength of resolution. He realised today that suffering was not the result of sin but a test of character. He had come to terms with his life, and realised that for some questions there were no answers.

He wrenched his mind away from the day ahead and began praying. He felt a moment of intense relief, forgetting what he had to face today. Georgie knew if he followed Mickey he would be walking back outside to the person he wanted to be rid of. If he didn't, he knew what the horrendous consequences would be.

Today would be the end; his unbreakable bond with his brother Mickey would shatter. He had committed the ultimate betrayal of his closeness and loyalty to his family and he had to confront it, it couldn't be put off any longer. Georgie sat with his head buried deep in his hands. Gut wrenching sobs filled the silent room. Hot tears rolled down his cheeks, he was stymied and defeated.

Mickey was planning a huge bonfire. But whose effigy would burn on it tonight?

Rosie

Rosie Richards stood in the long, narrow galley kitchen making tea for Lizzie and Georgie. Her bright emerald eyes watched the rain falling from the grey sombre skies as her tumbling curls cascaded playfully over her slender shoulders. Rosie had unique style and perfect taste. She was intelligent, gracious and sexy, gave off an energy and vitality in everything she did. She could talk easily with anyone, definitely had the gift of the gab, had no problem exchanging compliments or insults with a duke or a docker.

It had been years since she'd last been in Dagenham. Nothing much had changed; it was still a depressing pisshole of a place and was still filled with the same people. And as for the house, Rosie would much rather totally forget her time spent here. This was not a nostalgia trip. She wanted her horrific memories to stay put, deep in a dark place, but just being here was dragging her past from its dormant state. She couldn't change it, but she couldn't keep running from it either.

She gazed around her. Everything looked the same, smelled the same, and sounded the same. A deadly silence hung heavy over this oppressive house. Weighed down with time, fear still stalked every room, every hour, every day. How she hated it here. Her ugly, vivid memories would not be vanquished. Rosie shook; all her old insecurities came hurtling back. She didn't have to come to the house, but though she didn't want to, she knew she had to face her demons. She didn't feel scared to enter and walk through all the rooms, but she knew that each one held a different story with no fairytale happy endings.

Her head ached and her throat was dry. She felt like she was suffering from a massive hangover, but she hadn't had a drink last night, even though they'd all gone to the pub. She'd felt like going on a bender and forgetting everything, but she had to keep her head clear, not just because of Bobby Taylor and his incredible ability to wreck people's lives, but because she knew how difficult today would be for Lizzie. On the outside Lizzie was being very brave, but Rosie knew she was grieving for Bobby more than she would ever say. Not only had she lost someone she loved in the most shocking circumstances, but there was also the hideous trauma of Martin finding his dad's body. Rosie shook her head, pushing those unwanted images away.

Rosie had spent the last sixteen years of her life with rising intensity and ambition. The things that had happened had made her who she was. It had become her private nightmare, one that revisited her often, threatening her sanity, but Rosie had her strategy for survival in place. She had felt lost, adrift; it had taken her years to rebuild her life, though it had taken only one day to leave it. It seemed to Rosie that the central events of her life had happened here. She stubbed her cigarette in the ashtray, grinding the butt with suppressed anger. There were only two types of men – the dead and the deadly – and Rosie Richards wasn't going to be intimidated by any man again. She had been a young and naïve girl then, she was a woman now. Never again would she walk in anyone's shadow.

Her hands gripped the sink as she thought of the day she had left, the day she had promised herself that she would never return. She blinked back the tears as the memories came rushing back with a vengeance. She glanced at her watch; blimey, it was half past nine. She had to pull herself together. Everyone would be arriving soon and all the old faces would be walking through the door.

She wondered if Frankie Yates would be here. She didn't know if he was dead or alive. If he did show up it would be the first time she had seen his face since the night she had left. She swallowed deeply, realizing that she still loved him.

Rosie wondered what he thought of her, if he ever thought of her at all. Did he love her or hate her? Was he happily married to a wife who adored him? Did he have loads of kids? Fuck, fuck, fuck! She didn't know how she was going to handle this.

She straightened her new black dress and sighed deeply. It reminded her of the dress Frankie had bought for her years ago; he had always been buying her presents and spoiling her. She was so happy that day, so deliriously happy. She had felt like the Queen of Sheba. Rosie had held the dress against her, the soft silk against her face. It was so smooth. She had loved the tiny waist and the full skirt. She had felt wonderful going to church that morning. All eyes had looked at her, filled with envy. Her hair had been tied back in matching ribbons showing her finely formed profile, and she wore shoes to match her dress; they were a present from Frankie too. But her happiness hadn't lasted long. The moment she got back into the house, Bobby had followed her into the kitchen and started mouthing off.

'Look at the fucking state of you, dressing like a fucking whore for church. You put shame on the family you dirty slut.' Bobby's arrogant, handsome features scowled at her with pure hatred.

Rosie folded her arms haughtily. 'You talking to me?' She spoke with a fighting edge that she didn't really feel.

'What other dirty stinking little whore would I be talking to?' Bobby's voice was deadly quiet. He was standing in the doorway of the kitchen now, glaring at her.

Her face was full of contempt as she said, 'You don't impress me Mr Bobby, Bloody Taylor. You think you're something else don't ya? The big 'I am.'

He smiled a blatantly wicked smile. 'You're a dozy fucking whore. You really thought Lizzie would believe you, didn't ya?'

She laughed a bitter mocking laugh. 'You don't scare me any more, Bobby.'

Bobby smirked as he took a threatening step towards her.

'Don't I?' He stared at her, his eyes narrowing. 'You put up a good fight didn't ya?'– smiling smugly as he spoke – 'I know ya want me, you're gagging for it. What a shame that whore wife of mine disturbed us. I fancied a good fuck that night!' He laughed at her. 'Frankie told me what a good shag you are. But don't worry, I'll be in your knickers again soon. Back for a bit of your dirty minge.'

Rosie looked at him, acid burning in her eyes. 'Your arsehole could be dripping in diamonds and I'd never come near you. You're sick in the head.' She looked into his handsome face, repulsed. 'You're my sister's husband for fuck sake. Did you really think that I wanted you? You're having a laugh mate. You fucking repulse me, you're a sick perv.' She took a deep breath, 'You've fucked Lizzie's head up and she believes your sick lies, that I come on to you, that I fancy you. As if. I wouldn't come near you if you paid me.' She laughed sarcastically at him. 'It was you who came into my room and tried to rape me.' She looked deep into his eyes. 'I hate you,' – her voice strong – 'you're one nasty cunt. Frankie's gonna love it when I tell him all about you. What you done to me.' She leered at him. 'He'll cut your fucking bollocks off.'

'You cunt.' Bobby's rage was terrifying. He strode across the kitchen until they were face-to-face. She didn't back off. Rosie stared back at him, her eyes burning with hatred and spite. She wasn't a child any more, her figure was that of a woman's – high breasted, narrow waist and slender hips, but she was still young, and she was very, very angry.

Bobby saw her hand coming towards him to give him a slap; he grabbed her wrists in an iron tight grasp. She struggled with him for a few seconds.

'Come on then hit me, you're good at hitting women.' Her fine boned face, dominated by her angry eyes, stared at him. As he forced her to her knees, he kept hold of her wrists, gripping them tightly.

'That's where you belong you dirty whore. You should suck me off while you're down there – you know you want to!'

They were startled by someone banging on the front door. Bobby threw Rosie down onto the hard stone kitchen floor, smiled a cruel tormenting smile.

'You're a very silly girl, Rosie,' he snarled, as he lifted his chin and put his index finger across his throat, 'I ain't finished with you yet, cunt. You open your mouth and you're dead meat.' He strolled casually out to the front door.

Rosie smiled to herself, remembering the look on Bobby's face when Frankie had walked into the living room, giving Bobby a nod and a friendly smile. Bobby had grasped his hand and squeezed it firmly, returning the smile.

Bobby was pleased to be in the world of proper villains, not just tuppenny, ha'penny thieves. Frankie was a friendly man, but you had to earn his respect. He was a proud Cockney with solid principles.

Everything about him gleamed; his greased black hair, his sharp polished black shoes, his quick smile and his mistrustful dark eyes. Frankie was scared of no man. He didn't suffer fools gladly and could suss you out very quickly and he wasn't often wrong about people. He would be shocked when she told him about Bobby, what he was really like.

'Fuck me, you knock like the Old Bill,' laughed Bobby.

Frankie smiled as he turned towards Rosie and said, 'Now there's a sight for sore eyes.' His smile deepened. 'That dress was made for ya, darlin'.' He gave her an affectionate wink, holding his arms open wide. 'Come 'ere gorgeous.'

Bobby looked at Rosie, querulous with anger as she held Frankie tight. She smiled sweetly at him as she felt his hands on her waist. He pulled gently away from her, looking deep into her eyes. 'You all right girl?' Frankie spoke with concern in his voice.

Rosie forced a wide smile onto her face. 'Yeah, yeah course I am.' She smiled at Frankie but her eyes betrayed the sadness they held. She swallowed the bile searing in her throat, she could feel her knees trembling.

'Cheer up me ole darlin', he said. 'We ain't at a fucking funeral.' He raised his eyebrows. 'No one's upset you, have they Rosie?'

Rosie smiled as she drew her fingers through her hair. 'No. Course not. I'm all right, Frankie, honestly, just a bit tired that's all. I'll get ya a drink. What do ya want?'

He looked deep into her eyes, certain that something was bothering her. There was something she wasn't telling him. Frankie would find out and kill anyone who hurt or upset her. 'Whiskey.'

Rosie turned and walked towards the kitchen.

'I'll give ya a hand Rosie.' Out of the corner of her eye she saw Frankie picking up the empty glasses on the table, but his eyes were on Bobby, a deep intense, questioning stare. Bobby was watching the floor. She looked away as Frankie turned and followed her into the kitchen.

'Rosie what's a matter, you don't seem ya self?' His voice strong, he wanted to know what was wrong with her. This was so unlike her. 'Who's fucking upset ya? Come on babe tell me.'

She turned away from him, shielding the tears in her eyes. She wanted to tell him about Bobby, but it would have to wait till tonight when they were on their own. She just hoped and prayed to God that he wasn't taken in by Bobby with his vicious and spiteful lies. She knew how Frankie would react but she didn't care any more. The low life piece of scum deserved everything he got.

'Honestly, I'm OK, nothing's wrong. I had a late night out with the girls last night and I'm a bit tired that's all.' She opened a bottle of whiskey, and then reached for a glass from the draining board. 'I'll have a kip this afternoon and I'll be fine by tonight.'

Carefully, with her head cocked to the side, she poured a good measure of whiskey into both the glasses. 'I promise I won't be late. I'll be in the Cross Keys dead on eight o'clock.' Slowly turning, she passed a drink to Frankie. He raised his glass in the air and their eyes met.

'To us, Rosie.'

She raised her glass, 'To us, Frankie,' as their glasses clinked.

Rosie looked straight up at him. She loved him so much but Bobby had ruined everything. Frankie looked down at her with love in his eyes, as she placed her hands on both sides of his face, pulled his mouth down towards her to meet her soft lips. She kissed him quickly, then dropped her arms to her side and staring into his glistening blue eyes, she whispered softly, 'I love you Frankie, so much.' There was tightness in her throat; she was so scared that he wouldn't love her any more. There would be no Frankie and Rosie if he believed Bobby.

Frankie's big hands fell on her shoulders and he pulled her closer to him. They looked at each other. He spoke softly. 'I love you, Rosie, more than you'll ever know.' Then he kissed her gently. For a long moment they held each other tight. Rosie didn't know that Bobby had heard her every word.

All that day until she went to bed she could feel Bobby's eyes boring into her, running the length of her, from her face to her feet.

At seven thirty sharp she went out to meet Frankie, determined not to be late. She sat on the bar stool, a gin and tonic in her hand, a smile on her face, ready to dish the dirt on Bobby, ready to tell Frankie everything and watch as he put that nasty bastard in his place.

But he didn't show up. Her stomach sank as she waited and waited on the barstool. She knew he loved her and that their love had been real. Or had it? Surely if it had been real, Bobby wouldn't have been able to change his mind so quickly? But Bobby had a unique gift for twisting words, making people believe him, convincing them that what he said was the God's honest truth. And Frankie hadn't come. He hadn't come. And the longer she waited, the more she realised that it was all over, that she had to get out, get away.

Rosie went into her bedroom for the last time that night, sat on the edge of her narrow framed bed, shuddered. It was time to go, time to move on, time to start a new life. Her long slim legs stretched endlessly on the bed. She sat chewing her bitten nails, just thinking. She didn't know how she was going to get through all this, but she had managed so far because she had to. She felt weak with emotion. She would never trust another man again. She was so traumatised by it all. She never spoke about it again with anyone.

Rosie lay back on the soft white pillow, throwing one hand across her eyes trying to block out all her horror. Feeling the devastation wash over her, she sat upright on the bed, drew her legs close to her chest, arms folded around them, let her head sink down to rest on her trembling knees. She had to face her fears and rethink the rest of her life.

She sobbed quietly. Her lips moved silently in prayer begging Him to look after Lizzie, Sheila and all the kids.

'God, please look after them and keep them safe from harm,' Rosie shuddered. 'Why, God? Why did this all have to happen?'

She'd tried to talk to Lizzie, tell her what Bobby had done, but Lizzie had refused point blank to listen to her, just wouldn't believe a word she was saying. Lizzie retreated into her own fantasies, insisting that Bobby was a kind, loving man devoted to her and her family and Rosie was sick to say such an awful thing about him. Her denial mechanisms were insuperable.

Lizzie told Rosie that she was trying to destroy her marriage, hurt them all. She was nothing but a dirty whore, it was Rosie who was after Bobby, she couldn't keep her eyes and hands off him. She was always showing off and flirting with him, would never leave him alone – she was just an evil, manipulating bitch. A lying, horrible trollop. She wanted her out of her house and she never wanted to see her again. Lizzie said that Rosie was destroying her marriage and her life.

And so Lizzie carried on popping her pills, continued living in denial, wouldn't listen to the truth. Rosie knew that Bobby was sick in the head and so she felt compassion for Lizzie, who had to spend the rest of her life with that evil monster, but there was nothing she could do to help her.

Rosie knew Sheila, her sister, would be all right with Johnnie in Ireland. He was a decent, lovely man who cherished his wife, and was nothing but gentle with her. Sheila was onto a winner with Johnnie, he would always look after her and protect her.

Sheila was a loving supportive wife, had a lovely home, was always by her husband's side, always backed him up and had raised the boys perfectly. She was a good wife and mother, but despite Sheila's gentleness she wasn't shy or slow in coming forward. She could definitely handle herself. She knew Sheila would be devastated that she hadn't gone to her in Ireland, she had always told her that she would be welcome in her home any time. Rosie wished she could have talked to her about it and told her the truth. If only Rosie could have seen them, explained and told them how much she loved them all, but they all arse-licked around Bobby, so no one would believe her anyway.

She would never be allowed to leave. Bobby always kept his watchful eye on her – he knew who her friends were, where she went, who she was with. If it wasn't him watching her, it was one of his bunch of cronies. Unless she completely disappeared, Bobby would find her, and she would be a dead woman when he did. She hated him. She was sick of his presence, his dominance, his interference and control in her life. And now he had even managed to turn Frankie against her. She couldn't believe it; she thought Frankie was more of a man. She thought he loved her. How wrong she was. She couldn't stay anymore, and she would have to go a long way to escape Bobby's web of spies and liars.

She stood silently at the end of the bed smoothing her dress. She hated this house, which would never be a home. Her eyes strayed around the room for the last time. She must look to the future because she didn't want to think about the past. All that could be heard was the ticking of the clock on the window ledge. Rosie's face grew tense as she looked more and more frequently at the time, waiting for the right moment, when the whole world was asleep ...

She placed all her worldly belongings in the old tattered suitcase, slowly closed it, moving quickly before she lost courage to leave. She tiptoed to the front door and crept out into the cold, dark morning, tears she refused to let out glistening in her eyes. For one brief moment she contemplated going back and finding Frankie, but then it was gone. Suddenly she felt old and tired. She was on her own once again. She was walking away free, but every emotion she possessed was lost. She didn't care any more. She was leaving and never coming back. She had to keep going and get as far away as possible.

Walking slowly in a dreadful haze of pain, her footsteps grew heavier and heavier. Her hair hung loose down her back, blowing across her cold cheeks. Rosie felt a chill run through her, she had not really thought about the long-term consequences of leaving. What would she do if she couldn't find work or somewhere to live? The thought made her tremble with fear, but it could be no worse than it was here. The case weighed almost nothing, but her arms were aching. She stopped and put it on the ground, looked back along the Heathway. That was part of her past now, part of her unhappiness; she would never be able to forget. She was living for the day she would see Bobby Taylor pay for this. Yes! One day he would pay, she had told herself, and now that day had come ...

She wiped her hand over her face, brushed away her tears, forced her mind from the past and onto the day ahead. She'd better get her arse into gear and sort herself out. It was Bobby Taylor's funeral and she had serious responsibilities. She would see the day through, she had to. She would finish what Bobby had started, and see the bastard laid in the ground.

Mickey

Mickey got into his motor, stiff and tense. He could kill Sharon, the dozy bitch. The last thing he needed today was to waste time searching for her. But then he smiled, shifted his position until he was comfortable and relaxed a bit – at least it gave him another excuse to use his beautiful car. He pulled a B&H out of the packet and lit it, inhaling deeply.

It never rained but poured, he thought – Stevie Black, his mate, was back on the shit. Stevie's girlfriend Kay had rung him earlier this morning in hysterics, pleading and begging him for help. She was desperate. Stevie needed a bit of gear so he could go to Bobby's funeral, he couldn't function without it, she was scared he was going to die; she couldn't see Stevie in this horrible mess any longer. Mickey tutted, shook his head. He couldn't believe that he had actually made a few phone calls to arrange having a bit of brown delivered to Stevie, feeding him his filthy heroin habit.

He put the key in the ignition, smirking as he remembered the day Stevie had started at his school. He had stopped him getting a good hiding from a gang of kids, the local bullies. He had taken him home to clean him up and give him a bit of grub. He was so skinny he needed a bit of fattening up and he sorted him out some decent clobber. Mickey remembered how Stevie sang his praises to his mum for looking after him and saving him from having the seven bells of shit kicked out of him. He told his mum that Mickey was the only person who had done something for him and didn't expect or want anything back. Lizzie put her hand in her bag and pulled out a couple of bob to give to Mickey.

'Good boy, son, you and Stevie go treat yourselves,' she told Mickey, giving him an affectionate wink.

They had been best mates ever since and were always together, side by side. They made a formidable pair. Stevie became a permanent fixture in the Taylor household. Lizzie and Bobby loved him as one of their own. He was part of their family, they all thought the world of him. The only condition Mickey gave to Stevie was, 'Keep ya fucking hands off me sisters and you'll be all right mate.'

Stevie had a hard life, his dad had committed suicide when he was four and his mum was an alcoholic and a junkie. He never stood a chance. His life of crime started long before Mickey knew him. From an early age he was out choring with his mum, it just came natural to him. A piece of cake. But when his mum died, Stevie was taken into care and bounced between foster homes and kids' homes all his life, never stayed put in one place for long, he always had it away on his toes. He didn't settle anywhere, with anyone, always on the trot.

Mickey had seen how Stevie had changed – he was different lately – but he still couldn't believe he was back on heroin. He had lied to him and told Mickey that he was clean. It was only last year that he had gotten him into rehab and a detox to try and help him, to sort him out, but it seemed he was a lost cause.

Since Bobby had died, Stevie had been worse; he hadn't taken Bobby's death very well. He'd idolised him, looked up to him, loved him like the dad he'd never had. He would do anything for Bobby. As they got older it hadn't taken Bobby long to see the potential in the pair of them, he soon had them both working in the firm for him, ordering men around twice their age. Stevie was always working side by side with Mickey on the doors, collecting debts and settling old scores for Bobby. They rarely had to do anything to get money owed to them apart from ask. Mickey's name was on the streets and he became known as a dangerous fucker. No one apart from his family called him 'Mickey' any more. To everyone else he was simply known as 'Dangerous'.

Mickey sat on the soft cream leather seat lost in his own thoughts, remembering all the laughs him and Stevie used to have. The parties, the birds, the booze and the fights. They were both earning a nice few quid but Stevie spunked all his money on drugs. He was living with a decent bird that didn't want him just for his money and reputation, head over heels in love with him she was, worshipped the ground he walked on. If Stevie said to her jump, she'd ask how high. His flat on Thames View estate was the bollocks, a decent gaff, done up really nice with a thick white shag pile carpet, a black leather three piece and a top of the range television and stereo system. He had a decent set of wheels to run around in, a red MG sports. Stevie was doing all right for himself. He was making it, big time.

Mickey and Stevie were always out and about on a bender. Mickey didn't mind going on the piss but drugs were never his game – he hated drugs with a vengeance. A fag and a few drinks was enough for Mickey. He knew Stevie dabbled with a bit of this and that, but nothing too heavy, that's what he told himself, and Stevie never did drugs in Mickey's company, he knew it was more than he dared to do. But like many people, he had started small and ended up a dirty fucking smack head. Mickey swallowed deeply, stubbing out his cigarette in the car's ashtray; he was gutted, never again would he see the old Stevie he used to know. His best friend, his soulmate. They used to train together, spar together, run together, and have a pint together.

Mickey had noticed over the last few months the special bond between them seemed to be deteriorating fast. Stevie had changed big time. Mickey was gutted, he thought they had a deep respect for one another and didn't hide anything. How wrong he was.

He could remember it like yesterday when he first found out Stevie was on drugs. Mickey had needed to get hold of Stevie one night, a big job was on the boil and they had some important stuff to sort out, but Stevie wasn't answering his calls; no one had seen Stevie out and about that day. Mickey had been worried about him, drove over to his flat and let himself in with the spare key Stevie had given him. Mickey was shocked at what he saw. Stevie was lying on the floor stark bollock naked with a fucking huge needle sticking out of his thigh, jacking up on heroin and ketamine plus any other shit he could pump into his body. He was totally out of the game, hallucinating, laughing hysterically, tripping, on another planet, in another world, just complete madness.

This heap of shit he was looking at was his best mate; a fucking junkie, a heroin addict. His once fit body was covered with purple and red needle marks. What a fucking mess. Mickey had just lost it. He'd laid into him, punch after punch.

Mickey shook his head, fishing his lighter out of his pocket and lighting up another cigarette, carefully making sure no ash hit the leather seats. During the last year Stevie had become a contradiction of what the old Stevie stood for. There was nothing left, he'd lost everything. His girlfriend, his car, his home, his gold jewellery, his dignity, his self-respect. Every pound note he earned was spunked on that shit. It was killing him, and it was killing Mickey.

Stevie had always been proud of his body and had kept himself in good shape. He had had a great body rippling with power, solid muscle. Now he was an eight stone walking corpse, totally, completely and utterly fucked. Mickey smacked his fist on the steering wheel in frustration.

Mickey had vowed to kill the cunt who'd supplied him with the gear – Tony Barker – and he knew where to find the dirty piece of shit. He was serving it to kids his sisters' age and younger, who would end up like Stevie – no good, useless pieces of shit. Mickey was so protective, wouldn't hesitate to kill if anyone hurt any of his own. Stevie was family. This was personal.

That day last year, Mickey had driven over to the Gascoigne estate and parked up outside the high-rise block of flats where Barker, the drug dealer, lived, sat patiently and waited for a desperate customer to come along and knock on Barker's door.

Mickey knew the prick had at least ten locks on his door – if Tony saw his mush through the spyhole he'd never open it to him. Dangerous was well known. Mickey leaned back in the leather driver's seat and lit a cigarette, inhaling deeply, getting more and more agitated and wound up as each minute passed, waiting for a junkie to show up, his temples furiously pulsing. Then through the rear-view mirror Mickey spotted a well-known addict strolling along on his way up to the flat for his next bag of brown.

Mickey got out of the motor pretty lively and stalked calmly into the flats, adrenaline pumping through his fit body. The stench of piss and shit smacked him straight in the face as he walked through the doors, he wanted to chuck up as he felt the bile in his stomach beginning to rise. The putrid stink made him heave. Filthy shitty nappies lay scattered on the floor, faeces wiped on the walls, rubbish everywhere, graffiti, empty beer cans, broken bottles and dirty fucking needles and syringes littered the floor. What a fucking pisshole.

The dirty scumbag lived on the eighth floor. Mickey took the stairs two at a time, waited in the darkness of the corridor for the kid to come out of the lift and knock on the door. Mickey cracked his knuckles and clenched his fists as he stood rigid and tense. The predator waiting patiently for his prey. The young kid strolled out of the lift and along the corridor. Mickey watched him fidgeting at the door, shifting from left to right, desperate for his fix. Then he heard fumbling at the locks, the clicking and clunking of them unlocking. A smile appeared on his lips, warm with pleasure. Nothing would satisfy him more than to see this rotten low life suffer. He was as fucking bad as a nonce case, that piece of scum, a fucking scumbag heroin dealer.

The front door squeaked as it opened. The kid suddenly saw Mickey glaring at him from the shadows, and his face changed. Mickey could sense his fear, could smell it. 'Fuck off,' Mickey snarled at him. The boy legged it, shit scared, as Mickey barged violently through the front door, knocking the dealer back into the flat, clean across the small hallway.

Mickey walked over to him as he stood trembling against the wall. Crack. He head-butted the low life scum on the nose, smiling as he felt his bone crumble and the claret spray the walls. Mickey grabbed the cunt by the neck and smashed his huge fist into his face. His jaw cracked against his powerful knuckles as he was lifted from his feet; he reeled backwards, his limp body crashing against the concrete wall.

Mickey moved relentlessly towards him, grabbed a fistful of his hair, savagely twisted it around his hand, yanked his head violently back, forcing Tony to look at him, to stare into Mickey's eyes, eyes filled with anger and hate. This prick in front of him had destroyed his mate. Mickey's lips were drawn back into a snarl.

Mickey dragged him upright by the throat, his hands tight on his shirt collar as he pulled him closer. He stared at Tony, eyes rolling in pain. His jaw was broken and hanging out of place down the side of his face. Mickey took a deep satisfied breath. He could smell the scum – that malicious, gutless stench.

He glared at the cowering shitter in front of him, spat in his face as he gargled on his own blood, whimpering, begging and pleading with Mickey to stop. Slobbering like a fucking baby. Quivering, scared shitless. It only pissed Mickey off even more. Gasping for his breath, Tony screamed, 'No more,' through his smashed teeth. Mickey threw him violently back down onto the floor. He could feel his warm blood between his fingers.

'You cunt.'

Mickey's dark, dangerous eyes were twinkling as his boot smashed into Tony's ugly face.

'You no good ponce,' he said with another vicious kick in the bollocks. 'Dirty slag.' His mouth foaming. 'Low life.'

He kicked him again and again in the stomach and chest as Tony tried vainly to protect himself while all of Mickey's contempt, bitterness and hatred spilled out.

'You filthy fucking pig,' he said, his eyes twinkling with pure evil.

Mickey's mouth curled into a hateful smile. His face was cold and calculating. He reached down and grabbed Tony by the throat, forced his blood drenched head back against the wall.

Tony's features were smashed to pieces, his eyes dazed and colourless, as Mickey grabbed his lank greasy hair in his hands and repeatedly slammed his face into the wall. He threw him down again, leaned over him, his eyes twinkling with pure pleasure. 'Evil cunt.'

He stared into the demolished face underneath him and smiled. Time to finish the fucker. Mickey grabbed Tony by the ankles, dragged him out of the flat and along the landing, out towards the concrete stairs, leaving a messy trail of blood, gunk and slime behind him.

Mickey reached the stairs and paused. It was a long way down. Eight flights. He grinned with pleasure as he pulled the dirty piece of scum feet first down every step, his head cracking, smashing, splintering, banging all the way. Crack, crack, crack. One flight. Turn the corner. Crack, crack, crack, another flight …

When Mickey heard him die, heard him take his last breath, he felt better than he had in a long time. Tony deserved to die, and Mickey had done the world a favour by getting rid of that piece of crap.

He left him in a heap of blood and splintered bone at the bottom of the stairs, just another piece of rubbish for the bin men to take away, and strutted out of the high-rise block of flats towards his car with his firm shoulders pulled back and his head held high. He felt no fear, no remorse, just euphoria. He had taken one piece of shit out of this world.

But Tony was just the tip of the iceberg, the cunt who was giving Stevie the shit – there were others involved, weasely fuckers who were worming their way into the manor, selling their poison. His dad had allowed them in for some reason, let them spread their shit, but Mickey wasn't prepared to be so generous. He was going to take the fuckers out.

He knew who they were. Sean O'Sullivan, a family friend, and Robert Marshall, a prick who Sean had met inside. Mickey thought they were a pair of cunts, but Stevie swore they were both blinding blokes, both doing well for themselves, he told Mickey, earning a good wedge. He wouldn't have a bad word said about them. Nonetheless, Mickey had pulled Sean over one night in the pub and told him, 'Stevie's my best fucking mate. I love him like a brother, and if anything happens to him, I will hold you and that cunt Marshall fucking responsible, understand me?'

Sean had given Mickey his cocky grin. 'Course, Dangerous. He's my mate too, I'll look out for him,' but Mickey hadn't believed a fucking word of it. And Robert Marshall – he was even worse. From the moment Mickey had set eyes on Rob he hadn't trusted him one bit. Mickey had seen Rob out and about in different clubs and pubs lately, putting his face about, making himself busy, too busy for Mickey's liking. He hated the arsehole. He wouldn't piss on him if he was on fire. It was time to get them off the streets – off his streets …

A tap on the car window made him fucking jump. He glanced up – it was his mate Matt Feeley. Mickey rolled the window down. 'All right mate, I was in a world of me own then.' He pointed to his house. 'Go indoors and see me mum, there's a few in there already. Help ya self to a beer. I've just gotta shoot off somewhere. I won't be long.'

Matt patted him on the shoulder. 'OK, Dangerous, see ya soon.' Matt gave him a wink as he trotted off towards Mickey's house.

Mickey sighed deeply as he ran his fingers through his hair. He put the keys in the ignition then unlocked the passenger glove box. The .38 was safe, wrapped in a rag, with six rounds in a separate piece of cloth. Mickey moved them around and took out a brown envelope full of notes and put it in his coat pocket. He smiled to himself.

Satisfied, Mickey turned on the engine and pulled away fast onto the quiet road. Once he found Sharon and brought her home he could get on to the real business. The car gained speed as he splashed through the empty roads along the Heathway. He cruised along, weaving through the streets that he had known all his life. He loved the place, the friendliness of the people. He loved the pubs and the clubs. It was his home.

The events of the last couple of weeks had taken their toll. All the different things that had happened lately were swirling around in his mind. He was trying to piece it all together, make sense of it all. It wasn't just his dad's death – it had been brewing for a while. People were getting hurt; stabbed, blown apart, jobs were going tits up. Bobby's name was coming up too often, too close for comfort. Mickey had put the feelers out. He hadn't had a decent night's kip for weeks. He felt completely and utterly fucked.

He forced his mind away from the past and to the day ahead. Mickey had scores to settle. He had to keep his head clear, there was some shit going on out there. It was no fucking good sitting here feeling sorry for himself. He had serious responsibilities now. Suddenly he felt better, in control. He switched the radio on, turning it up full volume to take his mind off things. 'You'll never walk alone' blurted out. It was Bobby's favourite song. Mickey felt a lump in his throat. Suddenly feeling sick, he braked and pulled over to the side of the road, opened the car door and threw up.

Mickey smashed his fists on the steering wheel, screaming, 'You fucking cunt!' His shoulders stooped as his head bent on the steering wheel, his eyes raw with anger, disbelief, revenge and hurt.

When the tears finally came they were vicious. Mickey sobbed like a baby.

Sharon

Sharon Taylor and *Mags* Young staggered along the Heathway arm in arm, barefooted, their shoes dangling from their hands, splashing and jumping through the puddles like a pair of six year olds without a care in the world, singing Rod Stewart at the top of their voices.

'Wake up Maggie, I think I got something to say to you, it's late September and I really should be back at school.'

Sharon wiggled her slender hips from side to side, shaking her head backwards and forwards. Her long blonde hair waved in the cold wet wind. Mags clicked her fingers side to side in drunken rhythm.

'I know I keep you amused, but I feel I'm being used, Oh Maggie I couldn't have tried any more.'

Cocking their legs high in the air, oblivious to the world around them, they cavorted like Pan's People on Top of the Pops.

They'd been mates since infant school. Mags had always been a good friend to Sharon, always there when Sharon needed her and vice versa. Mags wasn't all tits and peroxide, the easy, convenient and willing slag that people thought she was. Sharon didn't know how she would have got along without her. Mags had gotten her out of trouble a few times and helped her through all the messes she had made. They told each other everything and shared their secrets. They would be friends forever. Mags was clever too, but she didn't give a toss about school and exams, she just wanted to leave school, start work and earn a few quid, find a rich bloke and have a good time. She lived next door to Sharon with her nan Betty, mum Jeanie and her two sisters, Patsy the eldest, Tracy the youngest.

'Look at the state of that.' Sharon pointed across the road to some old fat bird with her hair pulled tightly back off her face into a ponytail. The typical council estate face-lift.

'She's got TB.'

Mags looked at Sharon in confusion.   'What the fuck ya going on about? TB?'

Sharon gave a high raucous laugh. 'TB, Tits on her Belly.'

Mags laughed with her and hoisted her top up, juggling her huge tits in her hands. 'Oh, I've got a lovely bunch of coconuts dah, dah, dee, dah, dee, dah, dee, dah.'

They both fell about laughing. Neither of them could speak for a moment. They laughed so much tears were rolling down their faces. Sharon crossed her legs; she thought she was going to piss herself.

'Shal.you know ya knickers are like ya mates."

Sharon's eyebrows knitted together. 'Eh?'

'Well,' stated Mags, 'some crawl up ya arse, some are cheap and nasty, some are twisted, some are holey, some snap under pressure and then you've got ya favourites, and ya best ones.'

'Oh Mags ya silly bitch, ya really crack me up,' she said wiping the tears from her pretty face, trying not to laugh any more. Sharon plonked herself onto a wooden bench along the Heathway, tears of laughter still falling down her cold, rosy cheeks. Mags sat next to her still giggling in drunken stupor. Suddenly Sharon's tears of laughter turned to tears of pain and guilt and she flung her arms around Mags' slender neck. Sharon looked up at her friend; there was no longer a smile on her face or that sparkle in her eyes. Her eyes were downcast, sad and empty.

'I can't believe …' Sharon's voice was broken by her sobs, 'I got rid of me baby, Mags.' She spoke, struggling with her words, choked with grief and guilt.

Mags composed herself as she brushed away her own tears, then wrapped her arms around her best friend, who buried her head in her shoulders and painfully began to cry.   'Come 'ere girl, I'll always be 'ere for ya, don't ever forget that. I'll always be ya best mate.' Mags held her tight as she rocked backwards and forwards and patted her back softly.

Mags could feel Sharon's warm tears dampening her shoulders. She was gutted for Sharon, she couldn't stop her own tears from falling. Mags cried with her friend whose life had definitely gone tits up. She didn't know how she had gotten through it all. They sobbed in each other's arms. Sharon was crying for the baby that had been inside her, that had been part of her, that she had murdered in a sordid back street abortion. She trembled, consumed with terrible guilt. She hated Bobby, it was all his fault.

Sharon recalled the day, just a few weeks ago, when she found out she was pregnant. Fear had shot through her. Bobby would kill her if he found out she was knocked up. Sex was never discussed or spoken about in her house, it was a taboo subject, but she knew she couldn't have the baby and live – Bobby would have her killed, as well as the dad, the baby, even the midwife who delivered it. This was her worst nightmare. What the fuck was she going to do? How was she going to get out of this? She would have to go and see Paul Bailey, her bloke, and tell him. Surely he would know what to do? Everything would be all right, they could get married – they loved each other didn't they? She went to see him but couldn't believe what she had heard.

'You'll have to get rid of it, there's no other way babe,' he said looking into her sad eyes. He knew Bobby would have a price on his head and he would die the most slow and excruciatingly painful death imaginable if Bobby found out. 'What else can we do?' He pulled her close to him and put his arms around her, holding her tight.

Sharon shook her head from side to side, tears softly rolling down her cheeks. She wasn't hearing him right. She wanted his baby. She thought he loved her.

'Shal, ya know we can't get married or have the baby,' he sighed. 'Your ole man and ya brothers will have me dead and buried in Epping Forest if they ever find out.'

She couldn't stop shaking her head. She was shocked at what she heard. She wanted his baby, she loved him. She was so frightened, her voice quavered, 'I can't do it Paul.'

He told her he loved her, that she was doing the right thing and there was no other way. He knew a doctor who could perform the operation. She couldn't go to Rush Green Hospital – too many people knew her or her name, it would be too dodgy for them both. Bobby must never know. Paul told her that one day they would get married and have lots of kids; everything would be all right, but not right now. 'Don't worry, I'll be with ya all the way,' he said. Through her pain Sharon looked at Paul, her pale green eyes betraying the way she really felt. She sobbed in his arms as she agreed to the abortion.

It was a warm autumn day, a Saturday morning. Sharon and Paul thought this was the safest day of the week as Bobby wouldn't be around; he would be too busy sorting out the clubs and bar takings from the night before. Paul had always kept himself in good shape and was regularly at the gym on a Saturday morning; Sharon was always out with her friends, so Bobby wouldn't think it strange that she wasn't at home.

Paul drove to Barking. They never spoke a word to each other on the way, just complete silence, both of them lost in their own thoughts. They parked up in Longbridge Road and Sharon walked along in a dreadful cloak of sadness, her hands holding her belly, hot tears stinging her eyes.

Sharon was in a daze as Paul led her into a shabby little office with a horrible looking man, scruffy and dirty, who had the cheek to call himself a doctor. He stood in front of her and held out his hand, smiling at her, showing his crooked tobacco stained teeth. Reluctantly she shook his sweaty palm, noticing how filthy dirty his fingernails were. He turned as he spoke, 'Come this way,' motioning them to follow him.

Sharon followed the doctor, Paul behind Sharon. She couldn't go through with this, bile was rising deep inside of her. She felt hot one moment and cold the next, sweat dripping from her forehead. She wiped it away with the back of her hand.

Sharon was shit scared, she wanted to cry. Just looking at him made her want to vomit – she had to get away from this place, wanted to run away, go away forever.

'Paul, please I can't do this, take me home.' Her tear-filled eyes pleaded and begged him not to let her go through with it. He took her small hands gently into his and squeezed them tight, telling her that he loved her, and she was doing the right thing, then handed the doctor a roll of pound notes. The doctor turned away and began counting the money, then walked over and sat behind his desk, placing the cash in a drawer, before locking it and putting the key back in his trouser pocket.

He began moving and shifting things on his desk that was to be the operating table, making room for the tools of death. A long stainless steel instrument with rows of sharp ridges at the end, what looked like a huge crochet needle, and a long plastic tube. Sharon closed her eyes, this wasn't real, this was a bad dream and she would wake up soon. Opening her eyes she watched him getting everything ready.

Sharon lay on the desk, her legs wide apart on a saddle block, feeling like she wanted to die. There was no anaesthesia, just some strong painkillers. She lay motionless while the so-called doctor drove a sharp instrument deep inside her. She watched beads of sweat drip from his brow onto her as he squeezed the clamp, pulling really hard. Ripping her baby from her. She felt the cold steel instrument stabbing, scraping, prodding and pushing deep inside her. He squeezed the clamp, grasping and crushing her baby. Was it its arm, its leg, its spine? It was agony. She was a murderer.

Screams tore from her throat as the jagged-edged instrument yanked and pulled inside her. The pain was unbearable, she was being tortured, but she knew that what she was going through was nothing compared to what her baby was feeling. This was her punishment, her sin, she deserved it. She was bad and evil. Every slice and turn of the knife was like red-hot coals, such excruciating pain. Paul stood next to her as she gripped his hands tight.

'Paul, please help me, please help me,' she screamed at him as her tears and snot dripped down her face. Her young slender legs were propped up in the air and wide apart. She had never felt so embarrassed and ashamed in her life. She could feel something being yanked from inside her – first her baby, then the afterbirth. She was yelling, bawling, crying, screeching hysterically. She watched the doctor throw two red lumps into an old tin bucket and walk out the room.

Sharon sat upright feeling dizzy and light-headed. She looked down at her naked white thighs smeared with blood. Her stomach turned, she was heaving. She managed to get to the toilet before she threw up. The tin bucket was next to the toilet with her baby and the afterbirth waiting to be flushed away. A destruction of life. She was broken and degraded. A part of her died that day.

Through all of it she had begged Paul not to let her go through with the ordeal. He had the fucking cheek to stand there and watch her go through the pain and agony, telling her to stay calm, that she was doing the right thing.

After the abortion she tried getting in contact with him, but he wasn't taking her calls, she couldn't get hold of him. She hated him for putting her through the pain of the abortion. He didn't want to know her now – he had got into her knickers, got what he wanted and fucked off. The more she tried to find him the more he avoided her it seemed. She hated men, they were just after one thing, and as soon as they got it, they'd dispose of you like a piece of shit. He had lied to her, told her he loved her. Fuck men. She had her mates and she would use and abuse men like they did her.

A week before Bobby's death, Sharon and Mags were out at the Room at the Top, a nightclub in Ilford. She bumped into Darren Hendry, who was Paul's best mate. He stood next to her while she was waiting to be served at the bar. 'All right Shal? Can I have a quick word with ya?'

She smiled at him, 'Yeah course, what's a matter?'

'Shal, listen to me, Paul's nutty about ya and loves ya loads.' He took a mouthful of his pint.

'What the fuck you going on about?' She looked him straight in his eyes. 'Don't give me any bollocks. He fucked off without a word. He's probably shacked up with some old tart somewhere.' She took a large gulp of her drink. 'You've gotta fucking nerve standing 'ere telling me he loves me.' She hated Paul – he had made her get rid of the baby and then he got rid of her.

Darren swallowed deeply and looked gutted for her as he spoke, smoothing the hair from Sharon's tormented face and kissing her sympathetically on her forehead. 'He didn't want ya to know but ya dad paid him a visit …

~ ~ ~

Paul had just got back home from the pub, pissed after a few too many. He'd been drinking all day, drowning his sorrows, but he couldn't get her out of his mind, that look on her face when she begged him to take her home, not to let it happen, not to let her go through with it. That look would stay with him forever. He should have listened to her, but he didn't, he let her go through all that pain and suffering. He shivered at the thought. How could she ever forgive him?

He was sitting in his flat drinking a glass of whiskey when there was a loud knock on the door. He was so drunk, he just got up and answered it, not even thinking who it might be. By the time he saw Bobby Taylor in the doorway, an evil smile on his face, it was too late. His voice more than a whisper as he said, 'I wanna word with you,' and barged past Paul into the living room.

Paul closed the front door and then staggered in behind him. Bobby went straight to the bar in the corner of the room and poured himself a glass of scotch, stood sipping his drink as he took in all the details of Paul's flat. He walked menacingly up to him. Paul could feel his guts churning, wanted to run, wanted to vomit, wanted to be anywhere but standing face to face with Bobby Taylor.

'Nice place you've got 'ere Paul.'

Paul raised his glass, hand shaking, forced a word out of his dry throat. 'Cheers.'

Bobby stared deep into Paul's eyes, growling at him. 'Nice place to bring Sharon, my little girl, to. Nice place to shag the arse off her, you dirty little cunt.'

He slowly took the glass from Paul's hand, threw it against the wall, smashing it to pieces.

Paul knew he had to do something, say something, could see the poisonous anger building inside Bobby. 'Bobby it ain't like that,' protested Paul. 'I love her.'

Bobby seemed to think about this for a second, and for an instant Paul relaxed. Bobby swallowed his whiskey in one large gulp, suddenly grabbed Paul by the throat with one hand, smashed the glass into his face with the other. Paul dropped heavily to his knees, covering his face with his hands as blood seeped between his fingers. Bobby took a step forward, his face reddening with anger.

'You dirty cunt, fucking my daughter. You better stay away from her 'cos if you're ever anywhere near her sniffing around her drawers, I'll fucking kill you!' Bobby laughed as he grabbed Paul by his hair and repeatedly smashed his handsome face into the broken glass on the floor.

'Know what I'm gonna do?' he shouted, grinding Paul's face into the shards of broken glass. 'The dirty little whore needs to be taught a lesson. I'm gonna go home and I'll show the dirty slut what a good whore really does to a man. Then she'll be shop-soiled mate, and no one will wanna go near the filthy little bitch again anyway!' He laughed at Paul, lifted his head by the hair and smiled at his torn, blood soaked face. 'And when she sees your ugly face again, she won't wanna come near ya either.'

~ ~ ~

Sharon watched Darren walk away, felt the guilt wash over her. She had killed their baby, now Paul was seriously hurt because of her. Sobs racked her body. She hated Bobby but she hated herself more. Paul had been living in fear for his life, no wonder he gave her a knock-back. Sharon woke up most nights screaming, reliving the agony of that Saturday morning.

Mags cuddled Sharon closer, squeezed her tight to her. She hated seeing Sharon like this and there was nothing she could do to help ease her pain. Mags looked up at the winter sun as it disappeared behind the dark grey clouds. It looked as if the heavens were about to open.

'Come on Shal, let's get home and get ourselves sorted out before it pisses down.' Mags stood up and held her hands out to Sharon. They clasped hands and Mags pulled Sharon up from the bench. Sharon wiped her snotty nose with the back of her hand, sighed heavily, her heart aching.

They linked arms and began their sombre walk home. They stopped at the kerb to wait to cross the main road – a motor came roaring along the Heathway, roared past them, straight through a massive puddle right in front of them. The muddy rain arced up in a brown, muddy fountain, covered the pair of them. They were soaked from head to toe. They looked like they were in a wet t-shirt competition.

'Wanker!' Sharon hollered at the car, making the wanker sign with her hand. 'You fucking tosser!' she shouted, as she stuck her middle finger in the air yelling, 'Spin on that.'

The car screeched to a halt and some great big geezer jumped out of the motor and marched menacingly up the road towards them. They were both so pissed it was a minute before they realised who it was. Mags gave Sharon a quick nudge and whispered out the side of her mouth. 'Fuck me Shal, it's Dangerous – and he don't look very fucking happy.'

He was getting closer and closer, getting bigger and bigger with each step he took towards them. Mags sobered up as quick as lightning. He was a lairy fucker but she still fancied the arse off him, he was a bit of all right. But she knew he wasn't interested in her, he was with a bird called Mandy from Barking. They had been together for nine months so it was pretty serious.

'Get the fuck in the car the pair of ya,' he growled at them, his eyes twinkling with suppressed menace.

Sharon glanced wearily at him, trying to focus; she was totally out of it. She lit a cigarette, cocked her head to the side and studied his face in amusement, tossing back her drenched blonde hair off her pretty face. 'Fuck off.' Slurring her words, 'Who do you think you are, telling me what to do?' Pointing her long finger at him, she staggered forward, prodded him in the chest. 'You're not me dad, so fuck off.'

If looks could kill, Sharon knew she would be dead. Nobody told Mickey to fuck off twice. He grabbed her by the throat and pushed her head back against the wall. His strong hands were tight around her neck, his face close to hers. It scared her; he looked and sounded just like Bobby.

'You didn't hear me did ya? Get in the fucking car, now,' he ordered, shaking with rage. 'You dirty fucking tramp, look at the state of ya.' He pushed her roughly towards the car. She went arse over tit, falling heavily onto her knees on the pavement.

Sharon looked up at Mickey, screaming hysterically. 'I fucking hate you!' her face tight with rage. 'I wish it was you who was dead.' Her green eyes were moist with tears. 'You're a bigger cunt than him. You think you're the big I am? Ya know what Mickey, you're a big authority on fuck all.' Laughing at him, 'You even fucking get off on your own bollocks.'

'Do as you're fucking told and get in the car.'

Mags wanted to tell him to give it a rest. The poor girl was in mourning. She was bound to be upset and needed a good night out, but Mags decided to button her lip and keep her own counsel. She didn't want to be on the other end of Mickey's temper. She looked at Mickey. He was so handsome, with a gorgeous smile, yet looking at him now frightened the life out of her. His warm, friendly face was cold and callous. His soft brown eyes and soothing face suddenly changed. His face coloured slightly, his eyes were filled with anger and hate, half closed as he glared at Sharon. He was like Jekyll and Hyde, a deadly fucker. He could change from one to another in an instant. With Mickey's vicious temper, Mags thought Sharon had got off lightly.

Sharon and Mags looked at each other uneasily; nervously Mags struggled to help Sharon to her feet.

'Come on Shal, do as he says and get in the car.'

Sharon looked at Mags and then at Mickey, the pain and hurt in her eyes clearly evident. Her mascara was streaked all under her red, puffy eyes, her lipstick smudged round her lips. She looked like she was in 'Whatever Happened to Baby Jane'.

Mags and Sharon walked slowly to his car. Together, doing as they were told like naughty schoolgirls, heads down looking at the floor, they crawled silently into the back of Mickey's motor, travelled home without a word. But through it all, Sharon sat close to Mags, holding her hand as if she would never let go.

Sheila

Sheila emerged from a restless sleep, woken by the sound of the street door slamming shut. She felt like shit. For a moment she felt scared, she didn't know where she was. Then in an instant she knew, she was back at their old house in Dagenham. Johnnie had bought the place when they moved from Poplar, and Fat Jack had rented the house ever since Sheila, Johnnie and the boys had moved to Ireland. Johnnie was always backwards and forwards as he had a lot of work here with Bobby that needed looking after, so they'd all been staying with Fat Jack for the last couple of weeks, since just before Bobby's death.

She wished now that she could be back home in Ireland with her boys. Her boys. In this tangled web of a family they had always felt like hers, even before Sadie had been killed and she had adopted them. They were so young at the time that they didn't even remember their real parents, just like Sharon didn't remember that Sadie was her mum. With Sadie dead, murdered by that sick fuck Alfie, what else could they all do but rally round? Family took care of family, that's what all of the sisters had been brought up to believe, and so when one of them had died, the others had taken on their kids as though they were their own.

Sheila rubbed her eyes, she glanced at the bedside clock. It was an old relic that had been their mum and dad's, a wedding present, donkey's years old. 'Ten o'clock! Fuck!' Her voice was croaky and husky from too much drink and too many fags. Her heart throbbed furiously in her chest, her mouth was dry. She sighed deeply; she'd told Lizzie and Rosie that she would be there by now. Sheila felt tiredness wash over her. The mental conflict had kept her awake for hours; she'd lain in bed seething, aching with pain and misery.

Cautiously she raised her head from the soft pillows. Shit, it fucking hurt. Sheila tried moving but the whole of her body felt like it was made of lead. Her head felt heavy and tired, lethargy engulfed her. She slowly slid her left hand across to Johnnie's side of the bed – it was empty and cold. She instinctively glanced at the place beside her, where her husband should have been. Where was Johnnie? Then she vaguely remembered that Johnnie had arranged to meet Mickey at the office that morning to sort a few things out before the funeral in the afternoon.

Sheila smiled to herself – she was a young seventeen year old when she married Johnnie. He was everything she'd ever hoped for and more. She couldn't believe that in just a few weeks, on New Year's Eve, they'd have been married for twenty-five years. She loved him so much, they had a marriage filled with all the good things they had built and found over the years, a love they both cherished and respected. God, it only seemed like yesterday, it was scary how time passed by you by so quickly.

Sheila shuddered. Getting married was like death – you go in with your eyes closed, not knowing whether you're entering heaven or hell. Sheila knew where Lizzie had been all her married life, and realised how lucky she was to have Johnnie as her husband. He was the very opposite to Bobby Taylor, Lizzie's brutal, violent, aggressive, arrogant, demanding pig of a husband. She shivered. It hadn't taken her long to suss him out and see him for what he was. Her gut instinct had always told her that Bobby was no good, but Sheila had found out first-hand what an evil animal her sister had married. All Sheila had felt for him was hate. Bobby meant nothing to her and never would. Johnnie had always thought the sun shone out of Bobby's arse and would never have a bad word said against him. He would have killed Bobby if he'd known the truth.

Johnnie had slept like a baby all night, but she'd heard Fat Jack pacing the living room floor downstairs until the early hours of the morning. Something big was going down. Fat Jack never lost sleep over anyone, and it scared her. Sheila remembered the look on Johnnie's face last night in the pub; she knew something was wrong. She wouldn't ask, she knew he would tell her in his own time. She had a strange feeling it had something to do with Alfie Blake, and it frightened the life out of her.

Sheila lay back against the pillows and closed her weary eyes. She couldn't remember most of last night, she'd had too much to drink. Her mind was blank. She did remember telling Johnnie that she didn't want him getting involved with Mickey in finding out who was responsible for Bobby's death. She had told him that Bobby Taylor should have been hung, drawn and quartered years ago, that whoever was responsible had done the world a great fucking favour. If it was suicide, then it was the only decent thing Bobby Taylor had ever done for anyone in his entire life. He should have gone with the nine o'clock drop and not had this glorified pageant that Mickey had sorted out and spent a fortune on.

Delicately and slowly, Sheila got out of bed and wrapped her soft pink fleecy dressing gown around her slender naked body, sweeping her fingers through her untidy hair. She caught a glimpse of herself in the mirror; what a state she was in.

'Fuck,' she said as she put her hands deep into her dressing gown pockets and pulled out a packet of B&H. She felt so rough. Her hands were shaking as she lit a cigarette. Would the past ever be in the past? Bobby meant nothing to her then and he never had. All that had happened was a long time ago. She had learnt to tolerate Bobby for Lizzie's sake.

Sheila hated funerals. They always dragged up old times, memories good and bad. Just sitting and thinking, how we take so much in life for granted. Reflecting. Regretting. Questioning yourself, others, your life. Always realising too late that people are there one day and gone forever the next. No tomorrow to say sorry, goodbye, or I love you. The what ifs, the I should haves, the why didn't Is, the if onlys. Life, she thought to herself, what a fucking experience. How your world can change in a moment. Never ever knowing the mysteries of tomorrow.

Sheila paced up and down the bedroom, inhaling smoke deep into her lungs, trying to calm herself down. Her reflection in the mirror depressed her, what a mess she was.

She was here again after a good few years and fuck all had changed. The only difference was that on that fateful day years ago Johnnie was meeting Bobby and today it was Mickey. A clear and vivid picture of that was always in her mind. It was scary how time passed so quickly – it seemed like only yesterday that she had pleaded with Johnnie not to go away for a few days on a job. She didn't want to be alone in the house any more after what happened with Bobby. They had been arguing more and more, and it scared her.

'Please don't go tonight, Johnnie,' Sheila had begged, her voice heavy with emotion.

He sighed before answering her. 'I have to Sheila, I've got work to do, you know that. You want this as much as I do.'

'I take that as a no then?' Her voice was bitter, with a sadness in it that clutched her heart. She

Sandra Prior

couldn't tell him why she wanted him to stay, and it was tearing at her from inside.

Johnnie, with his dark hair and the good looks of the Irish, turned and walked slowly towards the window. She had thought that moving to Ireland was the equivalent of leaving London for the Garden of Eden. He'd laughed at that – she had only met his mother once, that was on their wedding day and she was on her best behaviour, Johnny had told her. If only he could see things from her point of view.

Johnnie could put the fear of God in the bravest of men. He'd gone into business with Bobby with his eyes wide open, knowing only too painfully about Harry Smith's shooting and Lenny Jackson's knifing. He didn't know then how many more corpses were on the way.

Sheila looked at Johnnie and noticed the expression on his face; she knew then that something big was going down. She knew the laws of the street, and she was scared. She loved Johnnie so much, he meant everything to her and she wanted him home at night, in bed next to her, close to her, safe, not in hospital, the nick or the mortuary. Her marriage to Johnnie had provided her with the best years of her life. He wasn't just her husband; he was her lover and her best friend. She had to get away from here. She hated being close to Bobby – he was always lurking in the shadows, his avaricious eyes following her everywhere.

Sheila and Johnnie had always wanted their special place in Ireland with their children. As she thought of them, a sharp pain spiralled deep inside her. She had wanted a baby so much it tugged at the core of her being, a sweet sadness mixed with all her other longings. Johnnie would get a proper job and he could have a reason to come home, not just work, work, work with Bobby. She trusted Johnnie completely and knew that he didn't play away from home – shit, if he ever did she would put a knife through his heart!

She drew impatiently on her cigarette. Sheila couldn't admit defeat. She wasn't pregnant again, and she knew how much Johnnie wanted a son of his own. In the early days, they had talked about moving to be near his mother, sisters and brothers. Their children would grow up surrounded by beautiful countryside with cows and sheep, fresh air and peace and quiet. Lush green grass and beautiful flowers, uncrowded, unspoilt, somewhere they could be happy and free. A big garden where their brood of children could play and wander in perfect safety. She could sit in front of a glowing fire reading lots of books, singing all the old songs and nursery rhymes. It would be wonderful. She could comfort them when they fell down, kiss them better and keep them safe from harm. She would have a family of her own who she could lavish her love on. For years, Sheila prayed daily for a baby to be inside her.

She remembered how she and Johnnie would lie in their bed with its big heavy wooden headboard. She was sure that the neighbours could hear them when they were at it during those long cold winter mornings, all cuddled up warm and cosy, draped in each other's arms, listening to the rain and the wind outside, safe and warm in their bed. They would make love constantly. Johnnie was a skilled and sensitive lover then and still was now. He'd never lost his touch.

They would share their hopes and dreams, whispering to one another when the world outside was still and silent. He would place his hands on her firm stomach as if their baby were already there. 'He'll be the most beautiful baby ever.'

Sheila had thought things would be just perfect, but Bobby was ruining all of that. She glanced at Johnnie that day and knew she had to get away from this cruel, sad, sadistic world they lived in.

'This is the last time. I promise hon, and then we'll be sailing across to the Emerald Isle, quick as a flash,' Johnnie answered in his cocky Irish lilt.

She had laughed sarcastically, 'That's bollocks Johnnie, and ya know it. How many times 'ave I heard ya say that?'

'For fuck sake Sheila, change the record. Hurry up and get your glad rags on or we'll be late for dinner.'

'You better run then darling,' she mocked. 'You can't keep ya master waiting.'

A cigarette hung cockily from her lips and a smirk spread across her face. 'Come on Johnnie,' she crowed, clapping her hands, 'chop chop. Chinese navy.'

She could remember clearly the way he looked at her that day. His face paled, but Sheila still carried on, she never knew when to button her lip.

'You're so far up Bobby Taylor's fucking arse, soon you'll be coming outta his tonsils!' she spat vehemently.

She saw his body stiffen at her words. He answered, frustration and anger sharp within him. 'Jesus fucking Christ, Sheila, I work my bollocks off for you, pay the rent, put food on the table and clothes on your fucking back. You get enough housekeeping to feed and clothe the fuckin' Red Army.' Silence. Glaring at her. 'I give you everything you ask for and more and you're still not fucking satisfied.'

Sheila exhaled loudly and angrily, her temper finally snapped. She smiled nastily at him. 'Well big boy, Mr Johnnie O'Reilly, the villain's friend.' Her hands resting firmly on her slender hips. 'I haven't got what I want and it seems you're not giving me what I want.'

She took a large gulp of her gin and screamed at him. 'I want a baby and there's fuck all wrong with me. So, sweetheart,' she said pointing her slim manicured finger at him, 'ya better start trying a bit fucking harder.'

She heard the bitterness in her voice and hated herself for it. Johnnie turned around and she flinched. So great was the contempt on his handsome face, she thought Johnnie was going to hit her. An expression of anger and fury dominated his good-looking features – he had such a thunderous countenance that it frightened her. She had never seen him look at her like that. Johnnie had a hot temper yes, but he had never laid a finger on her – a few walls and doors maybe, but never her. She knew her words had seared through him like a knife, then twisted. But he kept his clenched fists by his side, replied in a voice cold with hatred. 'Sheila, go fuck yourself.'

She knew she had gone too far, moved towards him pleading, 'Johnnie, please I'm so sorry, I didn't mean it. I love ya so much Johnnie I'm really sorry.' Her voice was full of pain and shame. She walked up to him and slid her arms around his waist and cuddled him. This always worked. In spite of the rows they had, they soon made up and things were back to normal again. They couldn't keep their hands off one another, their passion heightened through all of their trauma and difficulties. But not today. Her voice broke as she fought back tears, 'Please Johnnie, listen to me, I didn't mean it.'

She was sorry – she knew by the expression on his face that she had hurt him. He didn't respond, instead he pushed her away angrily, picked up his jacket and stormed out of the bedroom. The light died in his eyes. Hot tears pressed behind her eyes. She didn't know if they were for Johnnie or for herself.

She had punctured Johnnie's fierce ego and insulted his manhood and that was the last thing she wanted to do. But Johnnie would never talk about it; he would pretend everything was all right. She had prayed and prayed daily for a baby, but the months and years went by and still nothing. She must get pregnant soon. She hated her barren world. Everyone around her had babies, but not her. She wanted and needed to be surrounded by her own brood of children, she had waited years for her own family. Tears filled her eyes.

Sheila stood in the middle of her old bedroom and turned slowly around in a circle. So much had happened over the years. Sheila was left fighting back her tears, feeling hopeless and defeated again. The years might have flown by, time had gone so quickly, but though time can bring change, Sheila's feelings towards Bobby would never change. It was pure hatred for him that twisted and turned inside her every day; she would never forget what he had done to her.

Sheila felt a cloud of desperation sweep over her as the memories threatened to overwhelm her whole being. She didn't have time for this right now. Not today. She picked up her heavy gold hairbrush and hurled it across the room. It hit the wall and fell onto their double bed. Her throat tightened, tears prickled behind her eyes. 'Fuck, fuck, fuck!' she shouted, throwing herself on the bed.

She squeezed her eyes shut, trying to control her sobs. What a fuck up all their lives had been, and all because of one man, Bobby Taylor. An ache of unshed tears enveloped her. She seldom cried, she'd learnt that it didn't solve anything. She was glad Johnnie had left the house to meet Mickey; Sheila would never let him see her cry. She had to be strong and in control.

Sheila heard the street door opening, heavy footsteps stomping up the stairs.

'Auntie Sheila, it's me.' It was Terri, her voice soft and timid.

Terri put her head around the bedroom door. She had the beautiful skin of extreme youth and startling white teeth not yet scarred with years of abuse. Her eyes were normally cheeky and kind, but today they were filled with hurt and pain. 'Sheila! Are ya all right?' She could see the devastation in her auntie's face.

'Yeah, yeah I'm all right,' she replied, wiping her nose with the back of her hand. 'Sorry Terri, look at the state of me. I had a rough night and being back here's made me a little sentimental that's all.'

Sheila sighed inwardly as she moved her arms, beckoning Terri to come over to her. Terri smiled sadly at Sheila as she walked towards her. She was pale, hair uncombed, her eyes dark and hollow through lack of sleep. Last night's mascara was smudged heavily under her usually bright eyes. Her skin was dull, her mouth down and taunt. This was so unlike Sheila, she wouldn't answer the door or face anyone unless she was dolled up to the nines, her make-up always immaculate and never a hair out of place.

Terri sat on the bed next to her; Sheila put her arms around Terri and kissed the top of her head. She saw concern darken in her eyes and the coldness of her own fear mounted. Pressing her face to Terri's hair, Sheila felt her own warm tears slide down her cheeks. Silent prayers lingered in their minds. They were both crying but for different reasons.

Rosie

Rosie heard keys rattling in the front door. She felt a rush of intense relief. Thank fuck Sharon was home. Rosie had been up and down for most of the night pacing the floor worried about Sharon. She was waiting for Sheila to show up but she was late as usual, never on time. Rosie thought Sheila must have a bad hangover this morning as she had a right skin full in the pub last night – she must really be suffering.

As Rosie opened the door, Sharon tripped on the step and fell flat onto the hall floor. Mickey was right behind her. A look of relief washed over his face as his eyes met Rosie's. 'Take care of her, will ya Rosie? Dozy cow's still pissed as a newt.'

Rosie nodded. 'I'll get her cleaned up, don't ya worry.'

'Thanks.'

Mickey slammed the door behind him as he hurried out. Sharon looked up towards Rosie with a dazed, drunken smile on her pretty face. The smells of the night lingered on her clothing and on her body. She sat on the floor laughing loudly, her blonde hair flat on her head, dripping rat's tails. She was soaking wet and shivering. Last night's mascara smeared her eyes adding to the dark shadows. Her scarlet lipstick smudged all around her petite lips, her dazed and bloodshot eyes looked up at Rosie as she plonked herself against the wall for support. She opened her slender arms wide. Her voice slurred as she said, 'Auntie Rosshhie, come and gimme a shhnuggle, you're the only one who lovesshh me.'

Rosie looked at her with deep sadness in her eyes, knowing how vulnerable Sharon was. She held out her hands to her. She was a beautiful girl who had grown up hard and fast, not a child any more. It broke her heart to see her like this in drunken oblivion. Standing over her, she gazed down on this frightened, lonely and vulnerable young girl who was going through the most horrible crisis of her life. Rosie sighed deeply, shaking her head from side to side. Sharon looked like such a young and innocent child with her long blonde hair falling across her rosy cheeks. Rosie pulled Sharon up into her arms and gave her a gentle squeeze.

'Come on girlie, get up them stairs and sort ya self out before ya muvver sees ya.'

Sharon clutched Rosie's hand and grabbed the banister with the other, struggling unsteadily to her feet.

'You know I love ya don't ya, Rosie?' she slurred, staring up at Rosie and giggling. She stumbled forward planting a sloppy kiss on Rosie's nose, slobbering all over her as she spoke. 'Everyone's always telling me to sort me life out and enjoy me self. Well ya know what? I'm having a fucking good time.'

Rosie squeezed her hand gently, forcing a smile to her face, through the tears in her eyes. 'Come on, get upstairs and sober up. The priest will be here soon.'

Sharon stood still, looking at Rosie and raised her eyebrows in mock horror.

'A man of God in this house,' she said with a scornful laugh. 'What a fucking joke. The priests of the parish love us, the wonderful Taylor family 'cos we're making them rich. Fat Jack even fucking takes the parish priests to the bank with the church collection.'

Sharon's red blurry eyes sparkled as she gave Rosie a cocky wink. 'You wanna ask Georgie and Terri about Father Jim and why he's fucked off back to Ireland,' she said with a high raucous laugh.

Rosie watched Sharon's eyes, searching for the person who lived behind them. She swallowed down her tears; she could see the child beneath this young woman, frightened and alone, hiding behind a fierce bravado. 'Give it a rest Sharon; get up them stairs and get ya fucking arse into gear.' Hot tears stung her eyes; she turned away, what a fucking mess Sharon was in.

Sharon struggled to her feet, a cocky, drunken grin lighting up her face as Georgie, her eldest brother, appeared at the front room door. Days of dark stubble covered his tired face. He was a handsome, rugged man, quiet and respectful, lacking the natural aggression that was expected of him, but he was well known for his integrity and benevolence.

Rosie could see the bravado on his face; she admired him for the effort of it. Georgie and Mickey both looked like their dad, but had very different physiques. Mickey's body was powerful and muscular, the perfect boxer's build, while Georgie was tall and lean. The soft thickness of Georgie's dark hair, the boyish charm of his smile, and those serious deep dark eyes all added to his air of masculine appeal. He shook his head and sighed, watching Sharon wobbling backwards and forwards trying to balance on her platform shoes, paralytic. Georgie's bravado fell as he looked at them in utter misery.

Rosie smiled gently at him; he looked at her gratefully but couldn't return the smile. She could see the hurt in his eyes. She knew he had a lot on his mind, but she didn't know the half of it. 'Morning Georgie, there's a nice cuppa tea on the table for ya,' she said.

He looked like he needed something a lot stronger than a cup of tea. 'Cheers, Rosie.'

'You're meeting Mickey at the office before the funeral ain't ya?'

'I'm not going, Rosie.'

Rosie's voice was heavy with confusion. 'He's already there, waiting for ya to turn up.'

Georgie closed his eyes in distress, 'Something else has come up, but nothing for you to worry about,' he said with a loud sigh.

Rosie watched Sharon struggling up the stairs clinging to the banister, trying to focus on Georgie.

She stood still, sniggering as she looked from one to the other, standing face-to-face, staring at them both. The lifestyle the Taylor family led manufactured violence and danger. Rosie could tell by the look on her face that Sharon was determined that they wouldn't see the fear she felt inside.

'Don't fucking look at me like that Georgie, with that holier than thou look on ya smug face,' Sharon said laughing, pointing her long slender fingers at him. 'The official sinner, that's you!' She saw the hurt in his eyes and laughed louder. 'There's no holy light shining on you, Georgie boy!'

Sharon put her hand in her coat pocket and took out a can of cider. She pulled open the lid and took a large swig, spilling most of its contents down her chin. She wiped her mouth with the back of her hand. 'You might think you're God but I know you're a fucking Judas, so step forward with ya pocketful of lies. Tell the truth for once and stop pretending who you are.'

The bitterness in her voice wasn't lost on him. He didn't respond; the tears shone in his eyes. Rosie noticed how coldly Georgie had looked over at Sharon, like she was nothing, a two-bit whore. His disgust and the disappointment he felt was clear for them to see.

Sharon looked gutted. Her eyes flickering with rage, she licked her pert lips provocatively as a sarcastic smile appeared below her spiteful eyes. 'Oh Georgie boy, don't forget to say ya prayers.' She laughed high and mocking as she stormed into the bedroom, slamming the door viciously behind her. 'You're going to fucking need 'em,' she spat.

Georgie and Rosie looked at each other. Rosie saw the pain and sadness in his eyes – it was the same pain that she saw in the eyes of all the Taylor family. She squeezed his shoulder gently, swallowing down her tears as she spoke, 'Remember Georgie, when you're wondering what to do with ya life,' she said, pointing to her head. She moved her hand to her heart as she spoke softly. 'Take it from 'ere.'

Georgie looked at Rosie, his eyes unreadable. He kissed the tips of his fingers and put them to her soft lips. 'You're a good girl, Rosie.'

She gave him a quick and comforting squeeze. He turned and walked slowly to the kitchen, picked up a can of beer and lit a cigarette, then casually strolled out of the front door closing it firmly behind him. Rosie ran up the stairs behind Sharon. The enormity of what was going on hit her. She shivered. There would be murder tonight, she just knew it.

Mickey

Mickey strode into the Golden Palace restaurant, Fat Jack a step behind him. It was quiet at this time of day, just the sound of the cooks at the rear preparing the food for the day. The white tablecloths were already laid out for the lunchtime trade, the smell of grease and spices heavy in the air.

At the sound of Mickey's footsteps, Chen came hurrying out from behind the bar. He was in his late fifties, but looked far older, with a thin, cadaverous face, grey hair swept back into a widow's peak. "Ah, Mister Mickey! So sorry for your family!"

"Thanks, Chen."

Fat Jack whispered something to Mickey as they neared the back of the restaurant. Mickey stopped, looked at him. "You're serious?"

Fat Jack nodded. "As a fucking heart attack."

Mickey turned back to Chen, his face a mask of quiet fury. If Chen thought he was going to be a soft touch … "You owe us this month's money, Chen," said Mickey softly. Bobby's office had been in Chen's basement for donkey's years, and in exchange for the office space and a couple of grand a month, Bobby made sure that no other Chinese restaurants opened up anywhere near the Golden Palace.

"So sorry, Mister Mickey. It's been a bad month, all this rain …" He nodded back to the bar. A slim Chinese girl in a tight black skirt hurried out with a wodge of bills in her hand, held it out to Mickey.

"We have half the money, maybe have the other next week …" He looked pleadingly at Mickey. Mickey ignored the girl, ignored the money, turned to Jack. 'Did he ever pay me ole man late?'

Jack shook his head, his heavy jowls wobbling. "Never."

Mickey turned back to Chen, his eyes cold. "This is the first and last time you ever pay me late!" He looked at the girl. She was about sixteen, with long dark hair and a pretty face. Mickey's hand suddenly reached out and grabbed her wrist, pulled her towards him. "Each day you're late, you pay interest." He grabbed the girl, dragged her towards his office door.

"She's my daughter!" squealed Chen.

"I know!"

Chen started to step towards Mickey, but Jack put a meaty hand in his chest, stopped him in his tracks. Chen's protest collapsed as he watched Mickey drag his daughter into his office.

The office was small – a high backed chesterfield leather chair behind a large oak desk, a couple of old leather couches against the walls. Mickey stopped by the desk, looked at the girl. She was quite attractive if you liked that kind of thing. "On your knees!"

The girl's eyes went wide as she realized what Mickey intended. She didn't move.

"On your fucking knees, or I kill your ole man!" To emphasize his point, Mickey slid his knife from his pocket, slapped it down on the desk.

The girl took one look at the knife, dropped to her knees.

Mickey slowly unzipped his pants, smiled as her cool fingers wrapped around him, her warm mouth slid over the end of his cock. There were definitely perks to being the lord of the manor …

He thrust against her mouth, an orgy of lust and power surging through him, came in seconds, the tingling warmth radiating out through his limbs as he finished. He reached over, handed the girl a box of tissues. 'There you go sweetheart. Tell your old man that if he wants to take a few days coming up with the money, that's fine by me!'

She stood up, glared at him. 'Who the fuck you think you are?'

'Me?' Mickey grinned. 'Everyone know who I am. I'm fucking Dangerous, that's who I am!'

~ ~ ~

When the girl was gone, Mickey leaned back in his dad's chair. He looked deathly menacing in his carefully pressed black suit with his dark angry eyes as he looked around the office. All was quiet, but Georgie and Johnnie would be here soon, and he had serious business with both of them.

His fingers played with his gold sovereign ring on his left hand, then his initial ring – MRT – on the other. He was getting fidgety and finding it hard to sit still. He tried to resurrect his dad's final days, his final hours, his final moments. His deepest fear had been that Bobby might have shot himself, but never in his life could he see Bobby even thinking about killing himself, let alone actually doing it. And if Bobby didn't kill himself then who did, and why? Was it the start of a turf war, or was it closer to home? Was it one of the family?

Different things had happened lately, little things, big things. He racked his brains; he was trying to piece it all together before Bobby died. Who they were with, people they had met, places they had been. Deals that had gone down and ones that hadn't. A planned robbery had been delayed at the last minute because one of the boys never showed up. Other similar jobs were cancelled or put off. Bobby's income had plummeted over the past year. Some of Bobby's men were walking straight out on him to do jobs with other firms. Something wasn't right. None of it made sense.

Mickey had put the feelers out, his eyes and ears were everywhere. He had noticed that other organisations were still successful. His knuckles turned white he was gripping the arms of the chair so tight. Mickey's distrust and hatred was building up. He sat silently still, planning how he would exact his retribution. Mickey wanted blood and revenge for whoever was trying to fuck him up.

He couldn't be sure who was running it, but all roads seemed to be leading to the same two people – Sean and Rob's names were coming up way too often. Mickey picked up the phone and dialled Sean's number. On the third ring he answered the phone. Mickey didn't usually do business over the phone, but today was different. Today he had to get shit done.

'Sean.'

Sean recognised the voice 'Hello, Dangerous, what can I do for you?'

'I've got a parcel that needs to go to Suffolk this morning. It's very important. I want you and Rob to deliver it for me. You've done a lot of work for me ole man. He trusted ya both and had a lot of respect for ya.'

Mickey lit a cigarette, smirking, Bobby didn't have a lot of time for them; he thought they were a pair of wankers. 'It will be a nice little earner for ya mate.'

'Course Dangerous, whatever ya need, we're wiv ya.'

'Meet me at the yard within the hour. I've got you a motor here to get you up there. If you put your foot down you should get back in time for the funeral. Don't let me down Sean. This is very important.'

'We'll be right over.'

Sorted. Mickey hung up the phone, poured himself a large Pernod.

His uncle Johnnie should be here soon. He was a loyal man who would do anything to please Bobby. A decent bloke who everyone respected. He always supported his family and friends, they were important to him. His enemies feared for their lives, and time and time again he had proven to be loyal to Bobby and the firm.

Mickey's face grew more and more tense; the veins in his temples and neck pulsed, his teeth grinding. He glanced at his Rolex, sighing heavily; it was a present from Bobby on his eighteenth birthday. Georgie should have been here by now. Something was wrong, it didn't make sense, Georgie was never late, always punctual and on time. Mickey sat staring into space, his mind switched away from the unthinkable, the one thing he and Georgie never spoke about.

Mickey refilled his glass, swirling the liquid around. He lit another cigarette, inhaling deeply, dragging the smoke deep into his lungs. Mickey's presence created a stir in any room – he was the reincarnation of Bobby Taylor and certainly carried his genes. Mickey was good-looking and knew it. He was young, exciting and unpredictable. He lived a self-indulged hedonistic lifestyle, but was always loyal to his family and friends. His lean, strong, muscular body turned the heads of both men and women. He was extraordinarily attractive, but today he looked dangerous. Fucking dangerous. No one but his family called him Mickey any more. Dangerous was now his name. Power and control were his existence, his buzz, his amphetamine for life.

He gulped down the Pernod, emptying the glass, remembering vividly when they were just kids, the day he had learned his life's greatest lesson. Georgie was reading the Bible as usual. Mickey shook his head; he still couldn't understand how the fuck Georgie could believe in God and all the bullshit that went with it. It was all a load of old bollocks. What had God ever done for him or any of his family? Fuck all. There was no God in Mickey's life and never would be. Georgie was a soppy bastard, but he loved him.

He would never forget that horrible gasp of horror and the look of real fear that appeared on Georgie's face as they heard Bobby coming in from the pub, pissed again. Mickey never wanted to see that look on his brother's face ever again. They knew the sounds of the house. The stairs, floorboards, every door and every creak. The heavy drunken footsteps getting louder. Each noise told them where he was. They were always waiting and wondering what would happen next.

Mickey and Georgie had been in bed, tucked deep under the blankets, with Mickey's arms wrapped protectively around Georgie. They kept still and silent, pretending to be asleep, hoping that if they closed their eyes, he wouldn't be able to see them and it would all go away, they would vanish and become invisible. They would lie rigid and still, trying not to breathe, not to move, the two of them watching their world become more and more dangerous, night after night.

The door creaked slowly open, the landing light shone through the crack in the door. Then Bobby's huge shadow covered them with his darkness. He dragged the blankets off the bed, his face watching their every move as his ice cold eyes twinkled like the stars, bright and alive, dancing with pleasure. He grabbed Georgie by the throat, hoisted him out of the bed. Mickey took a deep breath as he heard the sharp crack as Bobby's huge left hand whacked Georgie, hurling him sideways against the chest of drawers, then a fierce right-hander smashed into Georgie's face, lifting him off his feet, knocking him to the floor. He curled up in a ball, covering his head, trying to protect himself as the claret gushed from his face.

Bobby turned, glaring at Mickey, and punched him in the face. Mickey didn't wince. He stumbled sideways, losing his footing, and then scrambled up quickly regaining his posture. Mickey squared his shoulders, took a deep breath and walked defiantly up to Bobby and stood in front of him. He'd had enough of this cunt he called his dad. Mickey looked Bobby in the eye, smiled and leaned forward closer, his arms open wide motioning Bobby towards him. He didn't remove his gaze from his dad's evil glare. Mickey had the same look in his eyes, his dad's twinkle, the twinkle that Lizzie had fallen in love with. Warm and loving, but the same twinkle that scared the shit out of you.

'Come on then you child-beating drunken cunt. If it wasn't for muvver you would be a fucking dead man by now,' Mickey hollered. 'Come on then prick, is that all ya can manage? Fucking hit me again, come on, do it.'

Bobby stood leering at him and snarled, 'You've made a very big mistake Mickey.'

Lizzie came rushing through the door begging and pleading with them to stop. As Mickey looked at his mum, Bobby threw a vicious left-hander. It caught him unaware and with such swiftness and force that Mickey fell to the floor cracking his head on the edge of the open bedroom door as he went down. He could feel the blood dripping down his face into his eyes, he couldn't see, his eyes were stinging. Bobby continued, cold and relentless. Mickey could taste the blood in his mouth as he ran his tongue along his cracked and broken teeth. Bobby's fists were merciless as punch after punch fell heavier and heavier. Mickey was doubled up on the floor gasping for breath, trying to get away.

Mickey finally scrambled back onto his feet and steamed towards his dad, blinded by the wet sticky blood pouring down his face. Mickey coughed, fresh blood and teeth sprayed from his mouth, splashing and splattering the walls. He thought he was going to die. He was dazed by the hiding he'd taken, his breathing was short and fast as the agonising pain seared in his stomach. He could hear his mum screaming at them to stop in the distance.

But Mickey had marked his card that day. If it hadn't been for his mum, the woman he respected and loved more than anything in the world, begging him not to hurt Bobby, then Bobby would have been a dead man long before now. But Mickey had promised his mum he wouldn't hurt him. Lizzie always defended Bobby, saying it was the drink, it was work, any excuse for him, always telling Mickey that Bobby was sorry and that he didn't mean it. Lizzie just blanked what he was doing to them all. Mickey took the licks and the good hidings, biding his time. He vowed to himself that he would get the no-good cunt, the day would come.

He shook his head, taking a very large gulp of his drink. His own fucking flesh and blood. There would be no white flag in Mickey's hands, he would go out fighting. He was used to it, could take it. Everyone had to take a good hiding and belting at some time in their life. The tears would always stay behind his eyes, he would never be weak and give Bobby or anyone else the pleasure of seeing him cry.

Eddie Jones, the next-door neighbour, must have heard Lizzie's screams as Bobby only stopped when Eddie appeared at the door and tried to drag Bobby off Mickey. Mr Jones must have wished he had never interfered as Bobby turned on him, frothing at the mouth like a rabid dog, a complete nutter. He dragged him outside into the street and around the corner, kneed him in the groin, smashing him in the head with his fist as he went down. He lifted his head by his hair and pulled his face to his knee, which was on the up. Fist after fist went into him as he lay there motionless, a blood-sodden body. Then Bobby's size ten Dr Marten stamped on his face, his head, his neck, his ribs, as he lay there sprawled on his back.

Mr Jones ended up in hospital for a long spell. No charges were brought – he told the Old Bill he was attacked on the way home from the boozer by a couple of blokes and Bobby Taylor scared them off, saved him. No-one dared testify against Bobby Taylor. The wall of silence. Nobody saw it, nobody heard it, and nobody spoke about it, therefore, it didn't happen, did it? Mr and Mrs Jones and their kids soon moved from the house, never to be seen in Dagenham again.

Mickey's knowledge of power and how to control it became his life's obsession. He knew his power over pain was stronger than pain itself, he simply didn't feel pain, not physical pain anyway. He would shout and swear with grief, and holler with anguish, and scream in anger and frustration, but if anyone punched him, whipped him, caned him, kicked him or slapped him, he would look at them and smile with that twinkle in his eye, just like Bobby, and make them tremble with fear. He had been walking in Bobby's shoes long before he was gone. Just being Bobby's son was a prerequisite for the job. Now it was official.

Sharon

Sharon staggered hiccupping into the bedroom she and Terri shared. She slammed the door shut behind her and leaned against it for support. She tried focusing – she needed to get into bed. Sharon felt like shit. Her sad, bloodshot eyes searched the room but all she could see was double of everything; the room was spinning, she felt dizzy and wanted to throw up. She wobbled backwards and forwards then tripped over a pair of shoes in the middle of the bedroom, falling flat on her face. 'Fuck that,' she spoke out loud, trying to get onto her feet. She managed to crawl slowly over to the window and heave herself up, gripping tight onto the windowsill.

She glanced bleary-eyed out of the window, wet with condensation, scribbled her name on the glass with her finger. She could remember when Terri and she were little – every Friday and Saturday night they would sit by the window with their bottles of Tizer and Bovril crisps, a treat from their mum if they were good girls. Even if they hadn't behaved themselves, Lizzie would still treat them anyway – she was as soft as shit, you could easily wrap Lizzie around your little finger.

They watched all the piss pots stagger and sway drunkenly home from the pubs and clubs, grabbing the lampposts and gates for support then chucking up in someone's front garden. Their legs would give way underneath them and they would fall knees over bollocks and stack it. Every Friday, Doreen does Dagenham, the local bike, would come along singing 'Show me the way to go home.' A Friday night never went by without them seeing her with someone attached to her arm. She would do anything for a beer, drunk and desperate. Doreen had had more pricks than a second-hand dartboard.

Sharon glanced at Terri's side of the room. It was always spotless and clean. She was the tidiest of anyone she knew, always had been organised and meticulous. Sharon's side always looked like a bomb had hit it. Sharon looked at Terri's bed; it didn't even look like it had been slept in. Terri wasn't there, as usual – the good little Catholic girl had gone to church again. She'd said yesterday she wanted to say her goodbyes and some prayers. What a load of old bollocks, she was hoping that Father Jim had returned from Ireland for Bobby's funeral, hoping she would see him at the church.

The sweet little Miss Innocent that everyone thought she was, the nice quiet little girl, Terri, the perfect daughter, the perfect embodiment of Lizzie's virtues. She even looked liked Lizzie, with her soft skin, wide blue eyes and long raven hair. She'd always been their mum's favourite and Lizzie always defended Terri. Anything and everything that happened was always Sharon's fault, never Terri's, she could never do a thing wrong in Lizzie's eyes. Prayers? Yes they all needed them now.

Sharon grinned drunkenly. Terri, the perfect one, had been shafting Father Jim. He was a bit of all right for a priest, she wouldn't mind shagging the arse off him herself; if it weren't for his dog collar you would never believe he was a priest. What a waste of a good man – he was always dressed in normal clothes, always dressed immaculately in the top named gear, he was really trendy. He was well liked by all of the people in the parish, young and old, raised a lot of money for charities and his parish.

Father Jim became a very close friend and confidante of Bobby's. She remembered how Bobby and the priest would often have very lengthy and private talks at home, long into the early hours of the morning. She wondered what they could be talking about. There must have been some special bond between them that encouraged Bobby's trust, Bobby never really trusted anyone but himself. There were some exceptions – some family and a few friends – and it seemed that Father Jim was one of them. But despite his worlds with the priest, Bobby went to bed with a gun underneath his pillow every night.

She wondered how Father Jim could just sit there chatting to Bobby knowing he was giving his daughter a good seeing to. The dirty old fucker, he must have been thirty odd, but he looked good for his age. Did he get on his hands and knees, asking and praying for forgiveness, promising not to do it again? Until the next time. And he had the fucking cheek to preach and tell her about her immoral and inappropriate behaviour.

Father Jim was an active fundraiser for the parish and the local community. Bobby would always give him an envelope full of money when he was organising or involved with a charity event. The local maternity unit, the hospice, the old people's home, the nuns and the convent schools and the Salvation Army. You name it; Bobby was involved somewhere along the line.

Every Christmas, Bobby would give him two envelopes filled with money. One for his own personal use, the other for the parish. Bobby had many strong and influential friends within the church; Father Jim had even paraded around the courts with Mickey. What a good, honest Catholic boy he was, from a good law-abiding family, who worked hard within the church and for the various charities the church supported. Father Jim had also saved Mickey from a few years inside, courtesy of the Queen, twice at Snaresbrook and once at the Old Bailey. She laughed to herself. Mickey had been breaking the law since before he had a hair on his bollocks. Mickey was so bent he wouldn't sleep straight even if he was nailed down.

Father Jim had been giving Sharon lessons at home and trying to calm and control this difficult and disruptive child. She knew they talked about her as if she was a nutter, a demented kid with severe psychological and behavioural problems. What a fucking cheek they had. She had been expelled from her local school for bunking off and getting caught smoking. She was always cheeky to the teachers, giving them loads of lip and disrupting the class. They couldn't accept her behaviour any longer and she was expelled. So what, it was no big deal.

Father Jim spent weeks at Bobby's expense shuttling backwards and forwards to the posh convent school miles away, trying to convince the school, its governors and other officials that she should be accepted in spite of her poor school record and behaviour. Father Jim did what he had to do, and with the additional help of a brown envelope she was soon accepted into the school.

Sharon didn't want to go; she hated it already and she hadn't even started there yet. She would do anything possible not to go, but Bobby would have none of it, he said he wanted the best for her. She screamed and shouted, but Bobby said she was going and that was that. No discussion, no compromise, whatever Bobby said, you did. There was no crying, no weakness, no laziness, no pleasure. Just duty, discipline and control with Bobby.

The school was isolated and miles away from home, she had to get a train and then get on the school bus from the station. She remembered her first day at the all girls' school as she entered the massive building dressed in the horrible sickly green uniform.

It was vile and disgusting. Sharon thought she looked a right prat in it; she would never let any of her mates in Dagenham see her dressed like that, they would right take the piss out of her. Her stomach turned over in somersaults. She just wanted to throw up and go back home to the comfort of her mum's arms. She had begged her dad not to send her to the school, she kicked and screamed, but Bobby told her he wanted the best for her and she was going. Her eyes flicked from side to side and up and down, her mouth was wide open trying to cope with it all. It was so big with gleaming oak floors, a long winding staircase leading to dark, cold corridors.

The school attracted people who had a few bob, and parents who were respectable and in proper jobs and proper lives. All the girls' dads were politicians, doctors or lawyers; they were all from wealthy and professional families. Their parents would have a fucking fit if they knew what her dad was involved in and got up to. Sharon detested the school and everyone in it, they were all silly posh tarts who'd had everything handed to them on a plate, they didn't have a clue about real life, the real world. She wasn't going to stay there, she was going to get herself expelled from this poxy school pretty lively.

She started really fucking about at school, her results were low and she was causing mayhem and chaos. She bunked off all the time. Bobby had Fat Jack drive her to school every day. He would watch her walk through the big iron gate, she would turn and wave goodbye with a beautiful smile on her face.

Satisfied that she was there inside the school, he would drive off. She would go into her class, get her registration mark and walk straight back out of the school gate.

Sharon had only been at the school a few weeks when Sister Mary, the snotty old cow of a headmistress, contacted Bobby and insisted that he came to the school immediately as it would be in his best interest if Sharon left the school. Bobby was in her office as quick as lightning. He wanted his daughter at this school and she was going to stay there. Bobby always got his own way.

She remembered walking into the office with her dad that day. Sister Mary sat behind her desk in the small stuffy office, which stank of mothballs. She was sitting stiff and upright, her hands clasped together resting on the desk in front of her, twiddling her thumbs. She made it clear without saying it directly that she knew exactly who and what Bobby was. She reminded him of the long unblemished history of the school, how important its reputation was, and what would happen if the school received any kind of bad publicity.

Not once did she say, 'I know you're a villain and your daughter should leave because of your reputation.' But Bobby now knew where she was heading and what game she was playing. He was no fool.

'I understand, Sister Mary, that my daughter Sharon has been having a very hard time here, hasn't she?' he asked in his best, put-on well-spoken voice.

Sister Mary nodded with a frown, still obsessively twiddling her thumbs, and looked at him as if to say, Mr Taylor, haven't you listened to a word? I don't want your daughter in my school.

'Sister Mary, what do you think we should do about this?' he continued. 'You know I want the best for Sharon. I'm willing to pay you to see that my daughter improves in her behaviour and her studies.'

Sister Mary, the crafty cow, lost no time in grasping the opening Bobby had provided for her. Sharon saw the slight smirk on her dad's handsome face. He could read a person like a book. He knew every person had a price, a want, a need. Bobby could have sold the Pope a double bed, he was a superb judge of character. Sister Mary didn't waste any time moving in on Bobby. 'Maybe Sharon's work could be brought to the school's achievement level and then she could stay at the school. Of course this would mean extra tuition and resources, which would be extremely costly.'

Sharon sat and watched Sister Mary – her eyes were wandering all over Bobby. She saw a slight smile appear on her stern face as she listened to him. Sharon wondered what Sister Mary was thinking as she studied Bobby. Did she think he was a good-looking and charming man? Or did men repulse her? Was she a lesbian? Did she ever think about having sex, what it was like, whether she was missing anything? She looked so miserable – a good seeing to was what she needed, that would put a smile on her miserable face. Maybe that's why she always looked so unhappy.

Would she be lying in her bed tonight thinking about Bobby fucking her? What a sobering thought, Bobby and Sister Mary shagging.

Sharon went back to school, but it didn't last long. Her form teacher, Miss Mahoney the stuck up bitch, carried out a class desk search and found twenty Dunhill International in Sharon's desk. The teacher tried to embarrass Sharon and make her look small in front of all of the class.

She made her stand up. Picked up the packet of cigarettes and showed the class. 'Filth, that's what these are. Pure filth.' Holding the packet in the air, 'Think it makes you look big do you Sharon, cool, hard. Well let me tell you its trashy, tarty and disgusting, just like the girl smoking them.' Silence fell over the room. 'They say you can take the girl out of Dagenham but not Dagenham out of the girl.'

Sharon looked her teacher in the eye and laughed at her. 'What a fucking cheek you've got to call me trashy, tarty and disgusting. I dunno who you think you are but I wouldn't wanna be your sweetheart not in a million years, especially when Mrs Hallmark finds out what you've been doing to her ole man in the library storeroom. You're the fucking disgusting trashy old tart.' Sharon walked out of the school and never went back.

That's when Father Jim began his boring private tuition with her at home. Terri, the lucky bitch, was studying the karma sutra with Father Jim and Sharon got stuck with maths, English, religion, history and geography.

But the private lessons stopped soon afterwards when Father Jim suddenly disappeared – apparently he'd gone back to Ireland. Sharon thought Bobby must have found out about Terri and Father Jim and he thought he'd better get back to Ireland before Bobby got to him first and killed him. Knowing what he knew about Bobby, he would have known what kind of death Bobby could give him. Sharon didn't tell Bobby about them and she knew Georgie would never open his mouth, but Bobby had eyes and ears everywhere.

Sharon climbed on top of her crumpled bed and closed her eyes – her head was spinning, she wanted to throw up. She would never know or understand her father. She remembered how it was when she was a little girl, she loved her daddy. He would take her to the library and get lots of books. He was a clever man and had always valued learning – he would make her recite poems and quotes, and when she went out with him she was always meeting new people. Bobby knew someone everywhere; he was so outgoing and friendly. Then things changed, but he was dead now and he couldn't hurt her any more. But she was so desperately lonely. She hated herself. What a fuck-up her life was. She loved him, she hated him, she was afraid of him. She was so confused.

She felt weak with emotion as she lay back on the soft white pillow, hot tears stinging her eyes – she blinked, trying to get rid of them. The potent odour of men, beer and smoke wafted from her, deep into her nostrils, laying bare their grubby reality, a life full of sordid horror, full of murders, ponces, whores, alcoholics, junkies and all the other pieces of shit they called family and friends. She felt the desperation wash over her, the events of the past few weeks showing with awful clarity upon her pretty face. Everything she had left was gone. Sharon knelt down by the side of her bed, shuddered. It was bloody freezing in the bedroom. She rummaged around under her bed amongst the rest of her tut and rubbish. Throwing out a pair of tights, a crisp packet, a chocolate wrapper, a pair of knickers, a half eaten bit of cake and a sock… There it was, finally. A bottle of vodka.

A smile appeared on Sharon's solemn face, she wasn't alone anymore. She opened the vodka and took a large swig, she felt better already. She was dreading today. She had loved him, wasn't that enough? She couldn't understand what he did or why – why had her loving father turned on her as she got older? She hadn't asked to grow up, to grow a pair of tits, to become a young woman, but with each passing month he had become colder and colder towards her. Instead of a smile and a cuddle he greeted her with harsh words, insults, sometimes even the back of his hand when she got cheeky or answered him back.

But through it all she loved him – he was her dad, what else could she do? But she hadn't had a chance to say goodbye and tell him how much she loved him or how sorry she was. It was all her fault they were in this mess – she shouldn't have wound him up, gone off the rails. Why? Why? Why did this have to happen? The selfish arrogant bastard, he hadn't thought about her and how she would get through it all.

Sharon slumped down into her bed, so desperately lonely. She sank deep under the covers with the blankets pulled tight under her chin, letting it all sink in. No matter what she did, she couldn't stop thinking about him. It wasn't just her he had turned on. How could he have done all that he did to each of them? To Lizzie, to Georgie, Mickey, Terri – to Martin. How could he do it to her? He'd loved her once, she was his daughter, his flesh and blood. The whys and ifs were endless and it really didn't matter anymore because he was dead and gone forever.

She blissfully swallowed the neat burning liquid, closing her eyes as she savoured the moment. It took away all her misery and pain. She lay motionless. Sharon had an overwhelming desire to be loved. The thing she lacked and so desperately needed was denied, gone. She picked up her bottle and hugged it protectively to her chest, spiralling into drunken oblivion. She lifted her bottle of vodka to the ceiling, smiling as tears rolled down her cheeks, sobs shaking her thin body. 'Thank fuck you're dead, I hope you burn in hell and suffer like me for all eternity!'

Then she buried her head deep into her warm pillow, wet with wasted tears. Rage, desperation and depression overwhelmed her, so raw and desperately lonely, sobbing quietly in her utter wretchedness.

Mickey

Mickey finished his drink in one gulp, stared at Johnnie O'Reilly as he strolled through the office door. Johnnie was a man of immense power and influence within the East End underworld, fit, sharp, with a good business head in their world of cheating and lying.

As a kid, Mickey had always looked up to Johnnie, loved seeing him when he came over from Ireland. He would always give him and the others money when no one was looking, or slip it in their coat pockets, put his finger to his lips indicating silence. Johnnie was never short of a few bob, always well-dressed in his Savile Row suits and black brogues. He was a good down-to-earth geezer, who you never took a liberty with. Mickey remembered feeling like the dog's bollocks when Johnnie used to sit him on his shoulders and walk round Romford market, striding though the busy stalls full of people, hollering and shouting, selling their goods.

Everyone knew Johnnie O'Reilly, and they'd always come home with loads of bags of food and other gear, though he hadn't put his hand in his pocket or spent a ha'penny. Sharon and Terri loved him too; they would run and jump on his lap, fighting for his attention. They all loved going over to Ireland for a holiday with Johnnie and Sheila. Johnnie always looked smart in his white starched shirt and tie as he sat and told stories about what he and Bobby used to get up to.

Mickey acknowledged him with a frown as he walked in. This was going to be hard. 'All right, Johnnie, what the fuck's going on?'

Johnnie shrugged. 'I told you last night I ain't got a clue what you're talking about.'

Mickey smiled and nodded, poured another large Pernod, pretending to give this some thought while staring into space behind Johnnie. He stood up, flicked imaginary dust from his strides while his ice cold eyes switched, and fixed on Johnnie. Then Mickey leaned over the table, hands on the end of it, face flushed, eyes intense. He pointed his finger at Johnnie.

'Listen you ugly cunt, don't take me for a mug. What's Sean O'Sullivan been mouthing about me ole man fucking up some big drugs deal?' He glared at Johnnie, 'And was he shagging Rob's missus?'

Taking another large gulp of his drink, he walked around the side of the desk, bringing his huge fist down onto the polished oak surface. 'Don't mug me off, you slag, not today. Not any fucking day. I want some fucking answers. Now.' His menacing eyes stared at Johnnie. He took a long slow breath. 'Who fucking set me ole man up? Who wanted him dead? Who the fuck are ya keeping quiet for?'

Johnnie shook his head slowly. 'Dangerous, I know as much as you do.'

Mickey shuddered in silence as his fists clenched and unclenched at his side. He calmly walked towards Johnnie; his eyes twinkled at him, burning through him, questioning him. Mickey stood erect, face-to-face with Johnnie, smiling as he pulled a .38 from his pocket and put it to Johnnie's temple. The dark metal gleamed dully in the grimy office.

Johnnie laughed, his eyes never losing their cold edge. 'Leave it out, Dangerous. I'm part of the family. I want the cunt who did this as much as you,' he replied calmly.

Still smiling, Mickey could feel the adrenaline pumping through his veins, that beautiful feeling of euphoria. He wiped his mouth with the back of his hand, and then shoved the gun's muzzle hard into Johnnie's ear with the other. 'Tell me who's fucking responsible.'

Still Johnnie didn't react. 'I've told you, I know nothing. Let's stop fucking around and get to your dad's funeral. Once today is out the way we'll sort it.'

'Tell me again Johnnie,' said Mickey, 'just to reassure me, that you know nothing.'

'I know nothing,' said Johnnie evenly.

Mickey's eyes narrowed in suspicion, he trusted no one. 'You sure Johnnie?'

Johnnie simply glared back at him, not a trace of fear in his eyes.

Click! Mickey pulled the trigger.

No bullet.

Mickey laughed, opened the gun, showing that it was unloaded. 'You've always been a lucky fucker, Johnnie,' he said, poking him hard in the chest. 'But some fucker killed me dad, and I just had to be certain I could trust you.' He held out his hand. 'Still mates?'

Johnnie grasped Mickey's hand and squeezed it firmly. 'Always.' Suddenly he pulled Mickey in close to him, their faces just inches apart. 'I'll give you that one for free,' he hissed, his eyes boring into Mickey. 'It's your dad's funeral and I know you're upset. But if you even pull a stunt like that again, the gun had better be loaded!'

Mickey pulled free, adjusted his cuffs and straightened his tie. 'I'm gonna find out who killed me fuckin' dad today, Johnnie.'

Just like that it was all over. Johnnie looked as though it had never happened. 'Of course.'

'I've got a job for you.'

'Whatever you need, Dangerous.'

Mickey leaned forwards, whispered something in his ear.

Johnnie's eyebrows went up in surprise, but by the time Mickey had finished speaking, his face showed no reaction or emotion at what Mickey had just told him. 'I'll take care of it.'

'Course you will.' Mickey looked at Johnnie with his dark eyes, the same look as Bobby as he pulled a packet of B&H from his pocket, lit a cigarette, drawing it in deeply. 'Don't ever doubt me Johnnie boy. No one, and I mean no one, fucks with this family.'

He threw the office keys onto the desk. He had to get moving. He hoped Betty and Jeanie had done a good job with the food. He had to see Pete to make sure the DJ was definitely coming and give him some money for the bar. He strolled casually towards the door and shouted over his shoulder to Johnnie.

'I gotta go, Johnnie.' He smiled. 'Everyone will fink you're in 'ere sucking me dick.' Mickey walked out of the office with a merry twinkle in his eyes.

Johnnie laughed as he watched him strut out. So like his ole man. 'You fucking wanker, Dangerous!' he called after him, shaking his head.

He perched on the edge of the desk, ran his hand through his thick, dark hair, poured a large glass of whiskey and gulped half of it down, then slumped back in the chair and lit a cigarette. Finally he raised his glass to the ceiling, 'To absent friends.'

Terri

'Come on.' Sheila held out her hand to Terri. 'I fink we both need a nice cuppa tea. Let's go downstairs. I'll put the kettle on, run a bath and I'll get meself ready. Then we can go to your house.'

They held hands and quietly walked downstairs. Sheila went into the kitchen and Terri walked into the front room, closing the door behind her. She sat beside the huge fire, holding her cold hands out to the heat. She began rubbing her hands together trying to warm herself up; she was bloody freezing. She stared into the flames, mesmerized by the glowing coals.

She spotted Caesar, Fat Jack's old Staffordshire bull terrier half asleep in his bed. 'Hello Caesar,' she said as she patted the side of her slim thighs. He stretched with a great big yawn and sauntered sleepily over to Terri, wagging his tail with excitement as she bent and stroked him. He jumped up to her, all eager for a fuss and a tickle. His large chocolate eyes were shining bright.

'Get down ya little rascal, look at the state of me.' Fat Jack must have already taken him out for his morning run over the chase, because his paws were covered in mud – it was smeared all over Terri's leg. Terri smiled tenderly at him.

'You little sod, get down.' She pointed to his basket. 'Back to bed.'

Caesar looked at her raised eyebrows as if saying, you just woke me up, got me out of my nice warm and cosy bed and that's all I get? He ambled lazily back, closed his eyes and snuggled back down into slumber.

Terri's anxious eyes watched the fire. She sat silent and still, staring at the flames spiralling high, hypnotically dancing in a violent rage, jumping fiercely, hissing and spitting. Just as Terri felt inside, so much anger and hate for herself, no confidence, no feeling, only pain, poignantly aware of her own self-victimization. She prodded the poker into the blazing fire. The fire overwhelmed her. Only emptiness remained.

Terri glanced up at the mantelpiece to a photo of Fat Jack and Caesar. He loved his dog so much – Caesar went everywhere with him, he was always by his side. Fat Jack had been Bobby's best mate for years; they'd met one another in prison. He was a great big lump of a geezer with a vicious right-hander. The sheer size and strength of him was phenomenal, but despite his enormous weight, he had a good-looking face with kindness in his eyes. His size overwhelmed you, as did the warmth of his friendliness and his broad infectious smile. He was a friendly, down-to-earth man with old-fashioned values. He wasn't a bully who enjoyed knocking people out for the fun of it, he was well respected with a reputation for being fair but firm – a proper gentleman from the old school. He was polite and thoughtful. Terri loved him loads.

Terri remembered when he used to pick her up and cuddle her when she was a little girl, lift her into his big strong arms, make her feel liked and important. She always felt safe when Fat Jack was around. All in all, Terri thought Fat Jack was a nice geezer. He was always with Bobby and spent a lot of time with all of her family, any occasion, birthdays and Christmases.

Terri loved Christmas, she loved the carols, decorating the Christmas tree, even the weather – those ice cold frosty mornings, the long dark evenings where the stars twinkled brightly in the cold dark night. And if it snowed, everything turned white and beautiful. It helped her to conjure up her little girl's fantasy Christmas. Terri would glimpse beyond the here and now and imagine and create her own winter wonderland capturing the pure magic of Christmas.

A season thick with love and kindness, a time to give your heart to everyone. A time for reflecting on friendship and love where unselfishness thrives. Those warm nostalgic images of family get-togethers at Christmas filtered through her mind, all huddled around a glowing open fire with the dog curled up right in front of her, all cosy and warm, or fast asleep, snoring with a Christmas hat placed on her head. All singing the familiar songs they all knew so well, the fire illuminating the room as the wind whistled sharp outside. Carol singers could be heard in the distance as Christmas bells chimed, the living room filled with shouts of happiness and glee, laughing and joking together, playing games. Love and laughter all round to give and receive, a quick kiss under the mistletoe, everyone together having lots of fun. Happy.

A spectacular Christmas wreath hung above the fireplace covered in holly and ivy, red poinsettia and gold pine cones, its crisp, clean, fresh fragrance filling the air. The loud cracking and banging of the Christmas crackers being pulled. The soft glow of the candles burning and those irresistible aromas wafting from the kitchen. The sweet fragrance in the air, the turkey and the beef roasting in the oven, mince pies and lots of sweets and cakes, all so wonderful and exciting.

A huge real Christmas tree decorated with golden bells and baubles, deep red ribbons overflowing on a tree with golden tinsel, glistening brightly, the lights twinkling and flickering softly and gently, giving a warm festive glow, a beautiful angel sitting on the top of the tree. Lots of presents piled high under the Christmas tree, beautifully wrapped with coloured beaded organza ribbons and bows; a row of hand-made Christmas stockings, their names embroidered on, hanging along the mantelpiece. The mince pies and a glass of sherry all ready to leave out for Santa, with some carrots and milk for his reindeer.

This was her warm and cosy dream that kept her safe from the outside world, that helped turn her darkness to light. All a fantasy …

She remembered as a little girl, another one of those Christmases when her daddy wasn't coming home. Terri knew he was inside, but Lizzie always told them he was at college or working away, never told them the truth of where he really was and why. Terri would look up to her mum, watching the tears roll down her cheeks.

'Is it 'cos I've been a naughty girl again Mummy? Is that why Daddy's gone away again?' Her bottom lip trembling. 'I know Daddy doesn't love me.'

Lizzie looked down at her from the butler sink with her red, tearful eyes. She wiped her wet hands on her apron, wiped the tears from her face, bent down and hugged Terri tight. Told her not to be silly, her daddy loved her, he was just away at college to learn new things, that's why she had to be a good girl at school and learn lots. Then she could tell daddy all she'd learnt when he came home. Lizzie stroked her hair away from her face and kissed her softly on her forehead.

Terri looked at her mum; she always looked so old and tired. Not like her auntie Sheila who always had a smile on her pretty face and looked so youthful and beautiful.

When Bobby was banged up, times were hard. Lizzie always worked to put food on the table and make sure they never went hungry. She always stretched what they had and would go without herself to feed the kids. She made sure they looked clean and tidy, even though they wore hand-me-downs and church jumble sale stuff. It was never easy for her. Lizzie would spend hours scrubbing the floors, cleaning the windows, and the front doorstep was always gleaming. Whenever she wasn't cleaning she was cooking.

Terri couldn't understand why some Christmases they had lots of toys and others nothing. Fat Jack was always there and tried to make Christmas better for them all when Bobby was away. Every year, he would dress up as Father Christmas, this fat, jolly white bearded man bellowing at the top of his voice and strolling jauntily around the living room. 'Ho! Ho! Ho!' His rosy cheeks and cherry red nose glowed with a broad bright smile, a great bundle of toys slung over his back overflowing from his huge Christmas sack. She couldn't wait to climb up on his lap and whisper into his ear her Christmas wishes. They never did come true. It was years before they realised it was him, but every year he still continued with his tradition of playing Father Christmas.

Terri felt a cold nose on her hand. Caesar had wandered over for a bit more fuss. She began stroking him again and glanced down into his eyes, tears filling her own as she thought of her beautiful dog Sheba, how she loved and still missed her so much. The house was never the same without Sheba around. She had been her soulmate, her friend and companion.

Sheba had always loved her, whether she laughed or cried, shouted or screamed. She always wagged her tail with excitement and pleasure when Terri was there. She would creep into Terri's bed every night and make herself comfortable in the crook of Terri's legs, and they'd keep one another snug and warm under the blankets on those cold winter nights. Terri would lie there at night wanting to move in the bed and get comfortable and fidget around a bit, but she didn't want to disturb Sheba when she was snoring blissfully. Terri grinned. She must have been mad, but she had loved Sheba dearly. There would never be another dog like her Sheba.

The cheeky little thing would sit under the table when they were eating their dinner and Terri would feed her when no one was watching. Sheba loved it; it was like their little secret, her daily treats. She followed Terri wherever she went. Sheba could be sound asleep on the floor, snoring her head off, but if Terri moved away or walked out of the room, Sheba was always there by her side. Even when she went to the toilet, Sheba followed her. She would lie next to her in bed at night, and Terri would press her wet face against her soft fur and rock herself to and fro while Sheba licked her salty tears from her face.

Terri and Sharon found her over Matchstick Island, a park they used to go to. Bobby used to sometimes take them over there when he was in a good mood and happy for a change, though that didn't happen very often. They would feed the ducks, then have a go on the swings and slide, laugh and have fun. A group of kids were tormenting and being really cruel and wicked to a puppy. Terri asked them to leave her alone and said she'd have the dog and take her home and look after her. They told her they would only give the horrible dog to her if she gave them her bike. She knew she would get a good hiding but she couldn't leave that poor little dog with those nasty kids.

She was only a pup, a bitzer, a bit of this and a bit of that, an adorable bundle of brown and white fluff with long floppy ears that bounced as she came galloping towards you. She jumped and frolicked like Bambi, her chocolate eyes full of fun and mischief. Every day when Terri came home from school, Sheba would be waiting in the front garden for her. She would run and come back to Terri with her toy or a shoe hanging from her mouth, standing erect and proud of herself, strolling over all cocky. She'd look at Terri with love and trust in her eyes – Sheba only wanted her love and companionship.

She used to run and stand behind Terri shivering and shaking when Bobby came home drunk, hollering and shouting. Terri knew when Bobby was a few doors away. Somehow, Sheba heard him, and she'd run upstairs and sit watching the front door from the top landing. Every night before she went to sleep, Terri would look up into the vast night sky scattered with thousands of stars sparkling brightly. One star was a little bit bigger and brighter than the rest. It was there every night and Terri knew it was her Sheba looking down on her. She would talk to Sheba and tell her how much she missed her and loved her. She was always in her thoughts and her heart.

'He's getting old now, him,' pointing over to Caesar, as Sheila handed Terri a nic hot cup of steaming tea.

'I know, I was just finking of Sheba, you remember her don't ya Auntie Sheila?'

Sheila looked at Terri and nodded. How could she ever forget Sheba? 'Yeah Terri, she was a lovely dog.' Changing the subject, she didn't want to think about that. Sheila noticed the bandage around Terri's arm. 'What ya done to ya arm, Terri?'

Terri looked at Sheila, her eyes innocently blank, 'Oh, that,' she gave a nervous laugh. 'I tripped up the front doorstep the other day and fell on a milk bottle.'

Sheila tutted, raising her eyebrows. 'You've always been a clumsy mare ain't ya?'

Terri nodded and laughed with Sheila, 'I know. I get it from muvver, she's always bumping into fings and falling over.'

'You're worried about some fing other than ya dad ain't ya?' Sheila said.

'No Sheila, honestly I'm all right,' said Terri forcing a smile.

Sheila wasn't remotely fooled by any of it. She smiled at Terri, looked into her niece's sad blue eyes.

Terri felt like that small girl again, crying behind her living room door, but she wasn't going to tell Sheila what was on her mind …

~ ~ ~

Bobby was back from the pub pissed as fuck. Terri was shit scared, she knew what was coming – she was gonna get a good hiding. Her auntie Sheila was over from Ireland for the school summer holidays with uncle Johnnie and her cousins, the terrible twins Danny and Kevin. It was lucky she was here as Lizzie was in hospital. She'd had a severe epileptic fit and had really hurt herself, and Sheila was helping to look after the kids.

Terri had finally found the courage to tell Sheila what her daddy had been doing to her, and Sheila had taken her straight to the police station where she'd had to tell PC Thomas what she'd told Sheila. The copper listened to her and Bobby was nicked, but she knew by the sceptical look on his face that he didn't believe her. He went into another room with Bobby, and she could hear them both laughing and joking together. They came into the room where she was and the copper still had tears in his eyes from his laughter. Then he spoke, 'Terri, you're a very naughty girl for lying, you could have got your dad in a lot of trouble; he could have gone to prison.' She saw Bobby wink at the copper; he smiled as he handed him an envelope. Bobby grabbed her hand and marched out of the police station.

He took her straight home – as soon as they were inside the door he pulled his gun out, warm from where it had been jammed down the front of his trousers, and shoved it in her mouth. 'You lying little cunt,' he snarled. 'You'll pay for this.' He forced her back against the wall. 'If you ever tell ya mum or anyone else, I will kill her, and then you.'

Terri knew he meant it, he wasn't joking. She was scared. She didn't want to die. She tried hard not to gag on the hard metal. He slowly withdrew the gun, his cold eyes still on her. 'I'm going down the pub. I'll deal with you when I get back!'

Terri sat watching and waiting for hours, just for him to come back, dreading each and every moment. She heard him coming up to the gate, ran upstairs to her bedroom. The street door opened as Bobby sauntered in, pissed as usual. Sheba ran down the stairs towards Bobby.

'Sheba, come here, Sheba,' Terri spoke softly but Sheba took no notice. She scurried happily towards Bobby. She sniffed around his feet, wagging her tail in anticipation and excitement, her eyes watching him with love and trust. Bobby bent down and stroked the top of her head.

'Cute little fing ain't ya, Sheba?' Sheba licked his face then rolled on her back waiting for her belly to be tickled. Bobby looked up the stairs at Terri as Sheba jumped around his feet, her tail wagging furiously around his ankles.

Bobby stroked her soft floppy ears; his eyes twinkled as he watched Terri, her face pale, drained of its natural colour.

'Good girl Sheba.' He picked her up playfully by the scruff of the neck.

'Please don't hurt her, daddy.' Her heart pounded in painful bursts as she walked slowly down the stairs. She was shitting herself. She might as well get this over and done with. She was gonna get a good beating, she wasn't gonna get away with it.

Bobby smiled, looking straight into her eyes, not listening to the words she spoke. 'Shame you wasn't a good girl, Terri,' he said as his menacing eyes twinkled in the dimness of the evening. His huge hands went around Sheba's chubby neck. 'Daddy could 'ave been in a lot of trouble 'cos of you, you lying little slag.'

'I'm so sorry daddy, I didn't mean it. I've told the policeman and everyone else that it wasn't true and I was lying. I promise I won't tell any more lies. I promise, I promise I'll be a good girl. I promise please, please don't hurt her.'

Sheba was yelping and screeching as his huge hands went around her neck, shaking her violently from side to side. She was frantic, whining and trying to struggle free from his grip.

Terri's bottom lip trembled. She bit down hard on her lip to try to stop the trembling. She wanted to shout and scream, tell him no, tell him to stop, but she was speechless with shock.

He held the dog in front of him, suddenly dropped her, kicked her straight in the stomach, splitting it in half, like a rugby player punting the ball downfield. The shrill scream Sheba gave was horrific. She went crashing against the wall and dropped onto the floor, blood pouring from her mouth and stomach. Terri grabbed a towel from the kitchen and held it close to Sheba trying to stop the blood. She mustn't die; she can't die.

Terri saw a shadow at the front door, then the key pulled through the letter box. Auntie Sheila steamed through the front door, her angry eyes looked at Terri, then moved quickly over to Bobby, filled with utter disgust, shaking her head from side to side as she saw Terri cradling the dying dog in her lap, blood everywhere. In an instant she understood what was happening. 'You evil cunt.'

Bobby turned round to Sheila, smashed the back of his hand across her mouth, a wicked smile on his handsome face.

'Watch ya fucking mouth, bitch.' He looked at her with contempt and laughed at her as the blood trickled from her lips onto her chin. 'Come back for a bit more of me have ya?' Bobby's hands gripped her shoulders, forced her back against the wall, holding her tight, no chance of escape.

She kept both her hands hidden, behind her back. 'Get your filthy fucking hands off me.' Hate and bitterness filled her every word.

'Lovely pair of tits you've got there Sheila.' She tried to struggle free but he had pinned her up against the wall. His heavy muscular body leant on her, one of his legs in the middle of hers. She could feel he had a hard on. One huge hand was around her neck, gripping tight, the other squeezed her firm breasts. Smirking, he leaned forward, licked his lips.

'Johnnie's a lucky fucker, you're a dirty whore in bed ain't ya?' His eyes were twinkling, alive with lust. 'You're a good fuck, Sheila, ya loved every minute of it, you were begging for more of me.'

He pushed his face close to hers trying to kiss her. Deep disgust and hate showed in Sheila's eyes. All the anger that she had for him that had built up over the years was etched on her face. The hatred she felt inside would live with her forever. She turned her face away. 'You'll pay for this one day, Bobby Taylor. You just wait and see.'

She had lived with the shame for all these years and told no one what her sister's husband had done to her. The horror of it all was too awful to speak about, to live with. She suddenly smacked him straight in the face with a wicked right-hander.

He glared at Sheila. 'You dirty fucking slag.' His eyes gazed over her with fresh lust, desire and hate. He was going to lay into Sheila, rip the clothes from her, give her a real good fucking – but she was ready for him. She kneed him in the bollocks, and suddenly brought her left hand out from behind her back – she had been ready for Bobby, had picked up a brick in the front garden.

The brick smashed down on his head, sent him staggering backwards, blood already spilling from his scalp, running down his face. For a second it looked as though he was about to fight back, then suddenly his legs gave way and he crumpled in a heap on the floor, out cold.

Terri watched it all, Sheba cradled in her arms. Looking down at her dying dog she hated Bobby more than anything in her life. Terri bit her lip so hard that spots of blood dripped onto her chin.

She sat holding Sheba close to her, praying to God. It seemed like hours she sat there with her but it was only minutes, sobbing in painful bursts. She watched the blood soak into the towel as she held it against Sheba's spewing stomach, her blood still warm and fresh on her fingers. The aroma was sickly sweet.

She hugged Sheba close and moaned into the soft folds of her neck. Her usually sparkling brown eyes were cloudy and dazed. Terri was gagging, going to throw up. She kissed Sheba's cold nose. Terri wasn't going to let her fall asleep alone into the dark, she would hold her, cuddle her, and make her better. She would get better. She would take her to the PDSA tomorrow, they would give her some medicine, everything would be all right.

'Wake up Sheba, open your eyes; wake up girl, come on, open your eyes. You've gotta wake up. Please don't die, please keep breathing. I'll look after ya and make ya better again. I'm sorry it's all my fault.'

Terri's face contorted with pain. 'Sheba, please don't die.' Sheba opened her glazed eyes and looked up at Terri. She couldn't move her head but Terri knew Sheba was looking at her. Terri whispered to her for the last time, 'I love you, Sheba.'

Terri watched Sheba take her last small breath with her head resting in her arms. Terri's head lay softly on Sheba. Terri quivered, frozen faced as her tears fell with a vengeance. Sheba's head was no longer warm and soft, but now heavy, limp and still. Terri hated Bobby. She would get him back for what he had done to her Sheba.

It was Georgie who finally got her bedroom door open, Sheila peering over his shoulder. They found her behind the door, her hands ripping at the roots of her hair, pulling out huge chunks, screaming hysterically. 'Sheba, my Sheba.'

Georgie grabbed hold of both of Terri's arms, trying to calm her down. Terri dropped to the floor like a rag doll. Georgie got down on the floor with Terri, lifted her to her feet, passed her to Sheila as she started to fall. Sheila reached forwards and drew her into her arms. Terri could smell her perfume – she smelt so clean and fresh. She reached up and put her arms around Sheila's neck holding her tightly; it felt so gentle and comforting. She could feel her heart beating and hear her soft and soothing breathing. Terri cried harder and harder, snuggled closer to Sheila and rested her head on her shoulder, sobbing into her neck as Sheila stroked Terri's hair. Neither of them could speak, their hearts heavy and full of pain. A single tear ran down Sheila's cheek.

The three of them stayed up all night digging a hole under the huge cherry tree at the bottom of the garden to bury Sheba. Exhausted, Sheila held her hand out; Terri gripped her tightly with one hand, grabbed Georgie's hand in her other. He closed his hand tight around Terri's as they walked together into the house, treading over her gutless drunken cunt of a dad, still out of the game at the bottom of the stairs. Georgie still hadn't said a word since he'd got home, but his soft brown eyes were full of tears – tears for Terri, hatred for Bobby.

Finally he spoke. 'Take her home with you, Sheila. She don't need to be around when this fucker wakes up.'

Sheila nodded. 'What you going to do with him?'

Georgie shook his head. 'I really don't know Sheil.'

They walked out, left him standing, staring down at his unconscious father, Sheila half fearing, half excited at what Georgie might do …

In the quietness of the night Sheila and Terri walked to Sheila's house, both dazed, arm in arm, but easy in one another's company. All was so quiet and still, everyone asleep in their beds, just the odd car every now and then shedding its light on them for a moment, cutting the darkness. They would carry this night with them for a long time.

Terri slept with Sheila that night, holding her close to her as Sheila lay behind her, with her arms wrapped tightly around her waist. Sheila's kind and beautiful face nestled into her hair and Terri could hear her soft breathing as she fell asleep. When Terri awoke the next morning with Sheila's arms still protectively around her, she realised that it was the first night in a long, long time that she hadn't had one of those horrible nightmares.

Mandy

Mandy Palmer glanced fondly at Pauline, her eldest sister, sitting at the table carefully applying her mascara. She smiled to herself, thinking how strange it was that however hard you tried, you still couldn't put your mascara on without opening your mouth.

Mandy looked into her sister's soft hazel eyes. Pauline was going to do her nut. Her mouth would be gawping wide open, not through meticulously putting on her mascara, but with shock, horror and disbelief at what Mandy was about to tell her. Mandy was shitting herself, knowing exactly the kind of reaction she would get and what Pauline was going to say.

Pauline Tate was an older version of Mandy, but with a hard look on her pretty face that told its own story. She was a little taller than Mandy and a bit wider – she'd put on a lot of weight since she'd had the four boys. Pauline was always on a diet, a different one every week, Weight Watchers, counting calories, weighing her food. The only diet that ever worked for her was the seafood diet. Pauline would see the food and just eat it. But since she found a doctor in Barking to buy slimming pills from she had lost nearly a stone in two weeks.

Pauline still looked good for her thirty-six years, her skin was soft and smooth and she didn't have a grey hair in sight. She was rushing around as usual trying to get herself ready, always in a hurry with a hundred and one things to do and never enough hours in the day. She was never punctual or on time – she'd be late for her own funeral, that woman.

Mandy knew that Pauline didn't think much of Mickey as brother-in-law material, but she liked him as her bouncer on the door and as a punter. He always had his hand in his pocket, was generous, would help anyone out if they were in trouble. He was well known and well liked. Pauline was always polite and nice to him, but when Mandy told Pauline that she was going out with him, Pauline had told her that she must be off her head getting involved with Mickey Taylor and his family – she'd live to regret it.

Mandy kept glancing out of the window, keeping her watchful eyes on her four young nephews playing on the swings in the beer garden downstairs. They were a bunch of little rascals. The rain had fallen in torrents last night and the muddy puddles were still evident on the ground. Pauline would do her nut if the boys came back up dirty and covered in mud – they were all dressed smart in their suits and ties looking like a little mafia mob.

It was going to be very busy in the pub today. Mickey was expecting a good turn out, he'd organised the entire funeral for Lizzie. Mandy thought Mickey was really strong and was taking it all very well. She'd tried talking to him about it and helping him in his grief – she hated to see Mickey hurting. His pain was her pain. He'd been very quiet, keeping it all to himself, buried deep inside. She wished he would talk to her, but everyone dealt with grief in their own way.

Mandy felt so sad and sorry for Mickey's mum and his brothers and sisters. Her eyes filled up as she thought of poor Martin, his little brother. He'd suffered the worst ordeal imaginable in his young life. She couldn't begin to understand how they must all be feeling. She shuddered. If anything happened to her mum and dad it would definitely send her over the edge; her mum and dad would always be around to love and protect her. They were a good, decent hard-working couple. They didn't have much money and had had to scrimp and scrape through a few times over the years, but they always had dinner on the table and their home looked clean and tidy. Her mum and dad and her seven sisters gave her all the love and happiness they could and more. She was lucky to come from a good, respectable, law-abiding family.

Her stomach turned, she felt sick thinking of how Bobby died and why. Mickey wouldn't have it that it was suicide, even though that's what the post-mortem said. Mandy didn't know what was worse – murder or suicide. Mickey wouldn't rest until he had all the answers. He was definitely on a mission with a lot to lose but a lot to gain. This scared her; she'd seen with her own eyes what Mickey was capable of.

She had stayed up till the early hours of the morning helping Pauline and Pete clear up after the fight last night. They'd spent most of the night scrubbing and cleaning blood from the walls and floor, tidying away the smashed glasses and all the mess, the broken tables and chairs. She was well and truly knackered; she could have done with going back to bed but there was no chance of that.

'Mand, are the boys all right out there?' Pauline said as she finished doing her make-up. 'They'd better not be dirty; I'll kill the little buggers if they are.'

But Mandy wasn't listening, didn't hear her. She sat silent and still, staring out of the window, daydreaming in a world of her own. Her thoughts lingered with Mickey and how she wanted to spend the rest of her life with him. Her long slim fingers fiddled with the gold chain and locket that Mickey had given her on their first date. He'd been so romantic – they were at the Steak House in Barking waiting for their food to come when he leaned over the table and cupped her chin in his hand and brushed his thumb over the outline of her lips. 'I've bought you a present.'

She felt her face flushing red; she was so embarrassed she couldn't speak. He looked at her with that amazing smile that made her heart race. 'Well, say something then Mand, even if it's only bollocks.'

She laughed with him. 'Thanks Mickey, you shouldn't have done that, but thanks,' she said as he handed her a small rectangle box wrapped in silver shining paper and with a white bow on the top. She stood up and leaned towards him and gave him a big kiss on the lips.

'Open it then, ya don't even know what it is, come on,' he said smiling at her.

Again she said, 'Thanks,' as she carefully unwrapped the present. It was a lovely gold belcher chain and an oval locket.

'Turn it over,' he said softly. She turned it over in her hand, engraved on the back was, 'Love Mickey xx.' Her eyes filled with tears of happiness, it was beautiful. He took the necklace and placed it around her neck. She put a lock of Mickey's hair inside the locket. It was so romantic. She loved the thought of him being close to her all the time. She also put a photo of them both inside, taken at the booth on Barking station, on their first night out together. She loved Mickey, she loved him so much. He was so kind and generous.

Her lean body tingled as she remembered the first night Mickey had asked her out. It was the most glorious spring day, not a cloud in the sky. As the sun warmed her face, she couldn't stop thinking of Mickey. She had fancied the arse off him for weeks – he always said hello, and had time for a quick chat, but did nothing that made her think he might fancy her. He was friendly to everyone he met. Mickey could have his choice of girls, all lovely looking, fantastic figures, nice clothes, flocking at his feet, flirting away, fluttering their false eyelashes at him. So what chance did she have? Mandy thought she wasn't pretty or clever, had a fat arse, a horrible figure, and as for tits, well God definitely forgot about her when he was giving them out. She was last in the queue as usual.

She knew he would be at the pub that day. He had organised a charity event for one of his friends, Jason Morrison. Jason had lost his younger brother to leukaemia; the poor little sod was only nine years old. The money raised went half each to cancer research and half to the children's ward at Oldchurch Hospital. Mickey and his mates collected the raffle prizes donated by the local shops and businesses. A meat voucher from the butchers; a beautiful bouquet of flowers; cuddly toy; bottle of champagne; whiskey; brandy; perfume; a record player and a weekend for two in Bognor. Lots of brilliant raffle prizes to be won. It was like the Generation Game.

A sponsored run had been arranged. You had to run once round the beer garden, drink a pint, and then run round again and again and again. Blokes and women were running round in the warm sunshine with their pints of beer still in their hand, drinking it on the way. Most of the contents spilt on the grass and mud, there were grown men and women slipping and sliding, dancing on the mud. It was comical just sitting there and watching them. Joe Mann won the contest – what a pisshead! He finished on twenty-two pints and collapsed on the finish line, but he sobered up a bit when he was hosed down with cold water!

One of Mickey's traveller friends brought a couple of his ponies down from the yard and they gave the kids pony rides all day. They loved it; they were in their element. She had never seen so many smiles and happy faces. A yard of ale contest too, it was all happening that day, everyone full of fun and mischief. The DJ played and everyone boogied around the beer garden, there was a hog roast turning on a spit and, next to it, steaks, burgers and sausages grilling on the barbeque. All the kids were in fancy dress, it was a warm and beautiful day, and everyone was dragged from their chairs to do the conga around the beer garden.

Shish the Turk, a good friend of Mickey's, volunteered to have all his hair shaved off by the local hairdresser. He was such a nice bloke who was scatty as arseholes. He was always laughing and joking. Shish would do anything for Mickey.

Even the Dagenham Post, the local paper, was there, taking photos of the event. It made a middle page spread the following week, with photos of the drunken antics of the day, applauding everyone who had worked hard organising the event, and in raising awareness of the charity and such a large amount of money. It was talked about for weeks after in the streets and the pubs.

Everyone was jolly and in good spirits. Sorrow for the family from all, but all happy that the sun was shining and loads of money was being raised for a good cause. The boy's mum gave a thank you speech, so heart wrenching, there wasn't a dry eye in the pub when she spoke. Mandy shivered. It didn't bear thinking about, a mother and father losing their child. It wouldn't matter whether they were five years old or fifty years old, they were still your baby. You never expect to outlive your children. What an awful tragedy.

The night was coming to an end, the DJ mellowing down the music and playing the slow songs. She saw Mickey walking confidently towards her and could feel butterflies in her stomach. Well, she hoped it was her he was coming to ask to dance. She gulped down her drink. 'Hello Mand,' he said as he kissed her on the cheek. 'Do ya wanna dance?'

His voice was so sexy. She was so shocked that she couldn't speak – she just nodded her head, thinking how good-looking he was.

Mickey held his strong hand out to hers. She clutched his hand as he led her to the dance floor in the middle of the beer garden with Percy Sledge singing 'When a man loves a woman.' Mickey's warm hands pulled her gently towards him, and he kissed her softly on the lips. His protective arms wrapped around her waist, his firm, hard body close to hers. She closed her eyes, her head resting against his cheek as they danced slowly. She could smell his aftershave, an expensive one. Her body tingled, she felt funny inside; she had never felt like this before. It was weird. So strange, but it felt so good.

As they danced she could feel his heart beating on her chest. His dark eyes gazed deep into hers, smiling. 'Do ya fancy coming out one night?'

An eager smile appeared on her pretty face. 'I'd love to Mickey,' she said, her eyes bright and alive. He liked her! She couldn't believe her luck – he wanted to take her out, wanted to see her again. Her body trembled with excitement. She wanted him more than anything in the world.

Mandy looked into his shining brown eyes. 'When?' Her voice was full of gratitude and joy.

Mickey put his gentle hands to her soft cheeks and pulled her face close to his and kissed her trembling lips. With a cheeky grin on his handsome face he looked deep into her eyes. 'How about tomorrow night?' His voice was so sweet and sexy.

She smiled at him, nodding her head, holding him tighter and closer. 'Great.'

As they danced, Mickey studied her. With her long chestnut hair falling over her slender shoulders, her intense brown eyes and innocent smile, she was so sexy. 'Tell ya what, Mandy, I'll give ya a lift home tonight if you're not staying here at the pub with your sister,' he murmured with his dark eyes gleaming in the dimness of the night.

She looked up at him, an appreciative smile on her face. 'A lift home would be great, Mickey.' She was so nervous.

At the end of the night Mickey pulled up outside her house, got out of the car, opened the door for her and helped her get out of the car. He was the perfect gentleman. He put his strong arms around her slim waist and walked her to the front gate.

'Night, Mickey,' she said with her eyes shining. 'It's been a great day, thanks. I've really enjoyed me self today.'

His voice was slow and very, very sexy as he spoke. 'Dream of me tonight.'

Mickey placed one hand gently on her chin and pulled her close. He laughed softly, cupped her cheek, then kissed her softly, whispering, 'I'll be dreaming of you tonight.'

They stood together for a while, just the two of them, his arms around her, Mandy's head nestled against him. She could feel and hear his soft breathing. The next moment, his lips were covering her face with his kisses. He was holding her slim body tighter to him, holding her silently. She was returning his kisses, she wanted him. Their eyes locked. Mandy knew she would always be his, and his only, it was her dream come true. He had captured her heart.

She wanted Mickey more than anything in the world. She was hungry for the pleasure he would give her, the feel of his huge hands on her soft skin, the moment when they gave themselves to each other for the first time. When he held her close it made her shiver inside. He made her feel different, alive, wanted. She felt so happy, that day would always be special in her memory. She smiled as she watched him stroll casually back to his car. He was so hot, she felt dizzy and light-headed, and it wasn't even the drink that was making her feel that way.

He turned and waved to her with a great big grin on his face. 'Night babe, sleep tight,' he called as he blew her a kiss. 'Eight o'clock tomorrow night.'

She stood and watched him drive away; waving at him till his car went out of sight. She couldn't wait to see him again, was so happy, so deliriously happy that Mickey Taylor wanted her.

Mandy walked slowly into her house, totally besotted, went straight up the stairs to her bedroom, her heart pounding fiercely in her chest. She fell in a heap onto her bed, giggling quietly to herself, trying not to make a noise. She rolled over, staring up at the ceiling, just thinking of Mickey. As she fell asleep all she could see was his smiling face. She gave a deep contented sigh. She was in love.

Pauline watched Mandy looking out of the window, in a world of her own for a good five minutes, wondered what she was thinking about. There was something bothering her, she could tell when things weren't right with Mandy. She couldn't hide much from her, Pauline knew her inside out. By the look on her face, she was worried about something and if it was anything to do with Mickey Taylor then it was likely to be trouble. Pauline walked slowly over and stood beside her youngest sister. She wasn't a baby any more, she was fast becoming a very beautiful young woman with all the complications and shit that went with growing up. She was in love with Mickey Taylor – or at least she thought she was. She was only young, too young to be that serious with a bloke. She should be out enjoying herself with her mates, having a good time.

Mandy had a loving nature with a gentle heart – she was a friendly young woman, very self-assured and strong-willed. Pauline wished she still had a figure like her sister's. Pauline prodded Mandy softly on the shoulder as she spoke. 'A penny for 'em.'

Mandy jumped with fright. 'Oh! Ya silly bitch, what did ya do that for? You frightened the life outta me.'

Pauline's eyebrows rose slightly as she smiled at her. 'You're in a world of ya own there Mand, what's a matter?'

Mandy looked sheepishly at Pauline as she put her soft hands to her firm stomach.

Pauline looked at her younger sister in disbelief. She stood in front of the window, her hands firmly on her hips, shook her head from side to side. 'I fucking knew it,' she said as she picked up her lager from the table, took a large gulp. 'The fuck is wrong with ya? Please tell me you're joking.'

Mandy Palmer laughed timidly. Smiling. A smile that made her look beautiful and happy. So very happy. A smile that showed how she felt. The love and passion she felt for Mickey Taylor was painful.

'I knew this would happen,' Pauline sighed deeply. 'I thought ya were on the pill?'

'I was, I mean I am, but I bloody well forgot to take it a couple of times.' Mandy spoke softly, her eyes downcast, staring at the floor.

Pauline ran her fingers through her hair. 'I thought you had your head screwed on.' She paced backwards and forwards. 'What does Mickey think of this then?' She shook her head in anger and pity.

'I ain't told him yet.' Mandy looked timidly at her.

'Good! You gotta get rid of it Mand. You're only young, you've got a life to live. You don't wanna end up in a high-rise on the Gascoigne estate, when a day out for the kids is a trip to the social security office.' Pauline had such high hopes for her sister, and now they were all gone. She was doing well at college, she could have gone to university and made something of herself, not be in debt up to her eyeballs, scrimping and scraping all her life. She should have nice clothes, go to nice restaurants, go to the theatre, afternoon country walks, visit the museum, see the world. Mickey Taylor would be just like his old man. She couldn't believe Mandy was sitting here quite calmly telling her she was having Mickey fucking Taylor's baby. How could she be so bloody stupid? 'The only thing you'll get if you have this baby and marry Mickey is fucking heartache,' she told her. 'Only you can choose what side of the street you wanna walk on girl.'

Mandy shook her head at her sister and sighed. 'Out of everyone I thought you would be happy for me, at least give me a bit of support.' She could never have an abortion – Mickey would kill her if he ever found out.

Pauline picked up her cigarettes from the table and put one to her lips. 'I could tell ya your fucking fortune Mand, but ya never listen, you know it all, you're always right and never wrong. Tunnel vision.'

She lit a match and inhaled deeply, blowing the match out with the smoke from her cigarette. 'I thought you might have learned your lessons from us lot. You wait and see, he's gonna be just like his dad. Do ya wanna have a life like his fucking muvver?' Anger was in her voice and her eyes as she looked at Mandy.

Mandy winced and closed her eyes, knowing she was hearing the truth about Lizzie getting a good hiding – but Mickey was nothing like his dad; he would never raise his hand to her. Mickey loved and cared about her. Every month he would send her a big bouquet of flowers, the card reading 'Love M xxx.' Mandy loved him so much, was sure that they would be together forever. They would get married, have a big wedding, and live in a lovely house with loads of kids filled with lots of love, laughter, hugging, kissing and having fun. Mickey would make a wonderful dad.

Pauline paced the floor, her voice tight with rage. 'You're off ya fucking head Mandy. Definitely not the sharpest knife in the drawer are ya girl?' she said, the sadness in her voice evident as she spoke. 'Do ya self a favour Mand, get rid of it.'

Mandy groaned inwardly, her face tight with anger, trying her hardest not to scream and shout at her sister. She got up from the chair, put her handbag over her shoulder, stormed out of the kitchen.

Mandy would show her sisters, and anyone else who interfered, what a decent bloke he was. Nobody knew him like she did. Mickey was a good bloke, a lovable rogue. Anyway, she didn't care what they thought. Pauline thought she knew everyone because she ran the place and saw and heard a lot.

Mandy's other sisters had made it abundantly clear that they didn't like Mickey. She wished they would all stop treating her like a baby and let her get on with her life. That didn't stop Mandy; it made her want him even more, she would have him no matter what it cost. Fuck them all; she was in love with Mickey Taylor.

Even Diane, Mandy's best mate, had looked at her in absolute horror and disbelief when she told her last night that she was pregnant. They were sitting in the pub. Diane rolled her eyes to the ceiling as she stood up and walked to the bar. 'I think I'll get us another drink.' She didn't have to tell her what she thought, Mandy already knew. Diane was thinking to herself, you stupid bitch Mandy. Can't you see what you're letting yourself in for?

Mandy sighed inwardly, why wouldn't everyone mind their own business? As long as it didn't hurt her, she didn't give a shit what anybody got up to. Why wouldn't people just leave her alone and let her get on with her own life? Mickey would be happy with her news, and if Mickey was happy, Mandy was happy.

'My cab's just pulled up. I'm gonna go to Mickey's. Tell him the good news.' Emphasising clearly the word 'good', Mandy strutted cockily out of the kitchen, slammed the door behind her, not caring if Pauline saw her anger.

Pauline slumped into a chair, fell into a deep brooding silence. How could Mandy be so bloody stupid? Hadn't the stupid bleedin' cow learnt her lesson from the rest of her sisters? All got pregnant young and had to get married. It wasn't for love nor money.

Pauline was like a mum, sister and friend all wrapped up in one to Mandy. They had a special bond between them, they could talk to each other about anything. Mandy practically lived with her. Pauline sighed, recalling her young years and falling in love. The rush of nostalgia brought tears to her eyes and she blinked rapidly, trying to pull herself together. It was too late for sorrow and self-pity, she had to make the most of it – after all, you only had one life.

She was gutted for Mandy, but how could she say that when she'd told her that she would always be there for her? Pauline knew there would be many times in the future when Mandy would come knocking on her door with her bags packed.

She could see it happening already, the life Mandy was walking into. She hated the way Mickey treated Mandy. He talked to her like a piece of shit, told her what she could do, what she couldn't wear – her skirts were too short, her tops too low, she had too much make-up on. He wouldn't let her go out with her mates – to him they were all no good, dirty old slappers.

She couldn't talk to any of her bloke friends who she knew from school and college. If she was walking along the road with him, or was in a pub and saw someone she knew, she would bow her head down, walk in another direction, turn away, not make any eye contact, anything so Mickey wouldn't see her looking or talking to another bloke. He was as jealous and possessive as fuck.

Mickey had even given Mandy's ex-boyfriend a good hiding and told him never to come near her again. Pauline felt really sorry for the poor bloke, he didn't deserve what he got from Mickey. She shuddered – she was serving behind the bar when it started. He was such a nice bloke, quiet and placid with not a bit of violence in him. He had a good job with a big firm in the City, and, more importantly, he earned a good salary. He hadn't had a good start in life, and had had his fair share of problems, but that didn't stop him wanting a bit more out of life. He earned his money the proper way, adored Mandy and would do anything for her, nothing was too much trouble. He looked after her, treated her well and with respect – she would have had a good decent life with him but no, Mandy wanted a bit of rough. She sure had it now...

Mickey was watching her from the bar as she talked to her ex-boyfriend outside the ladies' toilets, his jaw grinding as he glared at him, ready to rip his fucking head off. He snarled as that dickhead held his arms open to Mandy, as his eyes lingered over her very sexy body, as he pulled her close to him, then softly whispered something in her ear.

Mickey ran his fingers through his thick hair – the fucking wanker. They were looking into each other's eyes, laughing together. He held her gentle hands and pulled her close to him kissing her softly on her cheek. She gave him one of her smiles as she strolled into the ladies toilets. It was the smile that made Mickey's heart turn, he never wanted to take his eyes off her, she was beautiful, and she was his. He loved her. He loved everything about her; the way she talked, the way she sat, the way she looked at him with her gorgeous eyes, her smile, and her touch. He took a large gulp of his beer. That cheeky bastard was touching and mauling his bird, and he was going to pay for it.

Mickey banged his beer down on the bar and strolled menacingly towards Mandy's ex-boyfriend. Mickey's huge shadow covered him with darkness. No warning, just unprovoked violence, that was Mickey's way. He dragged him out of his chair, lifting him off his feet, his huge fist smashing into the side of his face. He fell sideways, crashed into the table, knocking all the drinks and glasses off as he fell to the floor. His shoulders slumped as he curled up in a ball covering his head, trying to do what he could to protect himself – smart enough to know what was coming, powerless to prevent it.

Mickey turned and looked down at him, glaring. His angry face raked him over from head to toe, watching him with his ice cold predator's eyes. He grabbed the collar of his coat, pulling him closer. 'Keep ya filthy hands off of her, do ya understand me?' Mickey looked him in the eye; smiled and leaned forward even closer. 'Did ya fucking hear me?'

Mandy's ex nodded sheepishly.

Mickey still wasn't done though – he kneed him in the bollocks, smashed him in the face again with a savage uppercut as he went down. He hit the floor hard, his body limp, half unconscious. Mickey smiled as he kicked him, hard body shots that made Mickey grunt with the effort. Finally he rolled him over onto his back with the toe of his black Doc Martens, surveyed his handiwork – split lip, teeth missing, broken nose, enough claret to paint a wall. Slowly, calmly, Mickey planted his massive boot on the geezer's face. 'If you ever look at her or go near her again I will fucking kill you.' Then he ground his boot into his face, smearing the blood and the dirt as he crushed his cheekbone.

Pauline tutted to herself, shaking her head from side to side. She knew Mandy would never have any kind of a life with Mickey, but Mandy was besotted with him. No-one could say anything about her Mickey, he was something special, and she adored him. Mickey Taylor was in control, and Mandy played by the rules – Mickey's rules. She was just the decorative, sweet smiling, obedient, dutiful bird hanging on the end of his arm. Mandy was blind to it all.

Pauline shivered. Mandy was walking straight into a life of living hell, she could have had her choice of blokes but the silly cow wanted Mickey Taylor. Now she was up the duff she would never be able to get rid of him, her life was mapped out for her already.

Pauline could see it all coming, the heartache, the tears. Dozy bitch. Mandy would look back one day and think to herself, I wish I'd listened to Pauline all those years ago, before things turned nasty with Mickey. Before she got a good hiding, before she couldn't look at him without feeling repulsed. Burping and farting in your face – sick and disgusting – his marshmallow dick slapped in her face. He'd fall asleep pissed on the toilet looking like a big fat Buddha in his dodgy Y-fronts, his huge sagging beer belly hanging between his hairy legs, covering his limp dick.

She should get out now, before she started listening to the same old shit over and over again. Before he filled her head with a load of old bollocks and the drunken spill came out of his mouth – the usual crap, things will be different, I'll change, I'm sorry, I didn't mean it, it won't happen again. Then, it's all your fault, you're a useless mother, no good in bed, the house is a shit hole, stripping her of emotion. She would hear the same old crap day after day, the same old bollocks over and over again, looking at that person that she had loved with so very different eyes. Get out now, she thought, before their love was lost. Pauline tutted to herself. Men were like the weather, nothing could be done to change them, they thought respect was lifting the toilet seat before taking a piss.

Pauline poured herself a can of lager and leaned back on the chair, closing her eyes for a moment. She didn't feel too bad when she woke up that morning, but now she was well and truly really poxed off. She lit a cigarette and shook her head dismally thinking of Mandy. She had always had a soft spot for her, she was the youngest of the family of eight girls but she wasn't a baby any more. Pauline sipped her glass of beer, her lowered lids shielding the tears glistening in her soft hazel eyes. Why wouldn't Mandy just listen for a change? But Mandy always knew best and wouldn't listen. She would learn one day, like all of us learn – the bloody hard way. Pauline had made many mistakes in her life and would no doubt make a few more, but she still hadn't learnt her lesson.

Since she was a little girl Pauline had dreamed of being on the stage. She would be rich and famous. She loved acting, singing and dancing. Her dream came true when she left school and won a scholarship for the London School of Drama and Dance. Then her dream ended. The first time she had had sex she got herself pregnant. She couldn't believe it – she was having a baby. She resented her boys sometimes and she had always wanted a little girl, but she never got what she wanted.

She blinked rapidly, trying to stop the tears, but she couldn't. They slid down her cheeks, dripped slowly into her beer, bitter tears for herself, for her regrets for the years she had wasted, and the things she had missed. It was true what her mum had said to her years ago, 'Well girl, you've made your bed now, you've gotta lay in it.'

She gripped tight on the gold crucifix chained around her neck and prayed to God for Mandy, whose life would never be the same again.

Mickey

Mickey really didn't want to come back home, didn't want anyone to know he was there, didn't want to see his mum, the way it was destroying her, but something was nagging at him, something about Bobby's last night …

He came round the back and climbed over the fence, like he had a thousand times when he was a kid, slipped in through the back door. Lizzie was in the living room, sitting in an armchair, very upright, her body held tight, as though waiting for something. She forced a smile to her face when she saw Mickey walk in. 'All right, son? Everything the way you want it?'

Mickey nodded, carefully closed the door behind him.

Lizzie's eyes were fixed on him – she knew his moods almost as well as he did, could tell when something was on his mind. She could see it right now, the way he held himself, the jaw locked tight, the slight tilt of his head, his hands held by his side, very still, but clenched tight into fists. 'Spit it out then.'

'I've got to know, mum. Got to know what happened that last night ... '

She cut across him. 'Got to know? Who says you got to know anything?'

'I'm the head of this family now. I've got to look out for everyone, keep the money flowing, keep the wolves from the door. And I've got to know who killed dad. So what happened that night?'

Lizzie snorted in disgust. 'What happened that night? You really want to know?' She met his cold hard stare. 'I'll tell you what happened that night. Your father came home, boozed up, stinking of some other woman's cunt, and raped me. Is that good enough for you?'

'That's not what I ... '

'Not what you wanted to hear? I'll bet.' Her eyes blazed at him. 'Ripped me out the bed, tore my nightdress off and raped me. But that wasn't enough for Mister Bobby Fucking Taylor, no sir. Then he had to beat the shit out of me, then he tried to drown me in the bath.'

Mickey looked away, sickened. Why had he let it go on for so long? Why hadn't he stepped in, done something? All his childhood feelings of helplessness washed over him – but Lizzie wasn't done.

'Would have succeeded too, if Martin hadn't jumped on his back. Brave little fucker. Saved my life that night ...' The tears flowed down her face. She sobbed, reached for a tissue and buried her face in it for a moment.

Mickey took a step towards her, but before he could say anything, before he could give her a consoling touch, she stared up at him. "He fell asleep in his motor. And then, then, finally, someone did what I've been wanting to do for almost twenty years. They took that gun and blew his fucking brains out!' She gave a sad smile. 'You want to know who did it, Mickey?' She shook her head. 'The list of suspects must be a mile long. He was the sickest, most vile bastard that ever walked God's green earth. The question is, why didn't you do it a long time ago?'

The question hit Mickey like a slap in the face. He reeled backwards, unable to take his eyes off his mother, then suddenly turned and ran from the room, out through the kitchen into the back yard. The cold, wet air stung his face. She was right. He was better than that. He knew what was going on, should have stopped it. He should be finding the bastard who killed his dad and shaking his hand, not vowing to kill him. And then, in the middle of his grief and torment, a face from the past flashed across his mind. Joseph Donnelly.

Never in his life would he forget the day that Joe had changed the way Mickey felt about himself forever. He had done Mickey a great favour that day ...

~ ~ ~

Mickey was twelve years old, and he was always frightened. Frightened of going to school, even more frightened of staying at home. Mickey woke up each day overcome with dread, his stomach turning somersaults. His walk to school every day was lonely and long. He trudged along the Heathway, shoulders hunched and eyes down. Each step he took was torture. He knew they would be waiting for him. Mickey felt that usual pain in his chest as he turned the corner and saw them; there was no way to avoid it. He was terrified and the fear made him sweat. He stopped, caught his breath, took it all in.

The bullies were waiting to terrorise him, torment him, mock him, embarrass him, push him, punch him, kick him, slap him and pinch him. They'd threaten to kill him. Tell his mates not to talk or play with him or they would get a good beating as well if they didn't do as they were told. He had been tormented every day for months, and it seemed as though it would go on forever.

Today was just another normal day, the same as yesterday, the same as the day before, like tomorrow and the day after would be. On Monday he had his dinner money nicked, so no dinner. Tuesday they took his school bag and Joseph Donnelly pissed in it. The rest of them watched, having a right belly laugh at Mickey's expense. On Wednesday they spat in his dinner. Thursday they ripped and tore his school uniform while he was getting a kicking, left him bloody, bruised and beaten. And now Friday, he knew that if he didn't give them the money they wanted ... Well, he knew exactly what was coming. He swallowed deeply. There they were, all eight of them, waiting for the kill. As he got closer he could hear the chants and the sniggers.

'Here he comes, Pikey Taylor.'

'There's the cry baby.'

Why did they pick on him? What had he done wrong? Was it his hair, his smile, his weight, his height, his clothes? Maybe the way he spoke, the way he walked? Why did they hit him, why wouldn't they just leave him alone? When was it all going to stop? He felt so alone and empty inside. There was no escape. He didn't know whether to run or cry, live or die. He hated the world and wished he had never been born.

Mickey put his head down and carried on walking. He looked up to see them walking menacingly towards him. His heart pounded heavily. Suddenly he turned the other way and started running as fast as he could – he knew it was no good, but fear gripped his heart.

They quickly gained on him, striding rapidly towards him, only a couple of paces away. He didn't stand a chance; they would just keep chasing him until they caught him. He could hear them hollering and shouting.

'Get the arsehole, don't let him get away.'

'He's gonna get a slap.'

'Get the money off him.'

Mickey had to stop. He was out of breath and couldn't run any more. He stood rooted to the spot, puffing and panting. His piercing brown eyes darted backwards and forwards between the line of bullies standing in front of him blocking his way. As they got closer, he could feel the terror well up inside.

They gathered around him, getting into position, shifting their weight from one foot to another, fists clenching and unclenching at their sides, shoulders connecting, nudging each other, waiting for the OK from Joseph Donnelly to give him a good kicking. They surrounded him, locking him in their circle. Mickey felt a bead of sweat run down the centre of his back. He looked for a gap to try to get out but there was no escape.

'Please leave me alone!' he yelled in despair, but they didn't listen.

They started pushing him backwards and forwards, laughing and jeering, spitting in his face, calling him names, every one of them enjoying every minute of his misery.

'Wanker!'

'Fleabag.'

'Arsehole.'

'Prick.'

One of the boys punched him straight in the stomach. Mickey doubled up in pain, gasping for air. He felt a hard blow to the side of his face and fell, banging his head as he hit the stony ground. A shadow fell across him as they surrounded him and began putting the boot in. The kicks and the punches rained down, coming from every direction. His vision began to blur and darken as his head started throbbing; he felt lost, dizzy. As Mickey lay curled up in a ball trying to protect himself, he prayed silently to the God he didn't believe in.

'Dear God, please can you help me, please do something, anything. I promise I'll always be a good boy and go to church every Sunday and go to confession. I'm sorry for all the sins I've committed. Please can you save me and make it all stop. Amen.'

Then suddenly it stopped. It was hard to make out the words spewing from the bullies' mouths. Mickey looked up, his face covered in snot and tears. One voice grew louder, a voice Mickey knew well, ringing in his ears. It was a rich voice, warm and soft, sliding effortlessly around every phrase, each dramatic sentence of a story it was never tired of telling. He could hear his mum's voice reading a passage from Jane Eyre, her voice filled with power, self worth, dignity, realism, drama and passion.

'When we are struck at without a reason, we should strike back again very hard; I am sure we should — so hard as to teach the person who struck us never to do it again.'

Mickey looked up from the dirty pavement at his tormentors; there was a banging in his head. Something inside him just clicked. And at that moment he realized, understood like never before that he was on his own, responsible for himself. No one was ever going to help him; he had to help himself.

He felt different, weird. He could feel a strange tingling sensation in his toes that moved slowly all over his body. He felt like the world's strongest man. He was on a high, fuelled by adrenaline and hate. He felt good; he wasn't going to take this shit no more from no one, not from these bullies, or his dad or anyone else.

Mickey managed to get to his feet without his face showing them anything. He was seething inside with all the feelings he'd kept bottled up for years; the horror of it all, the anger and fury at his dad for doing this to them. The guilt for all the times that he had done nothing to help his mum, or his brother and sisters when they needed him to save them from his dad's hands. A turmoil of emotions churned away inside him. He would never forget the fear on his mum's face, her panic stricken eyes pleading with Mickey to save her – and he'd done nothing.

He was a coward then, he didn't have the bottle – but today was a different story. Never again would he be scared or run away from anyone or anything.

Mickey lashed out for all the times his dad and the bullies had taken the piss out of him. For every punch, slap and kick. For each time he was frightened, each time he had cried. All the times he had bled. All the times he'd been hurt. Mickey's anger – raw, powerful and uncontrollable – was about to be released.

Joseph stared at Mickey. 'Where's the money?'

Mickey smiled. 'I ain't got none.'

'What do you mean you ain't got it?' Donnelly grinned, looked to his mates. This was going to be fun.

Mickey took a tentative step forward. He had no idea how he looked to them or what his face said about how he felt at that moment. He looked at their faces and saw hatred, excitement and expectation. But he also saw fear.

'This is your last chance, Taylor. Where's the money?'

Mickey shifted his weight slowly from one foot to the other and clenched his fists. He kept his face blank.

'You're a silly fucker, Taylor.' Joseph's eyes narrowed and he smirked. 'You think you're hard? Come on then.'

Mickey watched as they all laughed at him. They could have his schoolbag, his dinner money, whatever they wanted. Mickey would give them blood, but it wasn't going to be his, it would be theirs. And then he rushed at the dirty bastards.

Mickey slammed his fist into Joseph's face, floored him with a savage right hook. He kicked John Pugh to the ground. Turned and slammed his fist into Robert's nose. The gang were stunned, frozen in shock. Cool as you like Mickey walked up to Charlie and head-butted him – blood spurted everywhere. Crack. Another punch caught him in the jaw and knocked him to his knees. As he fell Mickey turned back to Joseph, still on his hands and knees. Mickey looked down at him, felt no pity, no compassion, just pure, cold hatred. He kneed him in the mouth and split his lip, kicked him hard in the bollocks. He slumped to the damp pavement, his face covered in blood.

The rest of the group shuffled backwards, scared by Mickey's unrestrained savagery. This was unlike anything they had ever seen before, a different world, a different person. They were kids. Mickey was an animal.

Mickey picked his school bag up from the pavement, swung it over his shoulder and walked into the school playground with a huge satisfied smile on his face. Those pricks wouldn't be strutting the streets and playground all puffed up like peacocks shaking their tail feathers any longer.

~ ~ ~

Mickey turned as the kitchen door opened. Lizzie stood in the doorway. 'I'm so sorry, son. I had no right to say that.'

Mickey walked across the sodden grass towards her, his feet sinking in the soft ground. 'It's all right, mum. It's just something I've got to do. Like you told me a long time ago – when we are struck at without a reason, we should strike back again very hard; I am sure we should — so hard as to teach the person who struck us never to do it again …' He paused in the doorway, gave her a gentle kiss on the cheek. 'When dad was killed, someone struck this family without a reason. And I'm pretty fucking sure that I should strike back hard …'

Alfie

Alfie sat alone at the bar, his dark eyes working their way around the pub, taking in every detail. Two young girls were running backwards and forwards from the kitchen armed with trays of chicken, beef, salmon, prawns, sausage rolls, pork pies. You name it, it was there, enough food to feed an army. Lizzie had spared no expense – anyone would think it was a fucking wedding they were at, not a funeral.

His eyes filled with tears, he choked on his drink. Bobby had been best man at his wedding. Alfie lit a cigarette, inhaled deeply, and then took another large swig of his brandy. It was strange being back in this boozer after all these years. He sat and watched the pub doors opening and closing, people in and out, coming and going. A bit like life, he thought to himself.

Everyone coming through the pub door was dressed in black. It was just beginning to fill up with people. All these people waiting to go to Bobby Taylor's funeral with their fond farewells and respect – what a load of bollocks, Bobby Taylor was nothing but a cunt. How ridiculous to even think of the original man he'd been. That man had been dead for years, same as himself. He swallowed his fifth brandy in one gulp, his foot tapping nervously on the heavy brass footrest around the bar as he waited with impatience for the poxy barmaid to stop chatting up the geezer at the end of the bar and get him his drink. He needed a bit of Dutch courage.

'Here darling, get us another one.' Alfie raised his empty glass into the air, swirling the ice around.

The dolly bird of a barmaid tottered along the bar in her high heels. 'Sorry about that, mate. I was just telling him,' she pointed behind her, 'how it all kicked off in here last night.' She took his empty glass. 'Same again?'

Alfie nodded, 'Make it a large one, darling.'

She continued, 'It was packed in here last night after Bobby Taylor's mass service; they do that with Catholics, have a mass the night before. Anyway, Mickey, one of his boys, put money over the bar for drinks on him all night. It was a really good night under the circumstances.'

She tottered off to get his drink still telling him the saga of the night before. 'There was this group of blokes in here, strangers, mob-handed, about twenty of 'em. The cheeky fuckers started getting really loud and noisy, upsetting a few people, getting right fucking stroppy and giving people the right bleeding hump.' She handed Alfie his refilled glass.

'Cheers luv.'

'I was serving these geezers and they refused to pay for their drinks, "Fuck off, it's down to them whose fucking party it is." They were giving me loads of grief. Mickey heard them. He came over and told the loud-mouthed geezer, "Pay the fucking lady, then fuck off." The bloke obviously didn't know who he was talking to 'cos he really started giving it some trap to Mickey, "You fucking wanker, fat ugly cunt," you should 'ave heard it.'

The barmaid took a drag on her cigarette and leaned forward giving Alfie an eyeful. 'Mickey just looked at him and smiled. "Do yourself a favour mate," he snarled at the geezer. "Pay the lady, apologise, and fuck off," he said pointing his finger at him. Then Mickey walked up to him, face-to-face. He poked his finger in his face. "Now do as you're fucking told, there's a good boy." Then the stupid geezer stuck his middle finger in the air, "Spin on that, you fat cunt," laughing in Mickey's face. His mates laughed with him taking the piss chanting, "You fat cunt, you fat cunt."

'Then boom, quick as you like, Mickey pulled a blade from his back pocket, sliced across the geezer's face from his lips to the top of his cheeks.' She took a large gulp of her drink. 'It made me feel fucking sick, the skin just peeled open, there was blood spewing everywhere, it was fucking horrible.'

She took another large gulp of her drink then carried on from where she'd left off. 'Then it all went ballistic.'

She refilled his glass giving him a cheeky wink, 'Have that one on the house mate.'

Alfie gave her a friendly nod and a smile. 'Cheers.' He raised his glass in the air.

'Before you knew it there were glasses, ashtrays and bottles flying all over the place. I had to duck a few times to miss the chairs and fucking ashtrays. It's a fucking liability working here.' She leaned forward moving her head closer to his and whispered. 'One geezer might even be dead. Four of 'em are in Oldchurch Hospital. No one's heard no more.'

Alfie swirled the ice around his glass and drank the remains. He glanced at the barmaid, passing her his empty glass, nodding with a sad smile on his troubled face. 'Same again.'

She took his glass and refilled it. 'Everyone will be coming back here after the burial. I hope no one upsets Mickey Taylor or any of his family today or there will be fucking trouble. He's a really nice bloke an' all Mickey, but when someone upsets him,' she said blowing smoke in the air, 'well, then he's a nasty piece of work.'

Alfie took his brandy from the bar and staggered slightly over to the table by the door and sat himself down. He felt half pissed. Alfie's mind wandered back over the years. Births, weddings, funerals, christenings, communions – any excuse for a good old piss-up and a party. Lizzie and Bobby's house in Poplar was always a hive of activity. A good few deals had gone down in that place, and many a pound note had passed through his hands in various deals. There was not much that hadn't happened in Bobby's house. There had been a few parties in his time. His mind was full of memories, good and bad. He remembered sitting in the boozers in the East End with Bobby many moons ago and it would all kick off. Talk about history repeating itself. What he had heard about Mickey was true, he was dangerous.

Alfie should have realised back then what a nasty bastard Bobby was. His thoughts turned to Sadie, his lovely wife. Thinking of the last time he saw her, the night she died. Yes, he did want her dead; he hated her, the lying, cheating, horrible, good for nothing whore. All women were the same. Whores. He wanted her to moan, beg, plead for her life. He wanted to see her cry, to hear her screams. She deserved it, like the stinking slut she was. He wanted to cut her beautiful lying face to pieces, gouge her deceitful eyes out and listen to her while she screamed for the mercy he would never give her. She deserved to suffer in hell in eternal torment for what she had done to him and the kids. No one would ever want her or look at her again. He would watch her die a slow agonising death with her throat cut and a silent scream coming from her dirty mouth. Why, why did she have to have an affair? He had asked himself that question so many times. The dirty old slag, screwing two men at a time.

He put his hand in his jacket pocket and pulled out a tablet bottle, took a couple of his pills. He needed to calm himself down, didn't trust himself, just like he didn't trust himself then when he found out that the woman he loved, the woman he'd married, the woman he trusted with his life, was making love with another man, touching another man, tasting him, her distrusting hands all over his body.

But not just any other man, his best friend, Bobby Taylor. The two people in his life who he loved, trusted and believed in. How could she put her head on the pillow at night? How could she close her eyes and sleep like a baby knowing she was shagging someone else, her sister's husband? It would destroy Lizzie. How could she look him in the eye, with a smile on her face and say, 'I love you Alfie Blake? I will love you forever.' Finishing with a kiss from her sweet lips filled with love, tenderness and passion.

If only Bobby had left his Sadie alone. If only he hadn't taken that job with Bobby at the yard in Stratford. If only he had been somebody else's mate and not Bobby's. If only he'd come from somewhere in Scotland and not fucking Poplar. The if onlys were endless.

It was sickening, just too painful, it hurt so much, and his heart had broken into thousands of pieces. The betrayed husband. How could he have been so fucking stupid, it was all going on right in front of his face, straight under his nose and he couldn't see it. They must have been laughing at him as they made love, all cosy and warm under the covers in his bed, telling one another their secrets. No wonder Bobby made sure Alfie was working away most of the time and not home with Sadie and the kids. Unfortunately, he had to work for Bobby, he needed the money – he had a wife and family to provide for.

He still loved her, still couldn't believe what she had done to him, just as he couldn't believe he'd been so lucky to have had such a beautiful wife in the first place. Sadie was so clever, so smart, just perfect, with her dazzling smile and glistening emerald eyes, and this breathless wonder was his, was in love with him, wanted him. They were courting for six months and then they were married. In the eight years they were married, he had given her everything he could, given her every piece of himself. He'd told her things that he had never told another soul in his life. Sadie and their children were his world, his reason for living – and all this time she had been lying to him, fucking Bobby Taylor.

Bobby who he'd thought was his mate. Bobby who had a good-looking wife with a good heart, who adored him, worshipped the ground he walked on and would do anything for him. But Bobby was never satisfied with what he had, he always wanted more and he always got what he wanted.

He remembered all the times they had spent at Bobby and Lizzie's, the parties, Lizzie's Sunday dinners, playing cards, Christmas and New Year all spent together. Lizzie was an excellent hostess, always running around making sure everyone was all right, that they were enjoying themselves and had plenty to drink and eat. They did have some good times together as a family, why did Sadie have to go and spoil everything?

Alfie wasn't expected home that night. The robbery they were supposed to do had been put off – a couple of boys had pulled out at the last minute – so he thought he'd come home early and surprise her. He had a great big bunch of flowers in his hand, a mixture of white lilies and red roses – her favourite flowers. They would bring a smile to her pretty face.

He put his key quietly in the door and crept slowly into the house, closing the door behind him. It was quiet, too quiet. Sadie must be upstairs putting the boys to bed. He peered in the crib, their little baby girl, his little angel, was fast asleep all tucked up cosy and warm. He walked out to the stairs and heard a noise, stood still and quiet, listening.

He crept up the stairs not making a sound, slowly opened the boys' bedroom door; they were curled up in their beds fast asleep. It wasn't the boys making that noise. Someone else was in the house. Alfie clenched and unclenched his fists. He stood outside his bedroom door and listened, putting his hand in his back pocket and pulling out a blade. Cautiously, he edged open the door slowly and peered inside. There they were. Sadie and Bobby both naked, their bodies entwined, Sadie lying there with Bobby on top of her perfect body, her flaming hair spread out on the pillow as he thrust his hips into her again and again. Sadie's face looked joyously into Bobby's as he made love to her, her hands clawing at his back harder and harder as they reached a climax. There, in his bed, in his house, Alfie looked at them both, finally seeing both of them for what they were. And after he'd killed her, Alfie had spent the next fifteen years of his life in Broadmoor, planning his revenge on Bobby.

He put his hands on the table for support to help himself stand up. He was well over the top, stood swaying side to side trying to get his act together. He needed a piss. He staggered to the toilet deciding whether to go to Bobby Taylor's funeral or not. He laughed drunkenly to himself – that would turn their cosy little families upside down. Bunch of idiots the lot of them. He would let them have the truth, Sharon was his little girl, his daughter not Bobby. Kevin and Danny his boys, his sons, not Johnny's.

He didn't know how he was going to handle this. If the truth be known, he was fucking shit scared. He had tried not to think about it until now, it was never gonna be easy, none of it. The funeral was one thing, but what went with it was something else. How he was going to handle that he still didn't know …

Georgie

Sitting on the front doorstep Georgie looked a sad, lost and lonely man finding a bit of comfort in a can of beer and a B&H held between his nicotine stained fingers. He was knackered and felt like shit. Mickey had been out on a job all night. It wasn't supposed to have happened till next week. So he hadn't gotten much sleep last night either. He thought about Sharon. How much did she know? Georgie took a last couple of drags inhaling deep into his lungs. He flicked the cigarette end onto the floor, stamped on it and twisted his shining black dealer boots on the butt.

Not for the first time that morning his thoughts turned to his dad. Georgie's fists clenched and unclenched involuntarily, sickened by his own thoughts of what he was and what he had done. Georgie closed his eyes, rubbed his hands over his weary face and then ran his fingers through his thick, dark head of hair. He slumped back against the front door, arms between his legs, head bowed. The sickening sweet smell of the huge wreaths, funeral sprays and bouquets wafted deep into his nostrils. He needed to breathe, needed to clear his head, get himself together before the ordeal ahead. He was going to tell Mickey everything when he got back from the office, he couldn't put it off any longer. He had to get this over and done with. He felt a soft prod on his strong shoulder.

'Georgie.'

Startled by the intrusion, he looked up, shading his eyes from the winter sun with his hand, saw his aunt Sheila.

He stood up, opened his arms wide.   'Auntie Sheila.' Into his sorrow came a touch of a smile gently lifting the corners of his mouth. They looked at each other for a second then Georgie stepped forward, gave her a tender hug.

'Hello mate.' Her eyes were filled with grief, but Georgie's were more so. 'I'm so sorry.' She just didn't know what else to say to him. There was nothing she could say or do that would make him feel any better.

She had been standing at the gate outside the house for a few minutes just watching Georgie, lost in his thoughts. He was a tall, good-looking man with a sweet and gentle smile. He'd been a great kid but Sheila saw no child in him now, only a very sad young man, struggling with this tragedy.

Georgie always used to be happy and smiling, a placid, easy-going child. He could read at the age of four, and at an age when most boys would be kicking a ball, jumping around and getting into lots of mischief, he only wanted to bury his nose in a book. He was a bit of a loner and very shy, and even now would just sit by the fire reading, nearly always the Bible. He seemed to have found his peace and sanctuary within the church.

Jinks, Sheila's old cat, a crisp white ball of fluff, would curl up on Georgie's lap and lie leisurely, purring in contentment. She would never forget the look on his face when Georgie first held Jinks, then just an eight week old kitten, in the palm of his tiny hand. Astonishment, wonder and kindness shone from his beautiful brown eyes. Georgie was always so kind, considerate and caring, which was hard to believe having a dad like Bobby.

As a kid, Georgie would listen to the news on the radio, read Shakespeare, even quote him. He was brilliant with maths and very intelligent, and Lizzie was so proud of him, her blue-eyed boy, full of old-fashioned charm. He would break a few hearts, that was for certain.

Sheila continued watching Georgie; the years had not changed him much. He still had a sweet, childlike look to his handsome face, still stood tall and erect, despite what had happened over the years. As the memories unfolded, her tears were close, but she pushed them back deep down inside. Life could be so fucking cruel.

'I'm all right Sheila,' Georgie sighed, his eyes betraying the way he really felt. 'Mum, Rosie and a few others are indoors,' he gestured to the front door behind him.

'How's ya mum?'

Georgie shrugged his shoulders. He wasn't in the mood for conversation, much as he loved Sheila. 'She had a bit of a funny turn earlier but Rosie sorted her out and calmed her down. She's not too bad now. I'm just waiting for Mickey and Johnnie to get back from the office, they should be here soon.'

Sheila nodded. 'I'm just indoors if you need me, Georgie.'

Georgie nodded his head and gave Sheila a sad smile. He moved aside to let her past – as he did she gave him another cuddle – then watched as she walked indoors to see Lizzie. She had no airs and graces, his aunt Sheila, she would never give away her age – always said, 'You're as old as you feel or as old as the man you feel.' She looked good for her age, still slim, slender and sexy. You took Sheila as you found her; you either loved her or hated her. She possessed a wicked sense of humour, but today wasn't a day for a barrel of belly laughs.

Sheila was his mum's older sister and over the years she had always looked after Lizzie. He loved her for it, and Sheila protected her boys with the ferocity of a lioness. Her world revolved around them and she wouldn't see them come to any harm. She never laid a finger on her twins, but took no nonsense from any woman or man. Georgie remembered one year when Sheila was over from Ireland for a few weeks. Kevin and Danny were playing out on their bikes – there was a woman who lived at the top of the road on the corner of the street, Mrs Hardy, who had nine kids.

They were a scruffy, noisy, horrible family, and Sheila never had any time for them. The silly woman was always shouting and screaming, always angry – every word that came spewing out of her mouth was a swear word.

One day, one of her kids took Kevin's bike. He was only six years old, but he went to the kid's house to get his bike back and the old misery came out of the house and clipped him round the ear, pushed him out of the gate, where he fell and grazed his knees. Kevin came home crying, 'They've nicked my bike and she gave me a whack round me head and pushed me over.'

Georgie could remember Sheila's dark, angry face – he knew she would punch the living daylights out of the old hag. She had a wicked right-hander.

She stormed out of the house and marched up the road ready for war, the kids running behind her, knocked on the street door. When Mrs Hardy answered it, she gave her a mighty left hook, sent her sprawling to the floor, out. 'You come near my kids again and I will fucking kill ya!' Sheila screamed as she stormed out the gate with Kevin's bike in her hands. She was a girl, his aunt Sheila. No one would tread on her toes.

Georgie felt fear wash over him, but he needed to forget himself and his own feelings for now, needed to think about his mum and how hard this all must be for her and how he was only going to make it worse. He didn't want to, but he always managed to fuck things up; nothing he did was ever right, but he couldn't keep it in, he had to tell them all.

He remembered how it all started so innocently. Sharon had been expelled from school and Father Jim had been giving her private lessons at home. Georgie, on Bobby's orders, had to see Father Jim on a weekly basis to see how Sharon was progressing with her school work and her behaviour. Georgie and Father Jim had a lot in common – history, art, religion, geography, politics – they used to have some very in-depth discussions. Georgie even confessed to him.

That evening was just another normal meeting with the priest about Sharon. It was Georgie's birthday so he took a couple of bottles of wine along with him. The mood was happy and jolly – it all began innocently enough. They drank wine and talked for hours about everything, including how Sharon was getting on with her school work, sitting quietly in Father Jim's office in the presbytery where they often talked privately. Nothing had ever happened before, but Georgie felt warm and strangely excited. Father Jim was a handsome man, gentle, kind and soft-spoken. His eyes were soft and understanding, and he was very athletic and fit with a firm body.

Georgie blamed it on the wine, but he knew he was attracted to Father Jim and had been for a long time – he had always known he was different. Georgie sat on the floor at his feet next to the warm, blazing fire while Father Jim looked down at him from his large leather chair and they continued talking.

Georgie felt Father Jim's soft hands on his shoulders, rubbing, massaging, and rolling, it felt so good and natural. He felt so calm, so relaxed, so content. Georgie looked up into his blue eyes and kissed him, a soft, light kiss. More kisses followed, his passion heightened, stirring – he wanted him, needed him. Then suddenly they were undressing, slowly and seductively, Georgie's fingers weaving through his soft hair, cradling his head as he urged him for more kisses. His mouth covered his fit body, his cheeks, his throat, his chest, his thighs, until finally they were both sated, content.

They were joined and happy, and for the first time in his life, Georgie was in love. They lay together, joined in front of the blazing fire, warm and still, Georgie's cheek resting on Father Jim's chest, listening to his soft breathing and soothing heartbeat. He could still smell him, taste him.

Then he felt his gentle fingers stroking his back, his hands travelling sensuously up and down his spine, from the nape of his neck to his firm bum. He was so tender when he touched him, Georgie's head fell back as he moaned and sighed, smiling in the dimness of the room as he looked at Father Jim's beautiful face. He felt like he could stay like this forever.

At no time during that night, or any time after, did he say that what they were doing was wrong. Georgie knew it was wrong, but it felt right. But both of them knew that no one must ever know what was going on between them – it would be a death sentence. They both knew the horrendous consequences for them both if Bobby ever found out. But despite that, their relationship continued to grow, and they had many more private meetings at the presbytery.

Then one night Father Jim came round to Bobby's house. Georgie had the house to himself that night, and their passion spilled out. After they'd finished making love, Georgie forgot to make the bed. As Father Jim was leaving the house, Terri came in, went straight upstairs. Suddenly, he heard her stomping down the stairs, standing in the door with a look of confusion on her face. 'Is this what I think it is Georgie? Are you shagging the priest?' she asked with a look of surprise and suspicion on her face.

Georgie looked at her with shock, then bowed his head, just looking at the floor. He couldn't answer her.

Terri stood and watched him, looked at him, then slowly turned and walked away.

'Who's shagging the priest then?' Sharon appeared from nowhere and stood at the kitchen door with a cheeky smirk on her face. Terri and Georgie were both stunned. They hadn't heard her coming through the street door.

'Who's shagging Father Jim? Come on tell me, what am I missing out on?'

Terri and Georgie both looked at Sharon. She had a filthy grin on her face. 'You dirty bitch Terri,' Sharon laughed. 'And you've got the fucking cheek to slag me off.' She gave a high raucous laugh. 'Fuck me, daddy's not gonna be very happy is he, when he finds out Father Jim's shafting his daughter.' She turned and glared at Georgie. 'I can't believe you're letting this happen.' She strutted out of the kitchen, laughing, and stomped up the stairs.

Then her voice booming down the stairs. 'Terri you tart, you even had the fucking cheek to go in mum and dad's fucking bed.'

Sharon didn't say any more, but soon after things cooled off between Father Jim and Georgie. Bobby stopped the private lessons with Sharon – there was no reason for Georgie to see him anymore – and Father Jim just disappeared.

Georgie was told he was back in Ireland, but he didn't believe it. If he was alive he would have somehow managed to get hold of him, let him know he was safe. Father Jim must be dead and he was to blame. What Sharon had said to Bobby he would never know, but he knew Terri wouldn't breathe a word. But then how could Sharon have told him anything – if she had, Bobby without a doubt would have killed them both.

In the distance Georgie could see Mickey's car tearing along the road. It was a sobering sight, his heart felt heavy, sick. This was the moment he had always dreaded, yet at the same time he was relieved. His feelings were all over the place, he didn't know if he was coming or going. Beads of sweat dripped down his forehead as he walked past the masses of flowers that covered the front garden towards the gate.

Georgie thought of his mum, what she would think. Bobby was her husband, and whatever Bobby was or wasn't, Lizzie had always loved Bobby and always would. Georgie was so worried about Lizzie and knew how difficult today was going to be for her.

She was putting on a brave face, but Georgie knew that what he was going to say was going to tear the family apart, break his mum's heart all over again. But Georgie had to do it, had to face the consequences, whatever they were.

Sheila

Sheila walked into the front room. The house was already filling up with people. She chatted easily to family and friends offering their sympathies and condolences, but out of the corner of her eye she could see Lizzie sitting in her chair by the fire, staring hypnotically into the flames. Sheila studied her face, comparing her to the last time she'd seen her. It broke Sheila's heart to see how much Lizzie had aged, and my God, she was so thin. The sight of Lizzie made her feel sad. How lonely she must have been living in this house for all these years with a husband who didn't give two fucks for her.

Sheila now felt guilty about leaving and going to live in Ireland – but she'd had to move to Ireland, though she hated the thought that Bobby had got exactly what he had wanted – Lizzie and the kids to himself with none of her family near. His to own, control, intimidate and manipulate. She'd hated the thought of being so far away, leaving Lizzie, and her kids – Lizzie needed her family but Bobby had brainwashed her and had managed to turn Lizzie against them all. Lizzie hadn't spoken to Sheila for a few years after the turn out with Terri.

Sheila felt no anger towards Lizzie, just pity. She felt sorry for her and wrote to her regularly, sending her letters and money via Betty, their next-door neighbour. Betty always kept schtum, she knew that loose lips sank ships – Lizzie was lucky to have her as a friend. Lizzie's kids would come over to Ireland and stay with them during school holidays, Sheila loved having them all there with her, all the kids got on so well, but Lizzie had never been to Ireland, Bobby wouldn't allow it. Sheila hoped she would come over now the bastard was gone.

Sheila was really worried about Lizzie with all her encompassing smiles and over-controlled calm. She had long ago said goodbye to the gleaming, vibrant, extrovert Lizzie, all that remained was a reclusive wreck. Why had God in his wisdom let this evil pig of a man into their lives? Lizzie had been captured the day she changed her name to fucking Taylor.

Lizzie had fought hard in her marriage and suffered for her own sanity. Her laughter was replaced with tears, pleasure replaced with pain. What a fucking waste. Sheila had never once heard Lizzie complain or slag Bobby off. She'd lied in court God knew how many times. Sheila knew she got a regular good hiding, but Lizzie was a superb actress and a good liar, she should have been on the fucking stage – she certainly fitted the bill with a name like Elizabeth Taylor.

Sheila glanced at Lizzie and noticed her hands were shaking. She knew she had been on high-powered tranquillisers for years and was still shovelling them down her throat in great handfuls, plus phenobarbitone for the epilepsy she had suffered from since she was a child. Sheila had known for years that Lizzie had latched onto Dr Baker in Ripple Road – she would send Rosie to him with a five pound note and a bottle of whiskey to fetch her prescription. He knew what she needed and alcohol was just what the doctor needed. He was an alcoholic and compulsive gambler, and would give you a prescription for anything you wanted – if you slipped him a few bob and a bottle of scotch, he'd sort you out. He came running whenever Bobby gave the nod. Sheila had lost count of the amount of times the doctor had been dragged out of the pub with his glass still in his hand.

With her tumbling hair and fine body, Lizzie could have soothed and eased the pain of any man, but she gave herself to Bobby totally, completely. Because she was lonely, she really needed someone to care for, to look after, but Bobby would never be any different as long as he had a hole in his arse. Sheila tried to tell her, but Lizzie never listened, she never wanted to hear the truth. Bobby had moulded Lizzie into what he wanted her to be, he had created her.

Sheila looked at Lizzie. The lines on her face were undisguised no matter how much make up she wore – she looked like an old woman. If her mum and dad could see her now they would be turning in their graves. Suddenly Sheila shuddered. Suffocation takes on many forms – she hated Bobby with a vengeance and the feeling had always been mutual. Sheila closed her eyes on the memory, on the pain, which had turned to anger and hate. But, she thought with a bitter smile, God pays you back in mysterious ways.

She tried to lock her memories away in her head but they were always there, jumping out at her, teasing her, talking to her, tapping her on the shoulder, knocking on the door, saying come play with me. Sheila had faced the most horrific experience in her life and had to relive the torture and agony when those flashbacks came. They were tormenting her now. Sometimes she felt like ending it all, ridding herself of those moments that came and caused her so much pain and anguish, but the memory of that awful night was vivid in her mind …

~ ~ ~

She'd awoken in the early morning darkness, bleeding and bruised. She tasted the blood and vomit on her swollen lips. Dazed and disorientated she slumped back against the blood stained pillow, naked and in agonising pain. Her head was sore, she felt sick. The stench of sex, beer and sick filled her and Johnnie's bedroom. Her stomach felt hollow, she was retching. She felt a heavy pounding in her head, her neck was stiff and sore.

Sheila's face turned deathly white as she looked down at her bruised and blood stained legs. Her mouth fell open, her eyes widened, her heart was pumping furiously in her chest as the impact of what had happened smacked her straight in the face. Her tits, stomach, thighs and face were covered with dry semen.

A convulsive sob left her lips. 'No! No!'

Her crisp white sheets were covered in large blood clots. She looked around her bedroom wincing in pain. Was he gone, was he still here? Was he coming back to finish her off? Fear filled her mind, panic rising deep within her. She was shocked, scared and angry. Angry with herself, for getting herself into such a state with the booze that she couldn't even remember coming home that night. She'd had a complete blackout.

But one thing she did remember was Bobby. He had hurt her, and he had hurt her again, and he had kept on hurting her.

He'd caught up with her just as she was getting home. She was drunk, delirious with happiness, excited to finally be pregnant, suspected nothing when Bobby wrapped his arms around her, helped her into the house. He was her husband's best mate, after all. 'Come on, love,' he'd said, 'let's get you home safe and sound.'

She had tottered into the house on her high heels, managed to get her coat off and draped over the banister, was surprised to find Bobby's strong arm around her waist, helping her up the stairs. 'I'm all right, Bobby,' she'd told him, 'I've got it from here.'

'Nah!' He kept a tight grip on her as they reached the top of the stairs. 'We need to get you in the bed.' He half-dragged her in through the bedroom door, shoved her towards the bed. She stumbled, fell, landed on the bed with her skirt up around her waist.

Bobby stood over her, admiring her slim legs. 'You're a looker, Sheila, and no mistake,' he muttered, his voice thick with booze and cigarettes. The twinkling grin lit up his eyes, 'And I'm going to give you a fucking you won't forget!'

Sheila tried to fight him off, but he was far too strong – he backhanded her with one thick hand while the other groped between her legs, his boozy breath in her face as he tried to kiss her.

The more she fought, the more he seemed to like it, tearing her dress off of her with his strong hands, thrusting himself into her again and again. 'I'm pregnant, I'm pregnant,' she wailed over and over again, but it made no difference.

How long it lasted she had no idea. Terror ran through her body at the thought of his hands mauling her, touching her, seeing her naked body, invading her. She locked herself in the bathroom, crying uncontrollably. Her foot slid gently on something wet and sticky and she looked down – a huge blood clot lay on the floor. Her baby.

She was in hell. She slid down the wall, an animal-like scream erupting from deep inside her. She ran a bath, it had to be scalding hot. She scrubbed and scrubbed away at her body until it was raw, trying to cleanse herself of the filth.

Scrubbing away his touch, his smell, his feel. Sheila was gagging – she turned and vomited over the edge of the bath. She sat curled up in the bath, her chin on her knees, her arms wrapped tight around her legs. She didn't know how long she sat there, but the scalding hot water was now freezing cold.

Sheila was shivering when she got out of the bath and began cleaning her teeth. She heard someone coming through the door. It was Johnnie, back from a job in the Midlands. Johnnie just took her in his arms, holding her tight. Questioning her, Johnnie kept asking her what had happened, what was wrong? She could only stare at him. Wordless. In shock. She didn't know what to say to him or how to say it. She knew how he'd react and that frightened her. Johnnie must never know. The worst thing she had to do was stand in front of her husband who loved her so much, and lie.

How could she tell the man she loved more than anything in the world that Bobby, one of his closest friends, had savagely raped her, made her lose their baby? She was heartbroken – she had waited for years to get pregnant. That night was meant to be special – a celebration. She couldn't wait for Johnnie to get home the next day and tell him their fantastic news. She'd been so excited, she couldn't keep her mouth shut, she had waited so long for this to happen, she was pregnant at last after all these years and she wanted the world to know. She'd told all her friends and family, and they were all so happy for her and Johnnie. They all knew Johnnie would be over the moon, thrilled to bits. She was four months pregnant, at last they would have a baby of their own to love and cherish. And now Bobby Taylor had destroyed it all.

She told Johnnie that she'd got a bit tipsy at the pub with the girls celebrating, that when she was nearly home when she was mugged and beaten up. They nicked her handbag. She said that she just remembered waking up and everything was dark and fuzzy. She couldn't tell him what they looked like as they grabbed her from behind.

And so Sheila drank to try and forget, to help ease her pain, to get rid of this unending grief. She knew she was drinking too much but it helped her get through the day, to take away the unhappiness she felt inside, overpowering her all the time. She would never be free but she had to survive and move forward. She wished it was a sick dream but sadly it was real, her secret.

~ ~ ~

Sheila walked into the kitchen to get herself a drink. She poured herself a large gin and orange, lit a cigarette and shook her head dismally, thinking how her sister bore no resemblance to the old Lizzie Richards she'd once known. Sheila thought for a moment that she saw a glimpse of hope in Lizzie's wide blue eyes, but then it was gone. She took a large gulp of her drink and then another, wondering how Lizzie would get through all this. Bobby's death was as horrific as Lizzie's life. If it weren't all so tragic, it would be laughable.

Mickey

Mickey pulled up a few doors away from his house, Fat Jack behind him in his flash new Mercedes. The traffic cones were lined out along the kerb to keep the road clear for the hearse and the cars that would be coming later.

Georgie could see Johnnie sitting in the back of Jack's motor, looking completely relaxed on the black leather upholstered seats. Mickey got out of his car. One hand went in his trouser pocket, the other swung as he took long strides making his way to the front gate where Georgie stood.

'Get in Fat Jack's motor,' Mickey ordered.

Georgie swallowed deeply. He could taste the danger, feel the sweat dripping from his armpits – his stomach turned. 'Mickey, I wanna have a quick word with ya, I've got something important to tell ya.'

Mickey just stared at him. 'We ain't got time now.' He spun on his heels, headed over to Fat Jack's car. 'Just get in the motor Georgie, we've got loads to do.' He paused, cleared his throat, his voice softer. 'Come on,' gesturing him towards the car. 'Get in, we ain't got all fucking day, mate.'

Georgie hauled himself to his feet, made his way out of the gate, pulling the collar of his coat up around his neck as he went, burying his hands deep in the pockets of his thick black mohair coat. It was bitterly cold. He looked at Mickey.

Mickey's eyes challenged him. 'What the fuck's going on?'

Georgie was petrified. He'd seen that look on Mickey's face many times and it always fucking scared him. He looked every bit as dangerous as he was.

Georgie couldn't find the words to say anything.

Mickey jumped in the front of Fat Jack's car, leaving his motor parked up outside his house, while Georgie climbed in the back with Johnnie. Fat Jack pulled out onto the road along the Heathway towards the pub where everyone was going after the funeral. Mickey wanted to make sure everything was pukka for this afternoon.

Mickey turned to look at Georgie, put his hand in his coat pocket, pulled out a packet of fags and handed a couple over the back to Johnnie. Johnnie lit his, but Georgie didn't fancy smoking, felt hot and sick. He put the cigarette behind his ear and handed the gold lighter to Johnnie.

Georgie shuddered. It wasn't going to be the nicotine that fucking killed him. He rolled down the window, sweat rolling from his forehead, and stared out, just looking straight ahead, the cold sharp wind blowing across his face.

Mickey stared at his brother. 'I've just got word that Alfie Blake is about, is planning on coming to the funeral.' He laughed mockingly, took a long drag of his cigarette. 'The saucy bastard. If he fucking thinks he can show his face 'ere, he's got another think coming.' He blew a big hoop with the smoke as he exhaled.

Georgie sat silent but fidgety as he watched the veins in Mickey's neck pulsating, heard his jaw clicking as his jawbone moved slowly up and down.

Mickey turned to them both as they sat in the back of the motor. 'You know what Johnnie, I've seen my fucking muvver cry so many times over what happened to Sadie. I can't believe the arsehole fucking cheek of the geezer.'

Mickey glared at Johnnie while pointing his finger at Georgie. 'Fucking tell him, Johnnie, tell him how much misery he caused to muvver and Sheila! And the bastard thinks he can show his fucking mush here!' He drew deeply on his B&H, stared menacingly into Johnnie's eyes. 'You're a fucking lying cunt Johnnie, you told us he was dead, hung himself in Broadmoor.'

Johnnie looked at Mickey. 'Well I'm as fucking surprised as you are. That's what we were told.' He met Mickey's eyes. 'We all did.' Bobby had told Johnnie that Alfie's death in Broadmoor had been sorted, back in the 1960s.

Mickey leaned back in the front seat shaking his head from side to side. Silence again for a moment. 'That cunt killed our aunt, murdered mum's sister, sliced her to fucking pieces.' He slammed his fist on the dashboard. 'They put it down to fucking manic depression through horrific war experiences. What a load of old bollocks.' Mickey snarled, 'Horrific, I'll show that cunt what horrific is.' His usually handsome face was now dark and demonic. His eyes were unreadable, his voice cold and menacing.

Georgie sighed inwardly. Mickey was definitely on one again.

'That cunt will be out permanently when I've finished with him,' spat Mickey.

Georgie and Johnnie kept silent in the back, their eyes meeting every so often, each with their own thoughts. Johnnie hoped he saw Alfie before Mickey did. If the truth came out it would be a fucking nightmare.

Fat Jack just kept driving along, singing, whistling and humming to the tune playing on Radio One. Mickey turned the radio off and glared at Fat Jack. 'Will you shut the fuck up?'

Fat Jack turned left, pulled into the pub car park. He circled it once, and then again. He parked up next to a green Rover.

Mickey turned to Johnnie. 'Take a look in there, Johnnie.' He pointed to the Rover parked next to them. 'Is that who I fink it is?'

Johnnie looked – it was Alfie. He nodded, 'That's the man Mickey. That's Alfie.' Johnnie started to climb out of the car. 'I'll deal with him; put the bastard in the ground where he belongs.'

'No!'

Mickey's voice was loud inside the car, left no room for argument.

'The fucker killed my aunt, then has the bollocks to show up today of all days?' He reached for the door handle. 'I'll deal with him.'

Mickey got out of the Merc, his eyes flickering everywhere, said nothing, just stood taking everything in. He turned around in a full circle, looking, surveying, watchful, predatory.

Johnnie and Georgie got out of the car as Mickey watched one police car drive by and then another. The sirens howled in the distance as they disappeared.

Mickey walked over to the green Rover and peered through the window, then opened the door and sat on the front seat. His huge shadow covered Alfie Blake, who was in the driver's seat staring at Mickey, the fear on his face clearly evident. His trembling hands gripped the steering wheel tight, 'What the fuck?'

Mickey held his hand out to him and Alfie took it to shake. Mickey clenched his hand menacingly, pulled Alfie close to him. 'Mickey Taylor. Remember me?'

'I know who you are,' whispered Alfie.

Mickey yanked him nearer. 'Got a lotta catching up to do ain't we?' His angry eyes bored into Alfie. 'You no-good piece of shit,' he spat with an expression of hatred on his face. He shoved him back violently onto the driver's seat as Johnnie and Georgie clambered into the back seat of his motor.

Mickey's face was close to Alfie's. 'This is me brother Georgie,' pointing his finer at him, then at Johnnie. 'You know Uncle Johnnie don't ya, Alfie?'

Alfie nodded his head, staring dumbly down at the steering wheel.

'Oi cunt, look at me!'

Alfie looked up, his eyes sad.

Mickey smiled coldly at him. 'Just do as you're told, Alfie, and drive the car to where I tell ya, understand?'

Alfie nodded his head once. 'Yeah.' He put the key in the ignition, his hands shaking with fright, started her up and drove out of the car park. Fat Jack followed in the big Merc.

Alfie's stomach turned, he was shitting himself, and he knew he was going to die. He drove through the traffic wondering how he was going to die, who was going to finish him off. It would be Mickey. He was sure it would be Mickey – he had that mad dangerous look in his eye that his dad had. Alfie just wanted it over and done with. He had nothing to lose. He would tell him everything, let him have the truth.

They drove to an old industrial estate in Dagenham East. Alfie's car rattled through the puddle filled driveway towards a derelict warehouse, the broken windows looking like smashed, rotten teeth.

'Pull round the back,' ordered Mickey.

Alfie parked his car by a rusting door, swinging uneasily on its hinges in the strong wind. Mickey got out of the car, stood tall and erect. He pulled his cuffs down and straightened his tie, took a deep breath then slipped his hand inside his coat, pulled out a shooter. He held the gun in his hand caressing it, fondling it gently, his eyes twinkling. Shrugging his shoulders, he walked round to the driver's door and opened it. 'Get out,' he ordered.

Alfie did as he was told. Mickey stood next to Alfie, towering above him. He shoved the barrel hard to Alfie's temple with his right hand and gripped his forearm with his left. He pressed the barrel harder. He was wondering if one shot was enough, or maybe two or three would be better just to make sure. He had never killed anyone with a gun before, this could be fun.

'Walk.' Mickey shoved Alfie towards the back door of the warehouse.

They all crowded in through the metal door, into a wasteland of broken packing crates, smashed bottles, the remains of a fire, blackened ashes on the bare concrete. Light filtered in through the broken skylights.

Alfie knew he wouldn't walk out of this place alive. Everything he had heard about Mickey was true, he was fucking dangerous. Was Mickey as sadistic as his dad, enough to make this killing as cruel as possible?

Georgie, Johnnie and Fat Jack crowded in as Mickey shoved Alfie onto an old wooden chair in the corner of the room. The only sound was the wind howling outside, the pigeons roosting high in the rafters of the dark, gloomy warehouse. Johnnie stood next to Alfie, who was slumped in the chair, his shoulders stooped.

His legs were wide apart, his arms dangling between his legs clenched together as if in prayer, his head bowed forward staring at the floor. Johnnie squeezed his shoulder out of respect, but Alfie shrugged his shoulders away from his grip.

Finally he looked up, met Mickey's mad eyes. For a second his courage failed him, but he knew he had to say his piece. Then he could die a happy man. 'Your old man was fucking Sadie!' he suddenly blurted out.

'You lying, fucking cunt!' roared Mickey, 'don't you blame him for what you did, you sick bastard!' But a glance at Johnnie's face told him that Alfie was telling the truth. He didn't care. He smashed his fist into the side of Alfie's head. 'How dare you come here on the day of his funeral to start telling lies about him?' Again he slammed his fist into Alfie's face.

Alfie looked up at him, blood dribbling from his mouth. 'I came home early from a job – they were in my bed, fucking like rabbits!'

Again Mickey's fist crashed into his face, sending Alfie and the chair tumbling to the ground. 'Get him up!'

Johnnie hauled Alfie upright. He was babbling the whole time. 'I'd rather her be dead than have that lying cunt fucking her!'

Every word he said was sending Mickey into more of a rage. He hauled Alfie to his feet by his jacket, nutted him right across the nose, once, twice, three times, dropped him in a heap on the floor.

But still Alfie wasn't done. 'That's when your mum and Sheila adopted my kids!' He spat the words out through his torn lips.

Mickey stopped, his fist cocked above Alfie's

upturned face. It was a smear of blood and broken teeth. 'What the fuck did you say?'

Alfie grinned through his shattered mouth. 'Thought you knew everything, didn't you?'

Mickey looked confused, turned to Johnnie. 'What the fuck is he talking about?'

'You going to tell him, Johnnie, or should I?' croaked Alfie.

Mickey slammed a brutal kick into Alfie's ribs, sent him sprawling across the floor. 'Johnnie? What is this turd talking about?'

When Johnnie spoke his voice was calm, measured. 'Sheila's boys, and your sister Sharon. They were adopted. They were Alfie and Sadie's …'

Mickey stared at him, gobsmacked. 'What the fuck?' He couldn't get his head around it. 'Why did no one tell me?'

'We didn't want the kids to know – about him … ' He nodded towards Alfie, trying to get to his hands and knees '… and Sadie.'

Mickey took a deep breath. This was a turn up and no fucking mistake. He nodded slowly, fixed his cold eyes on Johnnie and Georgie. 'Fair enough. What you just said stays in this room, right?'

Fat Jack, Johnnie and Georgie all nodded. 'Of course,' muttered Georgie.

'And this cunt …' Mickey glared down at Alfie, his face full of disdain. 'This cunt and his lies, never fucking existed!'

He suddenly took a step forward, anger reddening his face, smashed the gun into the side of Alfie's face.

Alfie tried to get up, but as his dazed eyes fought to focus on Mickey, he brought the gun down again, repeatedly pummelled him in the head. After the third or fourth blow, Alfie fell forward onto the cold, filthy floor, feeling nothing apart from the sticky sweet smelling blood trickling down his face.

Mickey stood over him, grinning, delivered a vicious kick in the bollocks. Alfie curled into a ball, his mind calm at last. He had said what he needed to say, and now he could lie here, on the dirty floor of a warehouse, a gun in his face and his life draining from him, and feel at peace.

Alfie looked up into Mickey's twinkling eyes. He wasn't scared any more, he was going some place else, to be with Sadie again. He sighed deeply. As he smiled he felt another blow. And again and again, the heavy butt of the gun slamming down on him. He didn't think he was going to get up again. He tried crawling to his feet, but his senses were dulled, and every time he tried to get up he was knocked back down with the gun.

He couldn't see, was blinded by the blood in his eyes as it poured down his face. Georgie threw himself towards Mickey and grabbed the gun from his hand, passed it to Johnnie as he dragged Mickey away from Alfie.

Georgie looked into his brother's mad eyes. 'Give it a fucking rest, Mickey. You've made your point.' He could tell by the way Alfie was twitching that he was halfway dead already.

But still Alfie smiled, through his shattered teeth and busted lips, infuriating Mickey. Mickey grabbed a chunk of wood from the floor, several nails sticking out of the end of it, repeatedly smashed it across Alfie's back as he lay blood-sodden and beaten on the ground.

Again Georgie tried to stop him, grabbed his arm. Mickey spun around on his heels and grabbed Georgie by the throat, pinning him up against the wall. 'Listen, you fucking wanker, don't ever try and tell me what to do, and never try and stop me.' He shook him angrily, 'Understand?'

'All right Mickey, I fucking understand,' Georgie spluttered. Mickey released his firm grasp from Georgie's neck, reached across and ripped the gun from Johnnie's hand.

BANG!!! BANG!!! Two bullets smashed into what was left of Alfie, blowing the top of his head off. Georgie gagged, a shock wave of nausea running through him, but Mickey smiled, slipped the hot gun back into his coat pocket. He could feel its weight against his side, comforting.

He turned and snarled at Johnnie. 'I fink we need to have a little chat later don't you, Johnnie? See if there's any other little secrets you've forgotten to tell me?'

Johnnie said nothing, just gazed sadly down at what remained of Alfie.

Mickey strolled out the warehouse with a spring in his step. He was on a high, adrenaline pumping through his veins. He felt good, very fucking good. He wondered if the bad feeling would come later.

Mickey put his arm around Georgie's shoulder as they walked back to the car with him. 'Ya didn't get blood on your shoes, did ya Georgie?'

Georgie said nothing.

Mickey suddenly stopped. Alfie's blood flecked his cheek, a reminder of the savage beating he had just delivered. 'What was it that ya was gonna tell me Georgie?'

Georgie's eyes met Mickey's. He gave a nervous laugh. 'You know what Mickey? I must be losing the plot, I've fucking forgot what I was gonna say.'

'Couldn't have been that fucking important then, mate,' he smiled at Georgie as he slapped him on the back affectionately. 'Come on mate. We better hurry up and get home.' He glanced at his Rolex. 'The funeral cars will be there in ten minutes.' He loved Georgie, he was a good bloke but he was as soft as shit.

They all got in Fat Jack's car and drove back to the house. Mickey and Georgie had each made their own choices that day.

Frankie and Rosie

Frankie Yates glanced around Lizzie and Bobby's house. It was full of different faces, old and new, all huddled in groups, all drinking and chatting away, telling each other their stories. But Frankie only had eyes for one person – all morning he hadn't been able to take his eyes off Rosie – he tried, but his gaze kept drifting back to her. He couldn't get her out of his head, even after all these years. He had listened to Bobby and Lizzie's reasons why she left but none of it had ever made sense to him. She had just disappeared sixteen years ago – no goodbye, nothing, just gone. All these years Frankie had wondered what it could have been or what he might have done to drive her away. She didn't just leave him; she had left her family, her friends and her home. The Rosie he knew wouldn't just disappear into thin air with no explanation.

He watched her as she stood tall by the fire, a confident stance and a bright smile on her face. She was still as lovely as he remembered her, with a lithe figure and slim waist. A little skinnier maybe, but just as beautiful as she was then, still sexy in her black dress and high-heeled black shoes, her auburn curls glinting like fire as the autumn sunshine caught them.

Her hair so long, he could see the curling ends below her firm bum. He grinned, remembering what a temper she had – it was as furious and fierce as her flaming hair. But right now she looked so sweet when she smiled, tall and proud, the very picture of a chic, stylish sophisticated Londoner.

Frankie watched her again, across the room, and suddenly she turned his way. Their eyes met, and they held the gaze for a long moment. He thought there was more than grief lurking in her dark eyes, there was heartache. Frankie waited till she was standing on her own and walked over to her. 'Rosie.' He spoke quietly, putting his hand out towards her.

She looked into his eyes as she drew her fingers through her hair, remembering the way he used to look at her with his gentle eyes and slow, warm smile. There was a moment's silence. Rosie looked stern and serious, and then a wide smile broke on her face as she put her hand out to meet his. 'Good to see ya, Frankie. It's been a long time.'

He nodded his head in agreement, 'It sure has girl.' He curled his strong fingers around hers, his eyes roving all over her face as he thought how much he had missed her. 'Come 'ere.' He pulled her close to him, embracing her, breathing in her perfume, feeling her warmth but sensing her resistance. He gazed into those wonderful green eyes and his heart lurched.

Rosie thought the years had been good to him. Frankie was still in good shape, his body was firm and strong. His piercing blue eyes looked deep and interesting, soft lines etched his smile. The man who stood in front of her was how she remembered him – he had always been a handsome man. She watched his face, nearly two decades later, remembering the warm smile that had first taken her breath away. There were slight crinkles on the corners of his eyes, his cheekbones looked a little deeper, but his hair was still thick and black, not a grey hair in sight. He was still as sexy as she remembered. Knowing and remembering the touch of his mouth, his hands, his fingertips, and the warmth of his body, she had a dreadful yearning for him all over again. Just the sight of him gave her butterflies in her stomach.

She leaned towards him and kissed him gently on his lips, his mouth warm, his scent familiar. He hugged her tight and close to him and she felt the excitement he always created within her. She stood there thinking and remembering, felt choked. With his strong arms around her she felt safe for the first time in sixteen years. She pressed her lips together, her eyes closed, then slowly shook her head. Christ, she didn't realise how much she had missed him. Within moments she felt so comfortable with Frankie, yet they had spent years apart. She thought for a moment about the reasons she had left here, the last sixteen years spent trying to rebuild her life.

There had been other men since Frankie – too many to count – but none of them had ever got through to her, none of them had ever come close to making her feel the way he did. Compared to Frankie they were weak, self-absorbed, almost effeminate. Frankie was one of the hardest men in London, yet when they were together he was kind and gentle. She had that feeling again, and in spite of her own protests, she wanted him, still fancied him. She had tried telling herself she would never ever fall into that trap again, but she couldn't help it. She wanted him to seduce her, love her, take her tenderly, passionately, beautifully, soft, hard, rough, playful. She did care, she wanted him.

He took her hands in his own, 'Rosie, you all right?' There was concern in his voice.

'Yeah, yeah course I am.' My God, she needed a fucking drink. She didn't know how she was going to handle this.

He spoke with an enormous grin on his handsome face. 'Where's that lovely smile of yours Rosie?'

She took a deep breath, forced enthusiasm into her voice, a wide gleaming smile on her pretty face that just melted his heart all over again. She gulped down the last drop of her whiskey. She needed another drink. It helped steady her nerves. Rosie lifted her empty glass towards him. 'I'm gonna get me self another drink. Do ya want one Frankie?'

'Yeah, I'll come wiv ya.'

She turned and walked out of the smoky, crowded living room through to the kitchen. Quietly, Frankie followed her. He stood at the kitchen door, observing her, watching her as she moved around the kitchen.

She could feel his eyes on her. She swung around, their eyes met, held for a long moment, wordless.

Rosie walked towards him and stopped a short distance away. She felt numb inside. It was just like years ago when she stood in this kitchen, the last time she had seen Frankie, just before she left Dagenham. Talk about déjà vu. 'What do ya want to drink Frankie, whiskey?' Her voice sounded nervous, cracked.

After a moment he nodded, 'Whiskey.'

She opened a bottle of Johnnie Walkers, then reached for a glass, turning away from him to shield the tears in her eyes. Nervously, she poured a large measure of scotch into their glasses. Slowly turning, she passed one to Frankie. She raised her glass in the air, 'Cheers, Frankie.'

They clinked their glasses, as Frankie replied, 'Cheers.' Their eyes locked. 'What to this time, Rosie?'

Frankie saw her trying to fight an assortment of emotions at once. Pain, anger, love, pleasure. Her eyes narrowed, her face tightened. Oh Frankie, Rosie thought. There were so many things she wanted to tell him with so many reasons not to. There were lots of questions she wanted to ask him, things she wanted him to tell her. How could he ever understand why she left? 'Frankie …' her tone was firm and even. The way she spoke his name had an edge to it. She was hurt.

'Ssh.' Frankie put his finger to her lips and spoke softly. 'Not now, not today.'

He turned away from her and poured another drink. 'I asked Bobby why ya left.'

Rosie's chest tightened. 'What did he say?'

He faced her again. Before he had a chance to answer her, she turned and walked away. Reaching out, he caught her by the arm. 'Calm down, Rosie.'

She looked at him with utter disbelief, anger boiling up inside her. How dare he tell her to calm down? She couldn't believe what she was hearing. She could hear her heart beating furiously in her chest. Her voice sardonic, 'That's why ya didn't meet me 'cos you believed Bobby's lies.' Her smile was melancholy. 'I thought you were more of a man Frankie. You really disappointed me.' She pulled away from him, silent and saddened.

'Rosie you've got it all wrong.'

'You're right Frankie. I got it wrong for all these years.'

He took a deep breath, ready to explain, but before he could speak to Rosie she turned and walked away. He pulled her back gently towards him, facing him.

She looked at him consumed with bitterness. 'Take your fucking hands off me, Frankie.'

He looked deep into her eyes. 'I was going to meet you that last night, Rosie, but someone set me up – I got nicked on a poxy job and spent six months banged up inside …'

Her face showed her shock. All these years she'd assumed he'd betrayed her, that he'd believed Bobby and left her in the lurch, and now … 'I can tell you who set you up, Frankie.'

She could see his eyes narrow, remembered just what a tough reputation he carried around with him.

'It was Bobby – he raped me Frankie, and when I told him I was gonna tell ya, he threatened to kill me …'

She could see the shock on his handsome face as her words sunk in, as the heartache of the sixteen years they had lost registered. She spoke quietly, 'I've thought about you so much.' She looked deep into his luminous blue eyes. 'I still do.'

He stayed silent for so long that she wondered if he was ever going to speak. For a long minute time seemed to stand still, the only sound she could hear was his soft, steady breathing, the grinding of his jaw. Finally he let out a long, pent up breath. 'Well that's a fucking shocker, and no mistake …'

He gazed past her, then finally let his eyes roam over her. 'There was a corner of me mind where I always had doubts …' His face was still cold, impassive. 'Well he's dead, and though there's many here to mark his passing, not many of them will mourn him.'

His eyes looked into hers, and then down onto her deep red lips, then her hair. His hand reached up and stroked her soft cheeks. 'What's done is done …'

She smiled at him, trying to stay in control, finding it hard to believe that within a few minutes of seeing Frankie again, she was prepared to throw up everything she had built in the past sixteen years. She put her lips to his and kissed him with tenderness.

He pulled her close to his hard and firm body. 'That's better Rosie,' giving her a confident and cocky smile.

Terri appeared suddenly behind them, moving quietly as always. 'Me mum wants a quick word wiv ya.'

Frankie turned towards Terri and gave a sympathetic nod of the head. 'Be wiv ya in a minute babe.'

As soon as Terri was out the room he grabbed her hand again. 'I left a message with Bobby that night,' he told her softly.

She made no reply, couldn't speak. She was angry, her eyes dark with emotion. In the silence they looked at each other. There was a deep sadness within them both, wishing that what had been inflicted upon them wasn't true.

'I never stopped loving you Rosie,' he sighed.

'I'll always love you Frankie,' as a single tear rolled down her cheek, she realised how much she had loved him.

He gently wiped her tear away, kissed her again, soft and gentle. He pulled her close to him. She held onto Frankie. After all the wasted years, she still had those old feelings for him. Rosie looked into his eyes, put her arms around his neck and softly pressed her lips to his. 'I love you, Frankie.'

Terri called them again.

'Come on, girl, we better see what ya sister wants.' Frankie took hold of Rosie's hand and they walked confidently arm in arm back into the living room to see Lizzie.

Mickey and Mandy

Mickey strolled into the saloon bar with Georgie and Johnnie following behind. Georgie walked straight up to the bar. Johnnie needed a piss and went into the men's toilets. Everyone greeted Mickey warily but with respect, each giving their condolences and sympathy to Mickey and Georgie on the sad death of their dad. They sat at their usual table at the end of the bar – close enough to the door for a quick exit, but next to the bar where their tools of the trade, coshes, knuckle-dusters, baseball bats, a shooter and knives were kept safely if needed. A thick cloud of dense cigarette smoke hung above their heads.

Mickey's eyes were all over the place, looking to see who was about and who wasn't. He strolled confidently over to the table of food. Betty Young, his next-door neighbour, and her daughter Jeanie, had cooked all the food – they'd been up all night cooking the joints of meat. His eyes glanced over the buffet, pleased to see that they had put on a good spread with a selection of cold meat, seafood, sausage rolls, quiche, salad, rice and a lot more. Loads of grub – they'd done an excellent job, his mum would be pleased. He must remember to bung them both an extra few quid for a job well done.

He felt a firm squeeze on his bum and turned round with a childlike grin on his face. 'Hello Mand,' he smiled. She looked the business. He held his arms open wide and she fell into them. He gave her a long, hard squeeze then planted a big kiss on her lips.

She looked up at him smiling, trying to hide her nervousness. 'Mickey, I wanna tell ya something.'

She looked lovely, so horny he felt himself hardening. She was wearing a black linen suit that looked like it had come off a catwalk, with black high heels that made her slender legs seem even longer. He gathered her up in his strong arms as his eyes lingered over her. 'Come 'ere gorgeous, what ya gotta tell me?'

She gently pulled away from him. 'Gimme just a minute – I'm dying to do a wee. I'm just gonna go to the loo, I won't be a minute.' She turned away towards the ladies.

Mickey grabbed Mandy by the arm and pulled her close to him, looking into her eyes as he whispered. 'I love you Mand. You know that don't ya?'

She smiled and began to blink rapidly, dumbly nodding her head. 'I love you too, Mickey.' He squeezed her shoulder tenderly, giving her a cocky wink.

She strolled to the toilet deliriously happy, she loved him so much. She took a deep breath; she couldn't believe he was hers, but she was still scared about telling him. Worried about what he would say, how he was going to react. Would he be as proud as punch? Maybe he didn't want to have kids and settle down. Would he hate her or would he love her even more? He could tell her to get rid of it, call her a stupid tart, say that she would be an unfit mother. Shit, she was fucking scared.

Mandy didn't actually need to pee – she needed time to gather up her courage, redo her make-up, sort her hair out. She had a good squirt of the Estée Lauder perfume Mickey had bought her – another of the many presents he was always giving her. She had to look her best when she told him – maybe this good news would help him through his grief.

Mickey looked around the bar – his local, his territory. He was a young man moving upwards, fast becoming a frightening face in the East End. A law unto himself, someone who wouldn't rest till he got what he wanted. Now that Bobby was dead it was Mickey's turn. He didn't give a fuck about no-one. His image, reputation and respect all held the same importance to him. Mickey was a fearless ally, but a deadly enemy prepared to do anything to defend his territory. His rule was trust no-one and take no chances.

The pub doors opened and everyone's head turned as Fat Jack entered. Mickey trusted Fat – he was a nice geezer, and he had also been one of Bobby's trusted inner circle. All Bobby's places needed looking after by trusted colleagues, people willing to give their undying loyalty to him, people who needed someone they could look up to. Bobby only employed people who would spit in the face of a copper or screw but still wanted someone to respect and tell them what to do. Bobby was the master of a pack of hungry dogs that would do anything for a pat on the head. And now that pack was in the hands of Mickey. How would he handle them?

Fat Jack settled into the bar next to Mickey as Mickey gave Pete, the guvnor, a wad of pound notes to put behind the bar for drinks after the funeral. Mickey's eyes flicked around the place, alert and watching, his back to the bar so that he could see who was coming and going. He wasn't going to be taken by surprise.

Out of the corner of his eye, Mickey saw Jimmy Cochrane strolling over towards him, pissed as fuck, staggering from side to side like the cock of the walk. Georgie and Fat Jack exchanged a wary glance – they knew it was going to kick off. Georgie groaned inwardly, but outwardly looked confident.

Jimmy Cochrane was well known around the East End, infamous among men who'd done time, a head case who left a trail of blood in his wake. He'd just finished four years of a six-year stretch for attempted murder and was proud of it. Some geezer had upset him at the gym he used – the bloke was on the floor lifting weights when Jimmy smashed him in the face with a twenty pound weight. The geezer was now a cabbage. He smirked at Mickey. 'Dangerous! How's it going mate?'

Jimmy smiled, standing in front of Mickey upright and erect. His eyes burned with defiance, not a slight sign of fear in his posture or his eyes. 'Sweet as a nut, Jimmy.'

This was a challenge, the first of many, and Mickey knew that how he handled this would make or break his reputation. Mickey picked up the bottle and took a large swig of Pernod, wiped his mouth with the back of his hand, smiled as he carefully put the bottle down on the bar. He'd already clocked the blade in Jimmy's hand, and quick as lightning Mickey kicked the knife from it, and grabbing Jimmy by the throat with his huge hand, stared into his face. 'Somebody should teach ya some respect and manners Jimmy,' he said through gritted teeth, 'coming at me with a knife when I'm here for me dad's fucking funeral!'

Mickey shoved Jimmy backwards, causing him to stumble and fall against the bar. He quickly regained his balance, took a step back, his voice filled with distaste and arrogance. He waved his hand as he spoke. 'Respect,' he laughed loudly, pointing his finger at Mickey. 'You're not worth a cup of cold piss. Just living off the reputation of your old man. You're a nobody, Dangerous. You're full of shit. How the fuck did Mandy end up with a tosser like you?' He looked around, made sure everyone was watching him, a grin creasing his cocky face. 'Mind you, she's got a lovely pair of tits, she has.' His hands went up towards his chest moving as if squeezing a pair of tits.

Mickey looked at Jimmy and shook his head. 'Fuck off Jimmy, you're beginning to piss me off.'

Jimmy laughed back at him. 'I'm not going nowhere, mate. You think people like Frankie will be working for you now your nonce of a dad's dead? You're just a fucking baby. People will be looking for a real man to take control – it's me who'll be running the streets now I'm back.' He sniggered, his eyes scanning the saloon bar. He poked his finger in Mickey's chest. 'You're just a little boy. Mandy needs a man. Now run off and play with your schoolmates while I go and give Mandy a good seeing to.' His hands rubbed his bollocks. 'She needs a good fuck.'

Silence dripped from the smoky yellow walls of the saloon bar.

Jimmy grinned. 'Dangerous, you don't even know why your cock gets hard mate.' Jimmy's scornful laugh filled the silence.

Mickey first looked at Fat Jack, then at Johnnie, then lastly at Georgie, his dark eyes twinkling. They all recognised that evil gleam in his eyes. They could feel his anger spiralling out of control, his eyes twinkling with pleasure, his handsome face growing dark and dangerous.

Jimmy was a hard man, but Mickey had two qualities that set him apart – he was fearless, and he was quick. Before Jimmy even saw it coming, Mickey's head slammed into his face, his forehead smashing his nose. Mickey smiled as he felt the bone crumble. As Jimmy's hands went to his face, blood splattering between his fingers, Mickey kicked him in the groin, then delivered a short uppercut to Jimmy's jaw as he bent over in pain.

As Jimmy's head flopped up like a rag doll, Mickey followed up with a powerful right cross to the side of his head.

Jimmy slammed against the bar as he went down, already half unconscious, but Mickey was just getting warmed up. A huge kick to the face lifted Jimmy's head from the floor, and even as he crashed down again Mickey's massive boot stamped down onto his head again and again.

As they surveyed Jimmy's crushed face, the pub shared a collective orgasm, a sharp intake of breath at the sudden and ruthless violence they were witnessing.

Jimmy lay in a pool of blood and shattered teeth. Mickey stepped over him, calmly picked up the knife that he had kicked out of Jimmy's hand, slipped it in his pocket as his angry eyes raked around the saloon bar, daring anyone to confront him. Finally he returned his gaze to Jimmy, gargling on his own blood. 'Get this piece of shit outside,' he told Fat Jack.

Fat Jack grabbed Jimmy's feet, dragged his beaten body out to the back of the pub. Mickey followed, leaving a path of bloody footsteps behind him.

The rain had stopped, but the ground was wet, the air fresh. Mickey carefully stepped in a puddle to clean the blood off his boots, then straddled Jimmy. He leaned over, grabbed a fistful of his lank hair, lifted his head up. 'Jimmy,' Mickey hissed. 'I don't think you're going to be fucking anyone.' He grinned. 'Want to know why? Coz you won't have a cock to play with.'

'Fuck off,' croaked Jimmy defiantly.

Mickey felt excitement rise up through him. 'No cock, no hard on!' he whispered with icy calmness. The knife was suddenly in his hand, slashing Jimmy's jeans open with one hand, ripping at the torn cloth with the other.

With a scream of fear, Jimmy clawed at Mickey's face, but Mickey slapped his weak hands away, calm and cold. Raising the knife again, Mickey looked into Jimmy's eyes – they were no longer defiant but filled with terror as Mickey grabbed his cock. 'You'll never be called daddy, you cunt.'

Mickey grabbed Jimmy's limp cock, pulled it upwards like a dead chicken's neck, and in one quick stroke, cut it free. The arterial blood spurted upwards, a red fountain quickly staining Jimmy's jeans, turning the muddy puddles red.

'Suck on this, you cunt!' snarled Mickey as he jammed the flaccid member into Jimmy's mouth. 'I hope you choke on it!'

And just like that Mickey's rage passed. He stood up slowly, his eyes wide with pleasure in a job well done, slowly lit a cigarette as Fat Jack dragged Jimmy's beaten body into the boot of his car to dump somewhere quiet. Jimmy would never be seen again, and no one would ever report him missing. The Church Elms had seen and heard nothing.

Mickey strolled casually back into the bar, his face wearing a satisfied smile. 'Drinks all round.'

Everyone raised their glasses, 'To Bobby Taylor.' The pub was now back in its boozy, funeral mellow mood. Mickey sat at the table like a High Court judge in flowery wig and flowing robes, holding centre stage, exacting justice Mickey Taylor style. The first challenge had been met.

Mandy tottered back into the bar on her high heels, looked down in surprise at the blood on the floor. 'Bloody hell, what happened in 'ere while I was gone?'

Mickey wrapped his arm around her waist, pulled her in close to him. 'Nothing important – just had to get rid of a bit of rubbish. Now what did you want to tell me?'

Mandy looked up into his dark eyes. There was a look to them that she had never seen before, and it scared her. As she stared at his face – the handsome face she loved – she noticed a smear of blood on his cheek. Her stomach suddenly felt weak, queasy. 'Get me a drink, won't you love?'

Lizzie

The funeral directors arrived in their traditional black suits, no expression on their faces. Solemn, still and stiff, like the corpses they carried. Lizzie's eyes were dry as her sad gaze drifted around the overcrowded, over-warm room. Everything was over the top, just like Bobby – overindulged, overfed, and overrated.

Lizzie spotted Mickey walking towards her, looked at the way he stood, with his head held high, pride shining from him. At that moment she couldn't love him any more than she already did. He was a good boy really – he'd helped her so much since Bobby's death, organised the funeral for her and made all the necessary arrangements. She couldn't have coped otherwise – he was being strong for all of them. Georgie and the girls weren't coping very well at all. Her heart went out to all her children, wishing she could take their pain away.

Lizzie stood up. She looked small and stylish in an elegant black dress. She wiped her eyes with a tissue clenched in her hand, then nervously straightened her dress, tugged at the pearl necklace Bobby had given her on their twelfth wedding anniversary, dainty pearl earrings to match. Her slim, slender hands fiddled with the pearls nervously, played with her long dark hair, hanging loose across her slender shoulders and straight down onto the back of her dress.

Lizzie sighed, closing her eyes for a minute, thinking about the ordeal ahead. She opened them again as Mickey hugged her and kissed her softly on her cheek, then put his arm around her shoulders, guided her gently through the crowds of people towards the front door. Georgie held Martin's hand and followed. Georgie had always been a good-looking boy, now he was a handsome young man with dancing dark eyes, but today they were sad and sombre, filled with pain. Terri and Sharon clung to one another, their arms entwined as they followed slowly behind.

There were crowds of people outside her house and along the road. All their eyes were on the horse-drawn cut glass carriage that carried the flower decked coffin. It was led by four elegant black horses, dressed with striking plumes in claret and blue, followed by five black shiny limousines.

Mickey guided Lizzie through the crowd, standing silent in the wintry drizzle. Many were there out of respect for Lizzie, even if she was the wife of the man they disapproved of. It was so quiet, so eerie, the men in their starched suits and black ties standing like mannequins, watching and waiting. There were so many faces she hadn't seen for donkey's years, family, friends, neighbours and associates, friends from the kids' schools, even some of the teachers were here. She couldn't quite believe the turn out, it didn't seem possible or even real. She wondered why they were all here.

Lizzie saw Arthur, the funeral man, the tail ender who never missed a burial and its wake. He was at every one he heard of, checking the Dagenham Post every week to see who'd died. Arthur was an old friend to each and every one of the dead. To Arthur, it meant a free piss-up and a bit of grub and he might find himself a rich widow. She gave his hand a quick squeeze before turning to Stevie. Lizzie kissed him softly on his cheek, his deadly white face so thin and gaunt. He was in a bad way.

Stevie clasped both her hands nervously, shifted his weight from foot to foot. 'I'm so sorry Lizzie,' his voice fragile and shaky.

Lizzie pulled him towards her and patted his back. 'Everything will be all right, love.' Stevie pulled away, choked with grief. Lizzie was worried about him. He hadn't taken Bobby's death very well.

She continued through the crowd, her gaze drifting, overwhelmed that there were so many people, so many faces, all suited and booted. She carried on shaking hands with everyone and thanking them for coming, all these different people, kids and housewives brushing shoulders with the hard men of gangland London. It was strange.

Mickey had his arm draped around her shoulders, steered her towards the black limousine. He was shocked at how old and frail she looked, he hadn't really noticed it before. They sat in the front car with Georgie, Sharon, Terri and Martin, while family and friends travelled behind in the other four cars. Lizzie turned to look behind her, at her house, as they drove away. All Lizzie's memories, good and bad, unfolded.

~ ~ ~

Blimey, it had been nearly sixteen years since they'd moved from Poplar…

~ ~ ~

It had been time to move on after the war; Lizzie could still remember the excitement in the air as they all climbed onto the lorry leaving Poplar. It was a new beginning, a new start, filled with new and exciting promises.

It was a beautiful spring day, the sun smiling through the white clouds. They sang all the old songs, 'Pack up your troubles in your old kit bag', 'On Mother Kelly's doorstep', 'Come round any old time and make yourself at home.' You name it, they sang it. They talked about their mum and dad, talked about Sadie, remembered the war and all the good times they had shared. They were all gloriously happy, laughing and joking as the car drove through the Blackwall tunnel and along the A13, then pulled up in front of their new three bedroom parlour type house, everything fresh and clean with bright red brickwork.

The smell of fresh paint was still lingering in the soft spring air as they stepped inside. It was lovely, with a kitchen, two rooms downstairs, a front room with a huge bay window that looked straight out onto the busy road – it was great, you could see who was coming up to the gate. Lizzie smiled to herself; she'd hidden from the rent man and the Provident lady many a time. The living room at the back of the house had views of the big back garden, which had a huge cherry tree at the bottom as well as a rhubarb patch. There was even a bathroom and a toilet indoors, pure luxury. They had never had an indoors loo before.

Their house was always the centre of activity, a place where friends and relaives would congregate and party. Lots of wheeling and dealing had gone on down there with Bobby and his mates.

She'd been happy at first, back in days of women chatting on the corner of the street and on the doorstep with the latest gossip, the street door open day or night, the kettle always on the go, watching the kids play on the green, kicking the football around, having fun. But gradually Bobby began to change – Sheila, Johnnie and the boys moved to Ireland and Rosie ran away.

Lizzie sighed inwardly; those days of love and laughter were long gone. She couldn't accept he was gone and never coming back. She shivered; Lizzie didn't know how she was going to live without Bobby. Her life had changed in a moment. She had lost everything, her life, her love, her dreams all demolished. All the things she had cherished, all the things that had kept her going for all these years were gone. But at the same time, for the first time in years she felt free – it was almost too much to bear.

She felt like a caged bird whose cage is suddenly opened – she knew she could escape, but she was almost too scared to. Much as she hated it, she was afraid she would miss the security that Bobby gave her, ruling her life, telling her what to do, what to wear, even what to think. Without him, she felt lost …

~ ~ ~

It took a good twenty minutes to get to the church, the hearse and carriage going at walking pace. Friends walked behind the hearse, and the cortege stopped outside the pub for a minute's silence. Lizzie just sat staring out of the window at nothing. Crowds lined the Heathway three deep, watching in silence, as if they were waiting for the town show to begin with the Dagenham Girl Pipers marching along with their grand performance. Some stood with their heads bowed.

Lizzie glanced at Mickey sitting next to her on the other side. She looked into his eyes. They were cold – was he dazed with grief, or was there something else going on behind that closed visage? As she sat staring at him, she noticed as if for the first time how much he was like Bobby. Everything about him was Bobby – the way he spoke, the way he sat, the way he cocked his head to the side, his brown eyes and perfectly sculptured handsome face. Even his voice so soft and calming, like his father's.

Lizzie shivered, feeling suddenly scared. It was as if Bobby were here, sitting right next to her. Surely they were going to someone else's funeral? It couldn't be Bobby's. She still couldn't believe he was dead. Mickey looked at her and gave her a wink, a bit of reassurance. A trace of a smile flickered on her face, she loved her Mickey – he was a good boy, underneath his tough exterior he had a good heart.

Sharon and Terri clung to one another and cried all the way to the church. Lizzie looked at Martin sitting next to her. Her beautiful little blue-eyed boy, her pride and joy, another Bobby look-alike. Everyone knew Martin. He was a loveable little rogue. He would stroll cockily down the street, wave his hand to everyone, 'All right, mate?' The old and the young acknowledged him – a little bleeder at times, but she loved him so much, he was her baby. She had to protect him now. No harm must ever come to him again. She felt hot tears stinging her eyes. The poor little sod had been through so much in his young life. She looked at his sad face, badly bruised and swollen, put her hand into his and clenched his hand tightly. 'Are ya all right?' He squeezed her hand back, nodded his head with a faint smile. The night Bobby died was vivid in his mind.

They'd had a big row, so Lizzie had ordered Martin to go next door to Betty. She always knew when it was gonna kick off with Bobby, knew just by that evil twinkle in his eyes. Martin didn't want to leave her but she begged and pleaded with him to go next door, telling him everything would be all right. He went to Betty's, who tucked him up safe and sound in her spare bedroom. She would make sure no harm came to him.

Leastways, Betty thought he was sound asleep, but Martin had tricked her, climbed out of the bedroom window, down the drainpipe, and crept into his house through the back door. It was still, dark, the arguing and fighting had stopped. He stood quietly at the bottom of the stairs and listened.

As his ears adjusted to the quiet, he could hear funny noises coming from upstairs. He walked slowly onto the stairs and listened, holding tight onto the banister. No lights were on so it was very dark as he walked quietly upstairs, making sure to step over the creaky floorboards.

As he got closer he could hear Bobby's voice, cold, chilling. 'Die you bitch, die whore,' coming from the bathroom. He could hear the bath water running.

Martin crept to the doorway, peeked through the crack – it was his mum, she was drowning, Bobby was trying to kill her. He was holding her head under the water, and she was gasping for air fighting for her life. Bobby was shouting at her, over and over again, 'Die bitch, die.'

Martin's face went red as he held his own breath, wishing his mum would breathe. She had to breathe again, she couldn't die. Martin heard her come up, desperately gasping for air. He took a deep breath himself. He listened harder, and heard loud splashes of water; he was pushing her head under again and again. Lizzie was struggling for her life; Bobby was going to kill her.

Martin had no time to think – he steamed through the bathroom door. Bobby had his hands wrapped around her throat, had her head under the water. Martin jumped on his dad's back, wrapped his legs around him as tight as he could, clung to his hair with his one hand and kept smashing his other fist into Bobby's face.

It was enough – Bobby stopped drowning his mum and turned his fury on Martin. He got a fucking good beating the night Bobby died, but it was worth it. By the time Bobby was done beating Martin, he'd staggered off, forgotten all about drowning Lizzie. They were burying that cunt today. He would always look after his mum; no one would ever hurt her again. No one.

Sharon

As the cars crawled towards the cemetery, Sharon sat silent, gripping Terri's hand. It had been weeks since she'd had that terrible abortion, but could still see it and feel the excruciating pain in her stomach, the hell that came after ...

She had just wanted to go home, go to bed, curl up and die. She hated Paul and Bobby so much, but most of all she hated herself. She got into bed, curled up into a ball and fell asleep. All of a sudden she woke up – it was dark, for a second she couldn't remember where she was, what had happened, but then the pain forced itself up through her conscience, grabbed at her stomach. But there was something else, that noise, those footsteps she had come to fear ...

Bobby came steaming into the bedroom, totally out of his face. She sat upright in bed, and pulled the blankets tight under her chin. The look on his face scared the life out of her. Her eyes filled with fright.

'There's the dirty stinking whore, you're fucking

pregnant ain't ya?' he screamed at her. His handsome face had become ugly and evil. His features were drawn and his dark eyes colourless and filled with hate.

'Who have ya been fucking, ya slag?' His mouth foamed, 'Or are ya just spreading your legs with anyone? You dirty slut. I bet ya don't even know whose cunt it is!'

She hated him, hated him so much hot burning tears filled her eyes. She screamed at him. 'I ain't fucking pregnant, so fuck off. I hate you.' Her eyes told him she meant what she said.

Bobby's hand lashed out, whacking Sharon's face with such force she fell sideways out of the bed onto the cold lino floor, dragging the blankets with her. She could feel the imprint of his hand already starting to bruise on the side of her cheek.

'Dad, please,' she said wringing her hands together in fear.

He stood over her, menacing.

'Dad, please stop it,' she said again, stuttering painfully.

'Stop it,' he spat, 'stop it? This is only the beginning,' laughing at her, laughing in her face. 'You rotten whore.' His lips were drawn back into a snarl. Grabbing her by the shoulders he dragged her upright, near to him, his face close to hers.

'Tell me you dirty fucking slag, was it good?' he growled, his eyes flashing venom. 'It's that fucking slag Paul ain't it. Did ya enjoy it? Cos I'm gonna enjoy killing the cunt when I find him.' He grabbed a chunk of her hair as though trying to uproot it from her scalp, yanking her head towards him, forcing her to look at him.

Tears blurred her eyes. His face was everywhere, she felt dizzy and light-headed. How did he know? Who told him? He knew everything – who she saw, who she spoke to, where she went, who she was with. She was never alone. Bobby's eyes and ears were everywhere. 'I ain't pregnant and I ain't done fuck all,' she told him, defiant. 'I couldn't have a fucking boyfriend if I wanted, no-one wants to come near me, everyone's fucking shit scared of you. So I ain't got no fucking chance and it's all your fault. I hate you so much, I wish you was dead. If you fucking touch him or hurt him, I promise I'll fucking kill you.'

A sarcastic grin appeared on his face. 'You're nothing but a dirty whore. You'll suffer for this!'

His big fist crashed into her temple, she fell backwards, her head crashed against the heavy dark wood headboard. She thought she was going to faint; she was feeling dizzy.

'No, Dad!' She blinked her rapidly swelling eye, looking through her dazed green eyes filled with tears of terror at the man who had once shown her love and affection. 'Leave me alone, please don't hurt me any more,' she screamed at him.

His huge hands came down around her slender neck; he glared at the cowering girl in front of him.

Gasping for breath, she croaked, 'No more please. Dad stop it.'

Bobby's mouth curled into a cold, hateful smile. 'A bit late to say stop it now, you dirty good for nothing slut.' His eyes twinkled above his cold, calculated smile, his face no longer handsome but evil and loveless. 'I'll show you a good time, you dirty whore. He'll never wanna come near you when I've finished with you,' he said as he threw her down on the bed.

She tried to wrap the blanket around her, but he ripped it from her hands. She wrapped her arms around her knees and stared at Bobby. Her eyes widened and her words came out filled with terror. 'No, Dad please. I'm your daughter for fuck sake. What have I done to make you hate me so much?'

Bobby heard her sharp intake of breath and a smile appeared on his lips.

Sharon's lovely face crumbled as she stared at her dad, his eyes flashing poison.

Bobby said nothing, just grabbed her by the arms and dragged her upright, gave a leering smile as he ripped her nightdress from her body. Huge crimson blood clots slithered down her slim white thighs, gushing from deep inside her, spewing all over the bedroom floor. 'You dirty, fucking whore!' he roared as he threw her down on the bed, climbed on top of her.

Dizziness' overwhelmed her; she was spinning round and round. It was dark, she was floating high in the sky, twisting and turning. Then complete and utter darkness.

She woke up in Georgie's arms. He was gently stroking her hair, murmuring, 'Wake up Sharon, please wake up!' His tears had soaked her face. When she opened her eyes he gasped. 'Thank fuck! I thought you were dead!'

She somehow forced a smile to her face. 'It will take more than that miserable cunt to kill me, Georgie ...'

Georgie nodded sadly – they didn't even need to say his name, they both knew who they were talking about ...

Georgie had hurried her out to his car, almost carrying her in the chill morning light, Sharon with a towel crammed between her legs to stem the bleeding. She remembered that all she could think about as they drove was that she was messing up one of her mum's best new towels.

At Oldchurch Hospital the doctor told her that the abortionist who performed the operation had butchered her insides, she would never hold a baby of her own in her arms.

Georgie held her hand as she lay in the cold bed, staring at the harsh fluorescent lights. Despite his warm presence, his soothing words, she still wished she had never been born, wished that Bobby Taylor had never been her father – for despite the darkness that had engulfed her, in a deep corner of her mind she knew exactly what her father had done that night, every filthy second of it ...

Lizzie

There was no one lonelier than Lizzie Taylor standing by the graveside on that cold, wet November afternoon. She'd watched Georgie, Mickey, Johnnie, Fat Jack, Stevie and Big Frankie carry Bobby into the church, little Martin walking in front with the funeral director, then carry him back out of the church on his final journey. Of what happened in church, she didn't remember a thing.

Her mournful eyes roamed the graveyard. So many people, their hearts pouring out to Lizzie and her children. She was a lovely woman whose family had suffered an awful tragedy, but every person who stood there remembered Bobby, with their own thoughts. A saint or a sinner? She could just imagine the stories going around, some funny, some frightening, some sinister.

Lizzie gazed at Georgie, standing tall and erect between Terri and Sharon. He was the softest of them; the most like her in many ways, but behind his deep brown eyes there were depths you could never guess at. Mickey, you knew exactly what you were getting, could predict exactly what he would do or say in most situations, but Georgie, he was a closed book. There were things going on in his mind that none of them would ever guess at.

She looked past Georgie to Mickey – he was stood behind Martin, his strong hands resting on Martin's shoulders. She could feel their sadness, joy, horror, sorrow and grief. Next to them stood Fat Jack, wiping the tears from his face as he watched his lifelong friend going into the ground. After all the years she'd known him, Lizzie couldn't make out if Fat Jack was good or twisted, ignorant or wise. He'd seen and heard so much – he always looked after Lizzie and the kids when Bobby was inside, was a good and loyal friend. She had cried on his shoulders many times, yet she had never heard Fat Jack say a bad word about Bobby. Whether that was from fear or admiration she would never know.

She could barely see them as tears sprang into her eyes. She could hear Terri sobbing uncontrollably. Sheila stood at the graveside with her shoulders hunched up, her head bowed down looking at the cold, damp ground, clasping Johnnie's strong hand. Danny and Kevin stood next to Johnnie, while Rosie stood stone faced next to them with not a tear in sight. Lizzie knew why and didn't expect anything different. Everyone was watching and waiting. He was finally going, gone forever.

Lizzie felt Martin's arms wrap tightly around her slender hips, his head pressed against her ribs. She looked tenderly into her youngest son's face, her eyes filled with tears of sorrow for all of her children. She touched his face with her soft hands and bent and kissed his cold, rosy cheek. She couldn't find any words to comfort him. She held him tight and close to her.

Mickey held her hand tight as she took a deep, raw breath. She was shaking so violently, the pain in her eyes was so raw. Her small figure, standing in front of him in the rain with her shoulders slumped, looked so alone, so vulnerable, the tears rolling down her cheeks. Mickey felt his own eyes welling up. He took her in his strong arms and held her for a long moment. His voice was low and soothing as he whispered 'I love you, Mum.' Lizzie shivered; those words meant everything to her. She put her arms around him, clutching him, holding him tight.

Mickey was scared she would go into hysterics; he'd been dreading this day. Mickey pulled her closer and she squeezed his big strong hand, gripping tight as if she was never going to let go. Her eyes never left her husband's huge coffin as the priest showered it with holy water and prayers, praying for the faithfully departed.

'Dear Lord, Jesus Christ, we pray for Bobby Taylor. Lord you know his soul, you made him, he is yours. Lord, in a moment of desperation blinded by despair he departed from us. Please Lord, by the merit of your cross and resurrection, humbly we ask for your mercy. Have mercy on his soul and help his family and friends. Heal them from this deep wound and

sorrow. Only you, the healer, can restore them and make them whole again. Amen.'

~ ~ ~

Lizzie started to sway as a feeling of faintness swept over her, and for a brief moment she could smell him – that malicious, gutless stench. Bobby always had one arm around her, the other digging the knife deep and twisting. He was here now, she could feel him touching, groping, and mauling her. She found it difficult to breathe, his overpowering presence was suffocating her and she could feel ice running through her veins. Bobby would be forever carved in her mind; she knew that she would be tormented day and night, forever doomed. It was her punishment and she deserved it. A reproach for her sins. She would never be free of him.

But Lizzie had to face life without her Bobby. She would never again hear his vile abuse or feel his fist smashing into her face. So where was the feeling of happiness she thought would come when she was free of him? She should have felt different knowing he was dead and she had her freedom, but she felt empty inside, a cold aching pain searing in her heart.

The truth was, she had been addicted to Bobby. She had needed, wanted and craved him. Bobby was her deadly poison, sly, cunning and baffling. She had fallen in love with his perfect exterior years ago, yet his dangerous interior had destroyed her soul. He had two faces, one he let others see, and the other he didn't. He had left behind him a legacy of death, destruction and misery, and the ghosts of the insulted, tormented and tortured lingered close by. The pain and the bloodshed hadn't died with him. She knew her memories would always be there and the scars would never heal.

Lizzie gave a horrible groan as his coffin was lowered into the ground. She grabbed hold of Mickey's coat as she fell to her knees on the damp, cold earth, sobbing in anguish. Her head sank deep into his mohair coat, crying bitter tears for herself and all of her children. If only she'd known then what she knew now, her life could have been so different. She could have saved her children from their pain and misery. 'Please God, help me,' she said in a strange voice, choking on her words. A shrill scream left her lips as she recalled the night Bobby died.

~ ~ ~

She'd lain awake in the darkness, like so many nights before, waiting and listening as she watched the shadows of the night roll across the ceiling. The house was quiet and still, peaceful, but then she heard the key on the string going through the letter box, the fumbling at the lock, the front door squeaking as it opened slowly. It was him – pissed again. She could hear each single drunken step on the stairs. The handle of the bedroom door turned slowly and then the door swung open violently, crashing loudly against the bedroom wall.

She lay in bed, rigid, still, trying not to breathe. Bobby stormed into the room, his vile smell, his dark shadow, his sounds filling the quiet room. Lizzie licked her suddenly dry lips, squeezed her eyes tightly, moved her lips in silent prayer, begging God to look after her. 'Please God, make him go away, fall asleep, anything. Please, please make him go away.' She wanted God, needed God. Why wasn't He listening to her? What had she done so wrong? 'Please make him stop hurting me.'

His footsteps grew nearer, and her heart roared in her chest, pounding rapidly. She could hear his knuckles cracking and fists clenching, he was warming up for the first punch. She felt the bile in her stomach beginning to rise, began trembling, bit down hard on her bottom lip. She looked up to the ceiling, trying not to scream or cry, blinking her eyes to keep the tears from spilling, blood dripping down her chin where she had bitten her lip so hard.

Then his mouth was against her neck, his unshaven face was close to hers, his dark rough stubble rubbing so hard against her soft cheeks that she could feel them burning. His hands tightened on the collar of her nightdress, pulling her closer to him. He burped in her face, and she could smell and taste him – women, sex, whiskey, fags and stale beer, the smell of Bobby Taylor. She gagged, nauseated by his presence, his stench, the retching coming from deep in her stomach as she clamped both her hands to her mouth, trying not to throw up. She knew what was coming, all his pent up frustrations were about to be released.

'Oi, cunt wake up.' Shaking and pulling her from side to side. 'I know you're not asleep.' He grabbed her hair from the back, dragging her face up to his, his red bulging angry eyes staring at her. 'Where the fuck is Rosie? How long has she been back here?'

'I don't know, Bobby.'

Bobby's hand whiplashed, stinging her soft, sad face. 'Tell me where she is, you no good piece of shit.' A slap to the left, then the right.

'I don't know Bobby.'

'Where the fuck is she?' he roared.

Slap to the left, right, left, right.

'Lying fucking whore.'

Lizzie screamed, 'I don't know!'

She could feel the imprint of his hands already starting to bruise. 'Please stop,' she said wringing her hands together in fear.

'Stop,' he spat, 'I've only just started, bitch.' He slammed his fist into her forehead, narrowly missing her eyes. 'Don't ever tell me what to fucking do! You're a no good piece of shit! You hear me?'

'Please, Bobby! No more,' she begged, whimpering like a dog. 'No, Bobby, no.'

Bobby's mouth curled into a cold, hateful smile as he launched his powerful fist into her face again.

His eyes twinkled above his cold, calculated smile, his face no longer handsome but evil and loveless. 'Where's that slag of a sister of yours? You're all fucking whores, you and your dirty sisters. I've fucked 'em all, ya know? Sadie was the best, I should have married her. They all fucking wanted me and kept coming back for more, I could fuck any one of them when I wanted. They were all up for a bit of me, couldn't keep their hands off me. But look at what I got fucking lumbered with. Look at the fucking state of you! You repulse me, make me feel sick.'

Tears drenched her face. 'P-please believe me,' she stuttered painfully. He grabbed her by the throat and pushed her head violently back against the wall at the end of the bed. She fell to her hands and knees, whimpering like a dog, begging and pleading with him to stop.

'That's where you belong you filthy whore,' he said with his mouth foaming.

She could feel her eye puffing up, the bruises throbbing. She turned around, her back against the wall, wishing she could be anywhere else but here right now.

'Don't fucking lie to me. Where's the dirty slut?'

Bobby's features were drawn and his dark eyes colourless. He poked his nicotine stained finger in her face, yelled, 'Tell me now!'

'Please Bobby, I don't know. Honestly, please believe me.' Stammering her words.

He stared into her face, poked his finger into her chest, 'You're fucking useless, look at the fucking state of you, you no good whore. You couldn't even take an overdose and get that right. I wish you were dead and so do the kids. They hate you as much as me. You useless piece of shit.'

He ripped her nightdress from her small frail frame and she heard his sharp intake of breath as his eyes raked over her naked body, her soul undressed. A smile appeared on his lips, warm with pleasure. Nothing satisfied him more than seeing her suffer. She was going to pay for her sins. Lizzie's terrified eyes widened, her words came out filled with terror. 'No, no, no.' She tried moving away from him. 'Please Bobby. No.'

He looked into her eyes, burning with lust and hate. Lizzie's lovely face crumpled as she stared at her husband, his eyes flashing poison. His sweet lips were drawn back into a snarl. Grabbing her by the shoulders he dragged her upright, near to him, his face close to hers. 'Tell me you dirty fucking pig,' he said with his eyes flashing venom. The way he looked at her, those eyes told her exactly what he was capable of. 'Where is she 'cos I'm gonna enjoy fucking her again.'

He grabbed a fistful of her hair, savagely twisting it around his hand, yanking her head back and forcing her to look at him. Tears blurred her eyes. 'You dirty whore.'

His huge fist smashed into Lizzie's face once again, and she reeled backwards, her limp body crashed against the heavy dark wood headboard. 'No, Bobby!' She looked up through a rapidly swelling eye at the man who she had married and loved, who at the beginning had shown her love and affection.

His huge hands came down around her slender neck as he glared at the cowering woman in front of him. Gasping for breath, Lizzie croaked, 'I'd never lie to you.' Years of painful experience had taught her when to shut up; she knew when it was checkmate. Bobby threw her violently back down onto the cold, damp lino.

She stared through her bruised eye into his face hovering above her. Lizzie tried to move but pain seared through her head and made her gasp. 'If I ever find out you've lied to me ...' His red eyes bulged with his inner twist of rage, lust and power.

He grinned, suddenly fell on top of her, so heavy that her ribs were crushed. His face was everywhere. She felt dizzy, light-headed, the room was spinning round and round and everything was in slow motion. The lights were so bright, flashing and falling like shooting stars. The room was getting smaller and smaller, closing in, she couldn't breathe. Her head felt as if it were made of rubber, a balloon getting bigger, tighter, stretching. Ready to explode. She slipped in and out of consciousness as waves of pain seared through her.

Bobby's rough hands started creeping all over her, groping, grabbing, touching and mauling her. His vulgar mouth moved up and down her, he forced her mouth open with his tongue as he pushed her legs open wide with his knees, sucking and biting her nipples until they bled.

Her fingers were white-knuckled on the crumpled blankets that had fallen to the floor, her heart hammering hard in her chest, her long slim legs trembling as she sobbed with terror. Please God, make him stop. I can't stop him, I want him to stop, too much pain. Everything is dark, everywhere black and fuzzy.

Bobby watched her writhe and twist beneath him. She tried to squirm away from him, but his strong arms gripped her wrists tightly, his face hard against hers. The evil was frozen in her screams that were never heard. He unzipped his trousers, pushed himself into her as hard as he could, enjoying the pleasure of giving her pain. Not making love to her, as a husband should, but raping her, a raw display of power to sate his swollen ego.

His strong arms not only held her down but also held down the hopes and dreams that she had clung to for so long. They broke the barriers of illusion that she used to protect herself and her marriage.

Lizzie wanted to scream but she couldn't, she just watched, detached from herself, from who she was, what was happening. It was just another body being beaten, mauled and humiliated. She wasn't that woman lying miserably on her back, moaning horribly as the most intimate parts of her body were attacked, that woman enduring and feeling her revulsion. She was someone else.

She could see Bobby's mouth moving – he was shouting and screaming but she couldn't hear him, the sound was just a loud buzzing in her ears. He fucked her like she was a piece of meat, enjoyed her humiliation, shuddered violently as he came all over her face, his face distorted with lust. Bobby exhaled in satisfaction, licking his lips as he looked down at Lizzie, lying with blood, tears, saliva, snot and semen dripping down her smashed and swollen face.

It was silent as she looked at his face through her dazed and bloodshot eyes. He rolled off her, pushed himself to his feet, then in one final gesture, completed his humiliation of her. He stood over her, swaying slightly, then slowly pissed all over her.

Finally satisfied, he crashed down on the bed, was asleep in seconds, snoring like a pig.

Lizzie lay in the darkness, wondering if she would ever find the strength and courage to leave him. She could feel the presence of his huge body, could hear him breathing, sleeping soundly on the bed above her. She turned her head, saddened and disgraced. Everything she had was gone, only loneliness remained. Lizzie had a love that would never know be met.

Lizzie had fallen in love with something very dangerous and her life would never be the same again, but she didn't say anything, she was used to the way he treated her. It wasn't his fault, it was the booze, he was sorry. She sat up and looked at his face, at those wild brown eyes that had mesmerised her. She touched his beautiful face, the face she had fallen in love with.

She shivered in the cold of the night. How could she be so fucking sick and stupid again? Abruptly, her sadness vanished and became anger. She hated him. She fought back the impulse to get a carving knife from the kitchen and rip his heart out and watch him drown in his own blood. Killing Bobby would be a release for them all. She wanted to hurt and torture him, wanted to watch him suffer a slow, withering agonising death, wanted him to grovel and beg her for his life, make him writhe in terror, horror, fear and feel pain as they all had felt. She wanted to feel the knife digging deep inside him, feel his wet, sticky, fresh blood. He would go to hell, she knew he would, he deserved to suffer eternal torment.

Lizzie knew she would be haunted for the rest of her life. How could her kids ever forgive her for putting them through all the pain and heartache they had suffered for so long at the hands of their own flesh and blood? She felt her own self disgust –she was their mum and she should have protected them.

Exhausted, Lizzie crawled naked across the damp lino to the bathroom. She sobbed hysterically as she sat in the bath washing the filth from her skin and the vulgar smell from her nostrils, sobbing uncontrollably, vowing to herself over and over that she would never let him treat them like this again …

~ ~ ~

Mickey watched his mum as she crumpled at his feet. He was gutted, she was in bits because she couldn't tear herself away from the graveside and leave her beloved husband alone in that huge dark coffin and go home without him. Mickey lifted his mum from the ground and held her close in his strong arms.

He bent down and picked up a handful of dirt and threw it on top of his dad's coffin, read the inscription, the stark reality. Bobby Taylor b. May 1930 d. October 1971 R.I.P.

Lizzie clung on to Mickey, needing his strength and security. But as the dirt slowly fell onto the coffin, she felt something snap, the final cord that had tethered her to Bobby for so long. For a moment she feared that she would simply drift away, like a helium balloon that breaks free, and drifts away on the wind, high up in the clouds.

As more and more dirt hit the coffin, Lizzie opened her eyes. Slowly, little by little, Bobby was disappearing. Mickey tried to pull her to her feet, but she resisted, just stared at the coffin, slowly vanishing beneath the dirt. 'I need to see this,' she whispered.

And then he was gone. The smell of clean, damp earth replaced the stench of Bobby Taylor. Lizzie wiped the back of her hand across her eyes, allowed Mickey to slowly help her to her feet.

Weak, frail, but free, she staggered away, let Mickey lead her back towards the waiting cars. Her head was down, no one could see her face, no one could see the faint smile that played at the corners of her mouth.

When they reached the cars, Lizzie stopped, watched as their friends drifted awkwardly away, not a word spoken, the only sounds their feet on the gravel and the steady drip of rain on the huge black umbrella that sheltered Lizzie.

And as the mourners passed, Mickey had his cold eyes on each and every one of them, certain, deep inside, at a place beyond reason, that his ole man's killer was at the graveside, watching as they laid him in the ground. Before the day was done Mickey would figure out who killed him. And then? Well let's just say he was feeling very fucking dangerous ...

Mickey

The pub was packed and noisy, chock-a-block with people who had been to the funeral. Most of them had been in since opening time and were half pissed already. Mickey undid his top button and loosened his tie as he walked around the pub with Georgie, doing the rounds, thanking everyone for coming and paying their respects. Mickey knew that Bobby would have been proud of such a decent send off and turnout, everyone getting good and proper drunk. That's the way Bobby would have wanted it.

Mickey made his way through the crowds, shaking hands, a quick chat, a comforting hug, a kiss on the cheek, lots of sympathetic smiles. Everyone watched Mickey with awe. He hadn't seen Mandy for a while, wondered where she was as his eyes flickered around the boozer.

Unbeknown to him, she'd been in the toilet throwing up since they got back from the cemetery. He smiled to himself as he spotted her in the corner standing at the table with Lizzie, his aunts and other family and friends. He was glad everyone got on well with Mandy and liked her. He strolled over to her, he could hear her laughing. He rested his chin on her shoulder, whispered in her ear. 'Hello babe, you all right?'

She turned to him, smiling, planted a kiss on his lips. 'Yeah I'm all right; I've just been talking to ya mum and a few of the girls. They're so funny, they crack me up.' He gave her that sexy smile that made her heart melt.

'She's a right one, Betty,' she laughed, 'she had me in fits. She was telling me when your aunt Sheila was in hospital, Betty went up to visit her with a carrier bag full of goodies. She gets out a bottle of orange juice – it was gin and orange. She also brought her down a toiletry set, sexy nightdress, a box of chocolates and a packet of fags. Anyone would think she was going away for a dirty weekend, not laid up in Rush Green Hospital.'

Mickey smiled at her. 'I know, she's as nutty as a fruitcake.' He cuddled her closer. 'I was worried about ya. I couldn't see ya. Where ya been? You all right?' He brushed her hair away from her eyes, squeezing her tight.

'Course everything's all right.' She gave him a peck on the cheek.

'What was you laughing about?'

She nodded towards Sheila and Betty. 'They were just telling me about the time a coach load of 'em went racing, Ladies Day at Ascot. All day they were there and none of 'em even saw a bloody horse.'

Betty heard what she was saying and picked up the story. 'We've had some laughs we have,' Betty told him, 'ya mum even came with us one year.' She lit a cigarette. 'We were all done up to the nines in our posh frocks and suits all parading around like we owned the place. You wouldn't have recognised us.' She took a gulp of her brandy. 'Fourteen of us had put a few bob away each week to pay for the coach and the food and drink. Jack, your dad's mate, was driving the mini bus. He must have wished he hadn't, the bleedin' state of us all on the way home.'

Betty laughed, a high raucous laugh, as she looked at Brenda Turner, pointing her finger in her direction.

'On the way there she went falling arse over tit spilling her beer all down her new dress. So what does she do? She takes it off and hangs it out the window to dry. Sitting there in the middle of the coach just in her drawers, giving everyone an eyeful. She got a few wolf whistles on the motorway.'

'I'm surprised she didn't cause a fucking accident,' laughed Mickey as Betty took a breather.

She took a swift gulp of her drink. 'One time, she went to see Doctor Baker, she had a terrible rash on the inside of both her thighs. Red raw they was. He told her, "Mrs Turner, the only advice I can give you is the next time someone's down between your legs make sure they have had a shave!"'

All the girls were laughing, she had them all in stitches, she should have been a comedian. The only trouble with Betty was she didn't know when to stop talking, you were lucky to get a word in edgeways when she started jawing. Someone else could tell you the story in five minutes, Betty would take five hours. She started chatting again.

'Then Sally Holloway,' she cocked her head over to the bar where Sally was standing with her old man, 'she was nearly pissing herself on the coach. We'd been in a traffic jam for ages. She gets off the bus and strolls casually into this very nice posh front garden. Beautifully laid lawn with lots of tropical plants and exotic flowers. It looked like Kew Gardens. Guess what she does?' Betty stood in the centre of her audience doing the actions. 'She hoists her dress up to her boobs, squats down and has a piss. She didn't give a fuck about who was watching. It was so funny I had tears rolling down me cheeks.' She took a puff on her cigarette and blew smoke as she spoke. 'We were lucky with the tit for tats. Bobby had a lorry load so we all got them on the cheap. We were all posh tarts for the day.'

'Was that where Sue met her ole man?' Mickey asked.

'Blimey, yeah it was. He ended up coming back on the coach with us pissed lot. We were all singing and dancing. I thought the driver was gonna have a flipping heart attack at the wheel. It turned out Tommy only came from Canning Town. They ended up married and have got three boys.'

She turned to Mickey.'A coach load of us are going again next year. Mandy's coming wiv us ain't ya?' Betty pulled her close. 'We're gonna give ya a taster of a good time girlie.'

Mickey grinned, taking a swig of his beer, thinking to himself, oh no she fucking ain't. He wouldn't let Mandy loose with that nutty lot. He didn't know what the fuck she'd get up to with them. Most of them were only out looking for a quick shag and an easy pound note. There wasn't a fucking lady between 'em.

Then he whispered softly in Mandy's ear, 'So what 'ave ya gotta tell me?'

Mandy looked into his eyes. She'd put it off earlier, frightened by the look in Mickey's eyes, but she had to tell him, wanted to tell him. 'Come 'ere.'

He bent forward towards her. 'Let's go outside, where it's quiet.'

They held hands as they walked away, leaving Sheila, Betty and the girls chatting, remembering the good times and the laughs they used to have.

Mandy thought it would take forever to get out of the pub. Everyone wanted to talk to Mickey, but eventually he managed to get away. He led Mandy out into the cold night air.

Mandy still had her glass in her hands. She threw her drink down her throat for courage, stood on tiptoes, put her arms around him inside his suit jacket and whispered in his ear. 'I'm having our baby, Mickey.'

He pushed her gently away from him, looked down at her with a massive grin on his lovely face. He was speechless with wonderment. His eyes were alive, dancing with pleasure and pride. He touched her face softly. She could feel the gentleness of his fingers as he stroked her cheek. 'Are ya sure, it's definite?'

She smiled and nodded her head.

He pulled her into his arms holding her close. No words, just silence. Then gently he held her away from him. They looked deep into each other's eyes, 'I love you, Mandy, and always will, ya know that don't ya?' he murmured with tenderness as he touched the side of her face.

She looked into his eyes, nodded.

Mickey kissed her, hard and hungry; he wanted her, needed her. She was his. He pulled her close. 'Me mum will be over the moon; it'll give her something to live for. She'll be a nan. I can't fucking believe it.'

They gazed at one another, laughing together. Mickey was in his element – powerful, virile, in control.

The pub doors opened and Stevie walked out. 'Oi, oi enough of that hanky panky.' He smiled at them. 'The pair of ya can't keep your bleedin' hands off each other.'

They both looked at him with happiness in their eyes. Mickey gestured him over. 'Steve, you will never fucking guess,' he said, his voice full of pride, 'I'm gonna be a fucking dad.'

Stevie took Mickey's hand and shook it. 'Congratulations, Mickey, me ole mate.' He put his arms around him and gave him a firm hug. 'Fuck me, Mickey, I never thought you had it in ya.' Laughing together.

'Fuck off ya cheeky bastard,' Mickey said as he slapped him playfully across the back.

Stevie pulled the two of them towards him, hugging them both. Tears filled his eyes. 'I'm so happy for ya both.'

Stevie kissed Mandy on the cheek. 'You'll make a blinding mum Mand, and you've got ya self a good un there, girl,' cocking his head towards Mickey.

Mickey had been a different bloke since he'd met Mandy. Stevie had watched the two of them, so wrapped up with one another, they weren't aware of the world around them. Stevie noticed the way they looked at each other, the way they touched each other. The look in their eyes, they were totally engrossed with one another, totally in love. They were good for each other and made a good couple. He hadn't seen Mickey this happy for a long, long time.

A car hooted in the road, they all turned as it pulled by the kerb next to them. It was Gary Parker, a friend of theirs, part of the trusted crew. He rolled down the window and shouted out, 'Dangerous, I need a word ...' He motioned Mickey towards him.

Mickey strolled over to the window and bent down. 'What's a matter Gary?'

Gary lowered. 'I've just had word that Sean and Rob were found shot, over at Hackney Marshes. A bullet through their heads.'

A wide satisfied smile appeared on Mickey's handsome face. 'Fuck me, couldn't have happened to two nicer blokes.'

Gary returned his grin. 'Thought you might like to know.'

As Mickey strolled back over, Steve grabbed hold of his arm. 'Dangerous, I've gotta shoot off for a while, I feel like shit. I wanna have a bath and liven up a bit. Gary's gonna drop me off home, I won't be long – I'll be back soon.'

Mickey stared at him, looking at a different man, a stranger. He knew exactly why Stevie was going home. Mickey was gutted. He loved Stevie, but he also hated him, hated what his best mate had become, what he'd done to himself. Mickey wanted to get hold of him, shake some sense into him, beat the fuck out of him. 'Whatever,' said Mickey.

'Dangerous, listen, I need to talk to ya about something,' Stevie said quietly. His eyes were unreadable.

Mickey pulled away, started to feel emotional, gutted. Whatever it was, he had a feeling it wouldn't be something he wanted to hear. But Stevie was his best mate … He glanced at his watch. 'I've gotta go and pick some fireworks up from Nicky Walker over at the Jolly Fisherman. I'll pop in to see ya on me way back. We can talk then, Stevie, all right?'

Stevie nodded and clenched Mickey's hand tight again. 'See ya soon,' Stevie said turning to Mandy and giving her a big hug filled with love. Hot tears filled his eyes. 'You take good care of ya self, Mand. You'll be all right wiv Dangerous. He'll always look after ya.'

Mickey and Mandy watched him get into the car with Gary, waved him goodbye.

Mickey would have a word with him later, but it wouldn't be the conversation that Stevie wanted. That cunt had to sort his fucking life out, he was completely fucked up. But Mickey would try and help him again, he had to, he couldn't see him like this any longer. He would sort out the rehab for him tomorrow, but this would be the last fucking time – if he fucked up again, Stevie would be on his own. Mickey wondered if Stevie would live to see his twenty-first birthday.

'Come on babe, let's go and tell me mum the good news, she's gonna be over the moon.' They strolled back into the pub arm in arm, gloriously happy and in love, as 'Who's sorry now' played on the jukebox.

Stevie

Stevie sat on a rotten, dirty mattress on the cold hard floor in the corner of the living room, alone in the quiet darkness of the night. He was scared, shaking, sweating and shivering as his eyes wandered around his home, taking in the relics of his life – his flat was empty, every possession he had was gone. He couldn't endure the pain and sadness any longer. Life was a funny thing, what was the whole meaning of it? Happiness, hurt, laughter, tears, love, destruction, joy? He wished he had all the answers. It seemed that our joy was the cause of all our pain. Nothing was ever as it seemed. Tears filled Stevie's eyes. He'd sold his soul to the devil and now he was paying the price.

He threw the syringe down next to him on the mattress then untied the belt around his thigh. His eyes moved to his bag of brown on the little table in front of him. A silver spoon, burnt foil, matches, lighters, Mogadon, methadone, Demerol, diazepam and a half empty bottle of scotch all stared back at him, talking to him, saying 'come and play with me. Let's party and have a good time.'

He'd tried so many times to knock it on the head, but he just couldn't. He had done it all – treatment centres, rehab, detox programmes, prison, hospital – nothing worked, he just couldn't do it. He didn't have a choice anymore, it was a need he couldn't live without. It was the first thing he thought of when he opened his eyes in the morning and the last thing he remembered at night as he drifted into unconsciousness. His life revolved around getting, using and finding more ways and means to get more and more and more. Nothing else mattered, just the big H – it helped him get rid of the misery he felt inside, made him feel good and helped him shut out all the things he didn't want to see, hear or feel, helped him survive and struggle through another day.

He sat staring, eyes wide open, seeing nothing. Stevie sobbed tears of fear, anger, sadness, weakness and rejection. He was broken and bitter and had forgotten what life was about and what it meant. Death was what he wanted, it was his release. He'd hurt so many people, people who loved and cared about him.

He picked up the packet of cigarettes that Lizzie had given to him earlier. His hands trembled as he lit a fag, inhaling deep into his lungs. He loved Lizzie, she was a good decent woman who had loved and looked after him ever since the day he walked into her house with Mickey all those years ago. Her presence was always around him – she'd hugged him, laughed with him, cried with him, listened to him, every day she gave him a bit of her time. He owed them all so much; the Taylor family had become Stevie's family.

Lizzie was always putting herself down and didn't think much of herself, but she was a special person worth her weight in gold and more. The kids were all so lucky to have her as their mum. He knew Mickey would always look after her and make sure she never went without. Stevie loved Mickey, he was a top notch bloke, Stevie had always wanted to be like him. Smart, trusting, loyal, kind, funny and clever, and he hated saying it, but he was a good-looking fucker as well! Everyone liked and respected Mickey, he was all the things Stevie wanted to be and knew he never could be.

Lizzie and her kids didn't deserve the life they had with that cunt Bobby, he had made their lives a living nightmare. The prick deserved to die – one bullet was all it took to shatter his skull, but one shot to the head wasn't enough to satisfy Stevie, it was too easy, too quick, it wasn't evil enough, painful enough or horrific enough for him.

That nasty bastard! Stevie had wanted to watch him crawl on his hands and knees and beg, beg for his life, beg for mercy. He wanted to see him suffer, hear him scream like a baby, feel the knife driving deep into his flesh. He wanted to smash a hammer into his handsome face until it was a mass of smashed bone, blood and pulp. This was the man who Stevie had loved like the dad he'd never had, the man he believed in, trusted, counted on and admired, the man people feared and respected. The man that had destroyed him ...

~ ~ ~

Bobby was good to him at the beginning. Stevie earned a lot of money working for him, and Bobby had looked after him good and proper, but he started taking the piss once he knew Stevie was on the gear. He started giving him all the shit jobs and he wasn't coming across with the wedge, but there was nothing Stevie could do or say, Bobby had him by the bollocks.

He knew Stevie was doing a bit of business with Rob and Sean and earning a nice bit of dough, and he didn't like it because Stevie was getting his money somewhere else and he didn't need Bobby anymore. One night Stevie was in a bad way and needed some gear – Bobby wasn't fucking stupid and he knew exactly what Stevie wanted, turned up at his flat, out of the blue.

Bobby put his arms around him, comforting him, just like he used to, then put his hand in his pocket and pulled out a bag of brown. 'This is what ya need, isn't it, son?'

Son, fucking son, that's what he called him.

But before Stevie could register what was happening, Bobby unzipped his flies, got hold of Stevie's hand and began rubbing it up and down his cock. Bobby had a fucking big hard on.

Stevie tried to pull his hand away. 'Bobby? No! I'm not like that!'

Bobby just glared at him. 'You're a fucking smack head – you'll do whatever I fucking tell you!' He dangled the bag of brown in front of his face. 'You want this, don't you?'

Stevie licked his lips, nodded. He wanted it so bad he could taste it. He would do anything for it, and Bobby knew it.

'So you do whatever I fucking tell you,' growled Bobby, 'and we're all happy!'

He grabbed Stevie by the throat, forced him to his knees. Bobby's cock stared him in the face. Once again Bobby dangled the bag, down in front of his dick. 'Suck it!'

Stevie closed his eyes. Everything was gone, everything he was, all his self respect, all his dignity, everything. He focused on the high he was going to get, the warm buzz he would feel as the poison coursed through his veins, took Bobby's cock in his mouth.

'Attaboy!' Bobby grabbed Stevie's thin, dirty hair, thrust against his mouth. The buzz of sex and power flowed through him, better than any high, any drug. 'You'll do just fine if you ever get put in the slammer!' he laughed.

Then just as suddenly he stopped, pulled his dick out, slammed his knee into Stevie's face. Stevie slumped back on the dirty floor, but Bobby was on him in an instant, clawing at his trousers.

Stevie tried to fight back, the taste of blood in his mouth, but Bobby was too strong. He ripped Stevie's trousers off, flipped him over onto his belly, crashed down on top of him. 'Now let's see how you like it up the jacksie!'

There was nothing Stevie could do; he was powerless as Bobby jammed his dick inside him. Stevie screamed in pain as the first thrust went in, but it was just music to Bobby's ears. Again and again he thrust, his face close to Stevie's, the smell of booze and cigarettes in Stevie's nose.

The bag of brown suddenly dangled in his face once more. 'All in a good cause, eh Stevie?'

~ ~ ~

Stevie wiped the tears away from his gaunt cheeks, picked up his pill bottle full of diazepam and poured the contents into the palm of his hand, popping them one at a time into his mouth, a swig of scotch to wash each one down. He picked up the letter he'd written earlier and read it over and over again. His eyes were getting heavier and heavier, the lines of anguish evident on his once handsome face, as he placed it inside the envelope he had addressed to Lizzie Taylor. He put it on the window ledge, turned his record player up full blast and lay down on the mattress listening to the Beatles.

~ ~ ~

Mickey strolled along the landing on his way towards Stevie's flat, put his hand in his pocket, pulled out the spare key he kept for emergencies. As he got to the door he noticed it was ajar. Cautiously, Mickey felt in his inside pocket, his gun was there. The door creaked slowly open, the landing light shining into the flat. He paused, drew a deep breath as he poked his head around the front door. He heaved at the fucking smell – the place stunk of piss and shit.

He couldn't see or hear anything apart from 'Strawberry Fields Forever' blaring from the stereo in the front room as he edged himself against the wall and moved slowly along the small dark hallway. 'Stevie, you all right mate?' he shouted into the flat. 'You in there?'

'Come in, make ya self at home me ole mucker,' Stevie hollered out.

Mickey carried on walking towards the living room, his angry eyes scanning, his face was set in a mask of disgust. It was several months since he had last visited Stevie's place, and he couldn't believe the change. This flat had been fit for a king, it was the nuts, now it wasn't fit for a fucking dog. Stevie was living in this fucking squalor, in a smack-head's shit hole.

Mickey stepped into his small front room and couldn't believe what he saw in front of him – his best fucking mate slumped in the corner of the room on a dirty, smelly, rotten mattress, gripping tight to an empty whiskey bottle, like a baby clutching his comfort blanket, rocking backwards and forwards. His cheekbones were drawn, his gaunt face waxen and deathly white, his eyes small and hollow, constricted with pinpoint pupils, like piss holes in the snow. He looked dead, like a corpse.

Mickey stood still in shock, staring at Stevie. There was a long silence as the song ended. Mickey couldn't take it all in, didn't realise it had gone this far. He paced back and forth, his head bent and his eyes twinkling dangerously. Shaking with rage, he turned and picked the record player up and threw it across the room. It crashed onto the floor splintering into pieces.

Mickey turned and screamed at Stevie. 'I don't fucking believe you, you've gotta sort ya self out, Stevie. Look at the fucking state of ya, I'm fucking ashamed to call ya me fucking mate. No wonder ya didn't want no fucker up here. You wanker.'

Mickey looked deep into Stevie's empty eyes. This was his best mate, they were like brothers. Why hadn't he talked to him, told him? He could have helped him. He would do anything for Stevie, he had to help him get better and out of this fucking mess.

'I'll get ya in rehab, same place as ya went last year, they'll sort ya out. You gotta do it mate.' He swallowed deeply, 'I want ya to be godfather to the baby. I can't have a fucking scag head can I? You've gotta do it. Do it for me Stevie, do it for Mandy. Do it for ya self.'

Stevie wet his lips and stared at him in silence. He dropped his hands between his knees and bowed his head. Mickey made it all sound so simple, so easy – he wished to God that it was. He'd tried so many times, over and over again, but nothing ever changed, he would never be free.

He stared up at Mickey. 'Ya just ain't got a fucking clue what it's like, have ya?' Stevie shook his head slowly. 'You've been so fucking loved up lately, ya ain't been looking so ya ain't seen what's been going on.' He poked himself in the chest with his finger. 'It's not just me – it was ya dad too. He was always popping loads of pills, out of his box most of the time. No wonder you've got fuck all in the bank account. He's got big debts, Dangerous, everywhere, and they're not all to do with fucking money. He's upset a lot of people, a lot of people have been getting seriously hurt 'cos of him. I'm talking big here. I ain't fucking joking. Your dad knew he was a dead man.'

Mickey paced up and down the room, his jaw moving up and down.

'Sean found out ya dad was shafting his missus. Bobby knew Sean would get him first, 'ave him dead and buried. Sean was ready to kill him. It was all arranged.'

Mickey shouted, 'Yeah? Well I fucking got there first – we wasted Sean today, so how do you fucking like that?'

'Ya think that's the end of it, Dangerous? It's just the beginning. I love ya and always have and always will. You've been a good fucking mate to me.' Stevie looked deep into Mickey's eyes. 'My only friend, you were always there for me, always saving me arse.' Stevie rolled his shirtsleeve up. 'But ya couldn't save me from this.' Track marks covered his arm. 'All I ever was, Dangerous, was a nobody, a nothing.'

Mickey's blood boiled in his veins. 'Will ya shut the fuck up and stop talking all that old bollocks? Pull ya fucking self together!'

Stevie just looked sad. 'You've looked after me all these years. You're the only person in me life who never wanted anything in return. Ya liked me for me.'

Mickey couldn't look at him. He just walked up and down the small front room in frenzy, shaking with anger, the fury frozen in his eyes.

Stevie continued. 'Every other cunt in the world wants a piece of me. Not ya mum, your brothers or your sisters, they're all right. They're good people. Ya wanna start fucking looking after ya mum and give her the respect she deserves.'

He leaned forward looking at Mickey, his smile had disappeared a long time ago and his eyes were dead. Stevie started crying uncontrollably. 'I'm a cunt, look at me, look at the fucking state of me. I wanna die. I don't wanna be here any more. Look at me, Dangerous!'

He ripped his shirt from his body and took his jeans off, stood stark bollock naked in front of Mickey. His body was bruised and bleeding, covered with needle marks, shoelaces tied round his upper arm. Mickey felt hot tears sting his eyes. Stevie looked like he had just got out of Belsen; it was horrific what Stevie had become, just sickening. Mickey was gutted. Where was the man he used to be?

'This is me life, Dangerous. Every day I need this shit, I can't live with it and I can't live without it. I ain't worth the steam of me own piss. I've hurt ya, ya mum, all ya family, everyone. Even Kay, my girl ...' A slight smile touched his lips as he mentioned her name. 'She loves me and I've broke her heart, she's in bits 'cos of all the grief I've caused her. Tell her I'm sorry and I love her loads, I didn't mean to hurt her.'

'What do ya fucking mean?' demanded Mickey 'Me tell her? I ain't no fucking messenger boy. She's your bird, you love her, so you fucking tell her.' Mickey took a gulp of whiskey from the bottle, picked Stevie's jeans and shirt up from the floor and threw them at him. 'Oi! Donkey fucking bollocks, get ya self fucking dressed.'

Stevie looked at him and gave a grim humourless smile, shaking his head. 'Dangerous, I'm living in fucking hell. I can't stop it, I wanna but I fucking can't,' he screamed as he fell to his knees, his shoulders heaving up and down. 'I wanna die. Don't ya understand me?' He sat on the cold, hard floor, blabbering and stuttering, his words not making any sense, distorted laughter, then hysteria washing over him. 'I'm so sorry,' he finally mumbled, still looking down on the floor.

Dangerous looked at him. 'Sorry? You will be if ya don't sort ya act out mate. You're sitting there crying like a big fucking baby, feeling sorry for ya self, wallowing in all this self-pity shit. The poor fucking me old bollocks. You got ya self into this mess and it's up to you to get out of it.' He glared at Stevie. 'All the crap I've had Stevie, but I ain't fucking moping about feeling fucking sorry for me self, popping loads of fucking pills and jacking up.' Mickey stood in the centre of the room with his arms in the air and turned slowly around.

'Look at ya self, look at this fucking piss hole. What's it all done for ya? Fuck all. It ain't made anything better has it? It's all still here and it ain't going nowhere till ya face it. Life's full of shit and always will be, but fucking crying and taking that gear ain't gonna make it all right.'

'Come on, Dangerous, fucking kill me! Kill me!' Stevie didn't care anymore, he didn't want to be here anymore, he just wanted to go away and die, be gone from this world forever, finally fall asleep and find some peace and quiet.

'Shut the fuck up, you silly cunt,' Mickey snarled at him, almost foaming at the mouth with rage. 'You're getting on me fucking nerves.'

'Kill me. I'm begging ya! Shoot me, put a knife through me, batter me to fuck, anything, just fucking kill me. You always said ya would do anything for me, didn't ya?'

Mickey looked at him, their eyes locked. 'You're really beginning to fuck me off, Stevie.'

'Don't ya understand what I'm saying? I can't live with me any more.'

Mickey stood up and walked over to him. 'Stop fucking crying, cunt.' He swallowed, took a deep breath, didn't know what to say or do. He pulled a packet of fags from his jacket pocket and lit a cigarette, inhaling deeply. 'It's all that fucking shit that's doing it, sending ya off ya rocker.' He kicked the table over, the beer splashed over the walls, whiskey and syringes crashed to the floor. Mickey's voice was cracked and vicious. 'You're talking about fucking dying – I've just buried me ole man and you're feeling fucking sorry for ya self? What the fuck's that all about?'

Stevie stared at Mickey, looked straight into his eyes. 'Ya know what, Dangerous? I loved ya dad, I trusted him, believed in him.' A long silence fell between them, both looking long and hard into each other's eyes. 'Listen to me.' Stevie started laughing. 'I killed him.'

Mickey punched him twice in the face, right then left, dragged him to his feet and nutted him between his eyes, breaking his nose. 'You dirty fucking cunt!' he shouted as he threw him back on the filthy mattress. 'You dirty fucking lying, smack head cunt!'

Tears, blood and snot rolled down Stevie's gaunt cheeks. He spat out blood as he spoke. 'Come on cunt, that's all you got? Fucking kill me!'

Mickey stepped towards Stevie, watching his every move with his killer eyes. He grabbed Stevie by the throat hoisting him up from his feet. Stevie took a deep breath as he felt the pain of his jaw cracking as Mickey's huge left hand smacked him straight in the face. He fell sideways, crashing on all fours onto the floor, his shoulders heavy and slumped as the blood gushed from his mouth.

Stevie managed to get to his feet, staggering and swaying, squared his shoulders and walked defiantly up to Mickey, stood in front of him. He looked him in the eye and smiled, showing his broken, bloody teeth as he leaned forward closer, his arms open wide motioning Mickey towards him. He didn't remove his gaze from Mickey's demonic glare. Mickey had that look of his dad in his eyes, that twinkle that fooled so many – caring and kind, but the same twinkle that scared the shit out of you.

'Come on then,' Stevie hollered. 'Come on then, ya ugly bastard. Is that all ya can manage? Fucking hit me again, come on do it.'

With a darkened expression and anger in his eyes Mickey stood leering at his mate, snarled. 'You're making a very big mistake Stevie. You've took the piss once too often, mate.'

'Come on, Dangerous, the big I am, fucking hit me, beat the fuck outta me. I killed him! I killed your old man!' Drugged and dazed, Stevie walked up to Mickey, was face-to-face. He felt warm, good.

'Ya better shut the fuck up, Stevie.'

'Or what, Dangerous?' He cocked his head and laughed.

Mickey stood still. For once in his life he was speechless.

Stevie continued. 'Well, come on then cunt,' motioning him towards him. 'Come on, kill me!'

'Don't fucking wind me up you bastard.' Mickey smashed his fist on the wall once, then again and again. His knuckles grazed and bleeding.

'Can't hack it can ya, Dangerous?'

'Shut it,' Mickey hissed. He raised his hands above his head. The pain seared through him, it was clear in his eyes. 'You've lost it, that shit is sending ya mad,' he spat in Stevie's face.

Stevie began laughing hysterically, walking round and round the small room, repeating, 'I killed him, murdered him!' Stevie folded his arms, challenging

Mickey. 'What are ya waiting for, just do it. Do it cunt, fucking kill me.'

Still Mickey stood frozen, unwilling to hear what Stevie was telling him. Could it be true?

'Dangerous, listen to me.' Stevie put his fingers to his temple, imitating a gun. 'I put the gun to his head and pulled the trigger. BANG. I watched his brains and pulp splatter on the dashboard, it was fucking handsome, his skull splintering, blown to fucking pieces, claret everywhere. The sweet smell of his blood as it sprayed all over me face, spilling all down the front of him. I watched his body jolting, shuddering, jerking and shaking like he'd had a fit. I watched him die. I fucking killed him.'

Stevie stood in front of him laughing loudly, his arm stretched out in front of him, his hand in the shape of a gun, pointing at Mickey. 'The bullet went straight through his head, into his skull from one side to the other. Blinding stuff. I left him with the gun in his hand.' He took a step closer to Mickey. 'You don't really believe all that suicide bollocks do ya? He was left-handed wasn't he? Funny how he shot himself in the head with his right then ain't it?'

Mickey screamed at him. 'Shut the fuck up!'

'This is the best bit, Dangerous. Ya wanna know why I did it? That cunt knew I was on the gear, he knew what I needed. Knew I would do anything to get a fix, anything. He poleaxed me up the jacksy mate. He made me suck his cock, he fucked me up the arse, and so I fucking killed him!' He fell to the floor on his knees.

'SHUT IT,' screamed Mickey. 'Ya dirty lying cunt,' he spat as his jaw moved up and down, his eyes flashing. He smashed his fist through the door panel.

Stevie laughed bitterly, 'It's simple, Dangerous, even you can get it. Your dad was a fucking nonce, a fucking perv. I wonder how many other geezers he was knobbing?'

Mickey felt an icy chill crawl up his spine. The truth was finally out there, and now he had to deal with it. There was no sympathy as he looked at Stevie, no compassion. Years of frenzy, anger, hatred, bitterness and betrayal rose in Mickey as he stalked slowly towards Stevie.

Stevie smiled as Mickey's fist smashed into him. He could see the look in Mickey's cold eyes, the same look his dad had, and knew that peace was coming. Mickey beat Stevie in sickness and disgust, beat him for his mother, for himself, for Stevie, for every fucker who had ever had the misfortune to cross paths with Bobby Fucking Taylor.

Mickey didn't stop until his fists were raw, his arms aching. He left Stevie in a pool of blood and vomit, a small, wasted body on the floor of his filthy flat. Just another junkie who had crossed the wrong person.

Mickey walked out into the cold night air, turned the collar on his coat up and shoved his hands deep into his pockets. It was bloody freezing.

Suddenly the fireworks exploded in the clear dark sky, a vast array of colour and light, banging, whizzing and screeching, bursting apart and scattering the darkness. Silver spirals, arrows flaring and falling, a kaleidoscope of light and colour. In the distance he could hear the cracking and spitting of the big bonfire blazing in the field opposite the flats as the kids stood huddled around, waiting for the fireworks to begin, waving their sparklers in the air and singing, 'Build a bonfire, and build a bonfire.'

Mickey was determined that Martin and the rest of the kids had a good night. Betty had made some toffee apples and toasted marshmallows, the potatoes, burgers and sausages were wrapped in foil ready to go on the bonfire, along with a guy that Martin had made.

As Mickey strolled out, some kids were sitting outside the flats touting for money. 'Penny for the guy!' they called out to him. Mickey threw a couple of bob in the tin on the floor. The kids' eyes lit up. 'Thanks mister,' they cried, before chanting, 'Remember, remember the fifth of November, gunpowder, treason and plot. We see no reason why gunpowder treason should ever be forgot.'

No reason that treason should ever be forgot? No fucking kidding thought Mickey. He walked back to his motor with a spring in his step. He wasn't proud of what he'd done, but he wasn't ashamed either. Sometimes you just had to do what was necessary. Stevie had been his best mate, but that was a long time ago – what he had just done was a mercy killing, snuffing out the flame of a life that had ended a long time ago.

A man walking by handed him a leaflet. Mickey

took it and got into the car, looked at the pamphlet – Watchtower magazine. Staring him straight in the face, the front cover read "And ye shall know the truth, and the truth shall make you free. John 8:32."

Mickey smiled as he rolled down the window, screwed the paper in a ball and threw it out. What a load of old bollocks.

He cranked the car, revved the engine, ready to get home. He had a boot full of fireworks – it was going to be an explosive night.

Lizzie

Lizzie woke in the darkness of the living room, her face lit by the soft glow from the fire and the television flickering in the corner. She'd dozed off in her chair earlier – she was knackered, it had been a long day. She could hear voices coming from the kitchen, Mickey and Georgie with a few of their mates.

Glancing at her watch she saw it was late evening. Mickey and Georgie had built a massive bonfire in the back garden and Mickey had got a job lot of fireworks from a mate of his over in Barking. Mickey loved it all; he was still a big kid himself, the bigger the fireworks the better. Family and friends had come round the house after the funeral for fireworks and it had turned out to be a good night under the circumstances. She was glad it was over, though – maybe now she could start to get her life together. She had to be strong now, there was no room in her life for weakness and regret.

Her tired eyes roamed around the living room, it looked like a bomb had hit it, empty bottles and cans of beer, overflowing ashtrays and glasses were everywhere. It was a bloody mess, but nothing that couldn't wait till the morning.

Lizzie looked at her children – Sharon was curled up in the armchair next to the fire, Terri was curled up on the settee with Martin, his head on her lap, both of them sound asleep. She could hear Martin's soft snoring.

As she stood up slowly and stretched, Mickey walked into the living room and looked at her, smiled. 'You all right, mum?' He gave her a comforting squeeze. 'Ya crashed out in the chair and I didn't wanna wake ya up. We're just having a few beers with the boys in the kitchen.'

They both pulled away and looked at one another as they heard a car pull up outside, its headlights running up the living room wall. Mickey was already on his way over to the front window, cautiously pulling the heavy curtain back, peering through the net curtain. It was the police, one plain-clothed officer and two uniforms making their way up to the gate.

Mickey turned to Lizzie, a pained expression on his face. 'It's the Old Bill, Mum.' It wasn't the first time the filth had come knocking on her door and she knew it wouldn't be the last. The times she had her foot in the door trying to stop them coming in, while whoever they were looking for had it away on their toes over the garden fence. 'I'll deal with them.'

Lizzie watched Mickey stroll out to the front door and open it, but despite his reassurances her face paled, she began shivering, a sickening feeling grabbing her gut. She glanced out to the hallway and could see the shadows of the policemen coming in behind Mickey. Her lips trembled and her eyes swam with fresh tears. She slumped back down in her chair, covered her face with her hands, began sobbing. Lizzie had thought she hadn't any more tears left to cry. What she was crying for she wasn't sure, but she was about to find out.

The three police officers followed Mickey into the living room. The kids were all awake now, all in the living room staring at the police with a look that said, what the fuck's happened now? No more bad news please, we can't cope with any more.

DC James walked in, held his hand out to her, remembering the night he came here informing her of Bobby's death. The filth were glad to see Bobby dead, but none of them wanted to be there, and they knew they weren't welcome in the Taylor household.

Lizzie stood up, composed herself, a sad smile on her face as he approached her and shook her hand. The plain-clothed officer stood silently for a moment looking into her pretty face. She looked well and truly worn out, the poor woman had been to hell and back with her husband. The detective took her arm gently, 'I think you'd better take a seat.'

The tension in the room was mounting. 'It's Stevie, ain't it?' Her voice trembled with emotion. Somehow she just knew.

He nodded, 'I'm sorry to tell you Mrs Taylor …' then a moment's silence. He swallowed before speaking again.

'Stephen Black is dead. He was found in his flat earlier this evening. A heroin overdose, he choked on his own vomit.'

Mickey shifted uneasily from one foot to the other, said nothing.

'We wouldn't have bothered you tonight, but he left this …'

Lizzie's hands shook as the detective handed her a long white envelope with her name on the front, written in Stevie's small, scrawny handwriting. She walked back to her armchair by the fire, feeling cold, dazed and in shock, glanced again at the letter, her hands shaking as she put it in her cardigan pocket. She couldn't believe he was dead. She took a deep lungful of breath, trying to stay calm. More death, more heartache, more pain. When would it all end?

Georgie handed her a steaming hot cup of tea. She nodded, whispered, 'Thanks.'

The policeman was talking to her. She could see his lips moving and see his hand gestures, but she couldn't hear a word he was saying. She sat still in her chair staring into the cup of tea, tightly clasped in her hands, was surprised when she looked up and saw Mickey ushering the Old Bill out the house. When she looked up again, Mickey was standing with his back to the fire, looking at all of them, wondering, knowing it was time. What were they all thinking?

Sharon, lost without her daddy, but with a look of defiance on her face.

Terri, the little girl lost, with her strange inner strength.

And Georgie, his thin frame seemingly battered by the events of the past few days, his shoulders hunched, eyes cast down.

'All right,' said Mickey quietly. 'It ends here, tonight, in this house.' He slid his hand through his hair. 'Stevie told me some things, things about dad that … Well let's just say they were hard to believe.'

'We could all tell ya stuff like that, Mickey!' It was Sharon, staring defiantly at him, her eyes still burning with hatred for Bobby.

'So what happened that night? What happened in this house?' He glared at them. 'Someone here knows, and we need to get it out, get it over with.'

He glared at his siblings, waiting for one of them to speak.

Silence.

'Well?'

'It's not them you need to be talking to.'

Mickey span around, shocked, stared at his mother.

'I'll tell you what happened. It's all I've been doing for days – thinking of poor Stevie and the night Bobby died …'

The story was easy to tell. It had played out in Lizzie's mind a hundred times.

Martin it was who had saved her life – the littlest one, but what a brave little fucker. If he hadn't come storming into the bathroom she would be a dead woman. She would have drowned; Bobby would have killed her.

Lizzie came out of the bathroom that night feeling like a different woman. Something had changed, she felt different, stronger. She didn't feel scared anymore. She didn't feel guilty or bad for what she was about to do. She felt better than she had in a long time, was ready to do what she should have done years ago. She wasn't afraid anymore and that feeling was good.

It wasn't what Bobby had done to her that had changed her – she'd experienced that a hundred times before. It was what he'd said, as he stood over her, leering down at her frail, naked body. 'What kind of a mother are you?' He spat the words out with contempt. 'You stand around with your pitiful cow eyes, pretending not to see what's going on around here? You make me sick!'

Lizzie said nothing, wanting him to just leave, go away. But he had more, more vitriol, more hatred, as though he had been storing it up for this night.

'I fucked all your sisters, you know that, right?'

She tried to keep it in, but she couldn't prevent the shock showing in her eyes.

Bobby saw it straight away, couldn't resist turning the knife. 'They all wanted it, all wanted me – but Sadie was the best, right little minx that one!'

Lizzie's eyes were wide with horror.

'Don't pretend that you don't know!' He stared at her, gradually realizing that her surprise was genuine. 'You really didn't, did you?' Her pain made him smile – it was his nourishment, his succour. 'I fucked your sisters, raped your daughters, beat up your sons – and you, you pathetic slag, you stood by and let me!' He laughed as he unzipped his trousers, pissed on her. 'That's what I think of you!'

The rape and the beating were routine, meant nothing compared to the words that were ringing in her ears. 'I fucked your sisters, raped your daughters, beat up your sons – and you, you pathetic slag, you stood by and let me!' He was right. But she wouldn't ever stand by again.

She had often sat quietly and planned and schemed how she was going to kill him, how she was going to make him suffer and beg for his life, tell her he was sorry for all that he had done. But she never found the strength or courage to do it. Until now. Now his time had come.

She crept slowly into the bedroom, crawled onto the bed and felt under the pillow. Fuck! Bobby was gone and so was the gun he kept there. But she knew where he would be – around the back of the house where he always parked the motor. It was his pride and joy, his E-type Jag. He was always out and about in it, out on the pull, thought he was a boy-racer cruising around the streets. Bobby had always cheated on her. He loved a bit of skirt and was always looking out for beauty queens, fair skin and smiles. She knew Bobby had shagged a few dirty slags in the back seat of his car – he had sex in it, he slept in it, and now he was going to die in it.

Things would be different, they would all be happy, all be safe, they could be a family again. There was so much to look forward to. Happy birthdays, wonderful Christmases, holidays, day trips, all those old family get-togethers.

The joyful memories of the past came rushing to her, the sights, the smells, the tastes. She would treasure those times, always. She so desperately wanted those happy days back again and now she could. There would be nothing to be scared of when Bobby was dead. They would all be free at last.

She put her coat around her shoulders and walked slowly into the kitchen. She felt calm and serene, felt good about herself, felt good about what she was about to do. They wouldn't have to suffer anymore, their troubles would be over. She had to do this for her children – it was the right thing to do. Maybe then they would love her, forgive her for all the pain and suffering she had put them through.

She took a carving knife from the drawer, placed it in her pocket inside her Coney fur coat, pulled the coat tight around her and walked out into the cold night.

Lizzie thought of all the bad things she'd done – Bobby was right, she was everything he had always said she was – lazy, dirty, ugly, stupid, a burden, a liar. Of no use to anyone or anything.

She was so sorry. She had let all of her children down, let her family down. Lizzie knew she was weak and selfish for putting herself first, not thinking about the pain she had caused them and the suffering they were going through, but she had never been able to accept the truth about Bobby. She couldn't even say what had happened, couldn't put it into words or tell herself the truth, it repulsed and sickened her so much she couldn't even go there. It was too disgusting.

She was scared to look it in the face. How could she have been so wrong about Bobby? She couldn't believe, wouldn't believe what he really was. She had tried but it was too painful, too disgusting to even think about. She had to forget it all, put a smile on her face and get on with it.

She would just think of something else, busy herself, and try to think of anything else but him and what kind of a man he really was. She would bury her head in the sand, do an ostrich and make out everything was all right and none of it was really happening. She was living in denial of her real life, in total oblivion. The pills helped her to forget, helped her to cope and manage to get through each day. She rubbed her head, it was thumping, the pain excruciating

She should have protected them at any cost. They must really hate her for putting them through their living hell. How could she ever repay them? She was so weak, she was as evil and wicked as Bobby for letting this happen to them.

The reality of it was too much to take in; she could never believe it was true, this man, who at the beginning had showered her with love and affection, gave her everything she wanted. Nothing was too much for him. Then things changed ...

How could she have been so sick and stupid? She hated herself. She had spent her life walking around in circles getting dizzier and dizzier. It was so confusing. She felt like she was going insane at times, became totally paranoid, nothing made sense anymore. What was she frightened of? How much more pain could she take before she finally did something about it?

Every time a thought of what he had done to her kids and her sisters crept into her head, she forced herself to stop thinking about it, push those ugly images far, far away and bury those disgusting thoughts deep into the recesses of her mind. Forget. Forget. Forget. That was the answer. But not now. Those days were over …

~ ~ ~

She stood close to Bobby's car, close to the man she had loved with all her being, close to the man who had destroyed so many lives. She could hear his heavy snoring and grunting, crashed out in his motor, his head resting on his arms, lying across the steering wheel. Lizzie walked calmly towards him, her eyes so focused on him, that she was almost at the car before she saw Stevie standing next to the car, the gun in his hand, pointing it at Bobby's head.

Lizzie took a deep breath. 'Stevie? Don't be silly, love, put the gun down.'

He turned and looked at her with his sad eyes.

She spoke again. 'Don't do it. He's not worth it.'

Steve shook his head, never took his eyes off Bobby. 'What's wrong with ya Lizzie? The cunt deserves to die. After what he's done to all of us? You should be glad to be getting rid of him.'

'Please listen to me, Stevie. You're young, you've got a life ahead of ya. Don't do it'

He slowly shook his head, said nothing, never took his eyes from Bobby.

'You'll end up doing life for that dirty pig and he ain't worth it,' she pleaded with him. 'Please give me the gun. Please, come on, for me Stevie. I'm begging ya.'

He finally looked at her, his eyes unreadable. 'You know what Lizzie? You don't know the half of it.' He turned slowly and put the gun to Bobby's temple. 'That cunt there paid for someone to kill Mickey. The car crash he had was no accident. Mickey was meant to die that day. He hated Mickey getting all the glory and fame with the boxing. Mickey was gonna make it big time but Bobby couldn't handle Mickey getting all the attention, no one was talking about him, he wasn't the face any more. It was Mickey's name on the streets not Bobby's, and he fucking hated it!'

Lizzie looked at Stevie, a shadow crossed her face. 'Give me the gun, Stevie.'

'No! The cunt's gonna die, deserves to die.' The tears were rolling down his cheeks. He looked like a little boy, young and vulnerable, a contrast to his fearsome reputation.

'Give me the gun.' She held her hand out to him. 'Stevie, listen to me, please don't do it. I love ya like one of me own. I want to see ya live your life not end up inside or at the mortuary. Stevie don't.' She held her hand out to him. 'Please, Stevie, give me the gun.'

He stood in front of her looking straight into her eyes, licked his finger and ran it along the barrel. He opened his mouth wide, placed the barrel of the gun on his tongue.

'No, Stevie, No!' she begged him. 'Please just put the gun down. Please.' They stood in silence for what seemed like an eternity.

Finally, his hands shaking, he lowered the gun. 'I fucking hate him, Lizzie.'

She held her arms wide open for him. 'Everything will be alright, Stevie.'

He stumbled towards her and wrapped his arms around her. They hugged each other tight as he sobbed on her shoulder.

Lizzie reached for his hand, tried to grab the gun, but as she did so a shadow passed behind her, cold fingers grabbed her wrist, a strong hand wrenched the gun from Stevie's hand.

Lizzie looked up in astonishment. 'No!'

The gun gleamed in the light from the kitchen window as it was jammed against Bobby's head through the open window of the car. 'Goodbye, cunt!'

For a moment time seemed to freeze. Stevie made a grab for the gun, Lizzie too, some insane last shred of loyalty for Bobby making her try and stop it. Three hands all reaching for the gun, all grasping the cold metal at the same time.

BANG.

The gunshot surprised them all. Lizzie staggered back, unable to believe it – even then she half expected Bobby to turn on them, beat and batter and berate them one last time. But no, he was slumped in his seat, his brains spread across the inside of his precious E-type.

Lizzie looked up into her son's eyes. There was no fear there, just a stone cold certainty.

'Go inside, mum. Ya don't need to see this.'

She nodded, shocked by his certainty, staggered back towards the kitchen door.

'You too, Stevie. Go home.'

Wordless, Stevie scrambled over the back fence, disappeared into the darkness.

And finally there was just the two of them. Bobby, dead in his car, and Georgie standing over him, his breath steaming in the cold night air. Calm as you like he wiped the gun on his coat, removing any fingerprints, then held it carefully in his hankie as he slipped it into Bobby's hand.

For years Georgie had watched as Bobby had taken them apart, one by one, destroyed his family little by little. He had said nothing, not reacted, seemingly oblivious to it all, but he was always watching, waiting for the moment, the time, when he would finally set things right.

But up until then he had never found the courage, had never found the extra resolve to finally take matters into his own hands. That was until he got the phone call from Father Patrick. 'You don't know me,' said the stranger, his strong Irish lilt a sudden reminder of Father Jim, 'but a mutual friend gave me your number, asked me to call you if anything happened to him ...'

Georgie felt himself choke up. 'Jim?'

'I'm afraid he's dead. He was found in a ditch on the edge of town. His throat had been cut ...'

Georgie didn't hear the rest of Father Patrick's words. Hot tears stained his cheeks, burned his throat as he cried, cried like he hadn't cried since he was a boy – since his dad had beaten him and Mickey half to death. Even before he'd put the phone down he knew what he would do, knew that he had to end it, now.

The gun nestled perfectly in Bobby's dead fingers. Satisfied with his work Georgie stood back, a faint smile on his handsome face. 'I hope you rot in hell, Bobby Taylor.'

~ ~ ~

The only sound was the logs crackling in the fire, burned down to glowing red embers.

Mickey looked back and forth between them, said nothing.

Lizzie looked at his dark, inscrutable eyes, wondered what he was thinking. He was so like his father in so many ways, but she couldn't believe that he would ever sink to the depths that Bobby had descended into as his life had unravelled.

Mickey sighed, glared at them one by one, until finally his eyes settled on Georgie. Georgie, his brother, the one he had always had to protect. Georgie's eyes met Mickey's, unblinking, unflinching. There was something there that Mickey had never seen before, something unsettling, scary even. For the first and only time in his life, Mickey blinked first.

'Bobby Taylor committed suicide, just like the police said,' said Mickey finally. His eyes were like chips of coal, black, shining in the firelight. 'And if any fucker ever whispers a word otherwise, I'll kill 'em with my own bare hands. Got it?'

One by one they nodded.

Mickey smiled. 'Right.' He leaned over and put his arms round Lizzie's shoulders, snuggled her close to him. 'Let's get ya up to bed, Mum. It's been a long old day.'

Lizzie looked at Mickey standing tall in front of her. He wasn't her little boy any more, he was a man. 'No, not yet. I wanna read Stevie's letter.'

Mickey looked at her with concern in his eyes. 'Leave it Mum, leave it till another time.'

She shook her head defiantly. The truth needed to be told, whatever will be, will be. 'We need to do this Mickey; we need to put everything behind us tonight, wipe the slate clean and start over.'

Everyone looked at Lizzie, all with different expressions on their faces. Sadness, confusion, fear, regret, compassion, hurt, all kinds of emotions rising to the surface.

Finally Mickey nodded.

Lizzie motioned for everyone to take a seat as she sat back in her chair, fluffing the cushion up behind her to make herself comfortable. She took a deep breath as she took the letter from her pocket, fumbled around with the envelope trying to open it. She slowly unfolded the thin sheet of paper, lit her cigarette and inhaled deep into her lungs, then read Stevie's letter aloud to her children.

To Lizzie, Mickey, Georgie, Sharon, Terri and Martin.

A moment's silence as she glanced around at her children all sitting wide-eyed and tremulous, staring at her, waiting for her to begin.

I just want to say to you all that I'm so sorry, please forgive me for what I have done. I wish things could have been different but there was no hope left. I had to go. I hope you understand why I did it.

Lizzie coughed, cleared her throat, continued.

Death is a release for me. I can't hurt myself or anyone else any more. I'm free from the bondage. There will be no more noises in my head. It all had to end. I had to be free of all the hurt and pain. I have no regrets for what I did, only for the things I didn't do.

She gave a heavy sigh, her heart pounding in painful bursts.

Be happy for me. I'm safe and at peace now. So don't cry, don't be sad.

Silence.

Lizzie, your kindness never ends. You have taught me so much in my life. You gave me love, showed me how to care, to share, I will always be grateful for that. You hugged me, laughed with me, cried with me, listened to me. Every day you gave me a bit of your time. You have shown me the importance of family, given me the important values in life, everything that my own mum couldn't. You always told me Lizzie, we make a living by what we get, we make a life by what we give. I've always remembered that.

Lizzie wiped her eyes with a bit of toilet paper she had rolled up in her pocket.

You're all very special to me. Look after each other, you've only got one family and it's precious. Don't ever let each other down, you all need each other. It's time to forgive and forget, move on, move forward and live for the moment. It's no good living in the past. Look after each other because none of us are here for long. This ain't no dress rehearsal, so don't waste your life like me. Keep your dreams, because when you lose your dreams, you die.

Her voice was cracking with emotion, she couldn't go on. She blew her nose and passed the letter to Georgie. He took it gently from her hand, pulled her close to him and gave her a reassuring hug. He walked up and down the room as he read, glancing at Mickey every so often, perched on the edge of the settee, his knees apart, his fists clenched, staring down at the floor. Not moving, not speaking. Nothing.

Thanks for being the family I never had. You've all touched my life. Keep me in your hearts and remember all the good times we shared, especially you Mickey. Ha, ha! You're a great mate and I love you, don't ever forget it.

Georgie dragged his hand through his dark thick hair.

I hope love, happiness and laughter will be with you all forever. I love you all and will forever have the happy memories you all gave me. You brought me laughter when I was dead inside.

Goodbye and God bless you all.

Stevie xxxxxx

PS. Cheers, Mickey. I knew you would do it for me. You've never let me down before.

Lizzie sighed heavily. Her face was devoid of any expression but her heart was filled with sadness. She remembered how the light used to shine from Stevie –

he was such a lovely and thoughtful young man, he hadn't even lived a life yet. What a fucking waste; Stevie had always lived for the moment and never ever counted the cost. Her eyes filled up, desperate anguish in her tears. She squeezed her eyes tightly shut trying to stop her tears. Poor Stevie, he'd died hopelessly lost. She must stop dwelling on the past, she had to mourn for her husband and Stevie then move on. She would be strong and do it with dignity, no room for regret. What's done is done. God promises us a safe landing, not a calm passage. If God brings it to us he will bring us through it. Stevie's soul was in a better place now; he deserved to be at peace. Lizzie had to live for the future and put the past firmly behind her.

She slowly climbed to her feet, her limbs feeling more tired than she could ever remember. One by one she kissed her kids goodnight – Martin, Sharon, Terri, Georgie, and finally Mickey. She gently stroked Mickey's face. The big man, the big I am, the new king of the manor. So young, and such a big burden to bear ... 'See you all in the morning ...'

Epilogue

Christmas Day 1971

Lizzie Taylor stood in front of the huge blazing fire holding her hands out to the heat, mesmerised by the glowing coals, so warm and inviting, their Christmas stockings – each embroidered with their names – hanging from the chimney breast. She was wearing a black well-cut suit, her make-up immaculate. Everyone was accustomed to seeing Lizzie in black since the death of Bobby, so today would be no different. She looked ten years younger than she had a few months ago, more like a sister to her girls than their mum. The kids had told her to stop wearing black but it was an every day ritual for her since Bobby had died, a reminder to herself of what she had endured.

But today, she looked different – instead of hurt in her eyes there was hope. Her skin had a soft healthy glow to it, she looked, happy, something she hadn't been for a long time. Her house would be a hive of activity today, all her family and friends were here celebrating Christmas. It had been years since they had all been together. She never thought she would see the day when she was surrounded with people she could talk to, people who cared about her and loved her. It made her feel good and her heart less heavy, she really was looking forward to the day ahead.

Lizzie glanced out of the window at the snow falling, softly, gracefully from the sky. A white Christmas. All the kids were out there throwing snowballs at each other, rolling around in the snow, legs and arms waving in the air, all with bright rosy cheeks and smiles on their faces. They had built a snowman, two big lumps of coal for his eyes, a carrot for his nose and one of Frankie's big cigars for his mouth.

Every roof in the street was covered in a blanket of white snow; the trees were glistening in the winter sun, sparkling and aglow. It was perfect, just like a Christmas card setting.

As she moved around the room she seemed to have a new life in her. A feeling of satisfaction swept over her as she glanced around her newly decorated and furnished living room. She smiled to herself – Mickey had made sure she was well looked after and never went without, and it looked really nice in here now. The house had been painted from top to bottom – Mickey and Georgie had sorted it out – they had mates in all trades from a plumber to a plasterer, a brickie to a chippie. It looked lovely, a new start, the bad memories of these rooms banished.

She sighed with contentment as she sat down quietly at the table. It was decorated beautifully with matching tableware, deep red serviettes, and a lovely Christmas centrepiece in the middle of the table. A real Christmas tree stood tall in the corner of the room, the Christmas tree lights twinkling and reflecting her tears of joy, all the gifts wrapped in ribbons and bows beneath the tree. The sweet aroma of beef, turkey and mince pies wafted in from the kitchen – she had been up for most of the night cooking and cleaning. Everything had to be perfect.

Lizzie sat and thought about her life, her marriage, her responsibilities and obligations. She didn't know what joys or sorrows lay ahead but what she did know was that at last she had her family back and they would always be there for each other, no matter what. She wouldn't change this day for the world.

She glanced at Sheila and they exchanged smiles. Sheila was chatting with Rosie and Frankie, while the twins were out in the garden with the others. Johnnie sat next to his wife, holding her hand, whispering playfully. They were always teasing and laughing with each other. Sheila still looked youthful and pretty, it was obvious that Sheila and Johnnie were still very much in love – they had a love you build, and cherish and look after, a love you want to live for or die for. They were a lovely couple.

It was their silver wedding anniversary on New Year's Eve and the family had all put a few bob together and organised a surprise party in the school hall. She knew it would be a fantastic night, a total surprise for them – Sheila and Johnnie didn't have a clue. They all made out it was a church party that was going on that night, it was all so exciting.

Martin came rushing in through the living room door and ran over to the Christmas tree, tucking straight into the chocolate decorations. He was a good kid that one, despite what he had been through. He was doing really well at boxing – Lizzie had tried to dissuade him but neither Mickey nor Martin were having any of it. She watched him, a mischievous grin on his cheeky face as he squared up to Mickey. 'Come on Mickey.' He jammed his hands into his new boxing gloves, shifting and shuffling around the living room. 'I can't believe you've got us tickets to see the Ali fight in London. I can't wait,' he said as he moved, blocked and slipped punches with Mickey.

Mickey gave him a beaming smile. 'That will be you one day, Martin, a world champion.' His eyes twinkled with pride.

Minutes later Terri and Sharon came running through the door with glowing red noses and pink cheeks. 'Cor that food smells lovely, mum,' they shouted. Georgie followed behind them swinging a bottle of Johnnie Walkers in his hand. He brushed the snow from his coat. 'It's bleedin' freezing out there,' he said, shivering. He held the bottle of scotch high in the air. 'Merry Christmas everyone.'

They toasted each other, 'Merry Christmas.'

Lizzie smiled as Mickey and Mandy shared a kiss underneath the mistletoe. She couldn't believe he would have a baby of his own soon. She shook her head in wonder, Mickey a dad. They were going to get married next year and they had already started making all the plans. Lizzie thought Mandy was a lovely girl; she was good for Mickey and she would make a good mum. Lizzie would have to get her knitting needles out, do a bit of knitting for the baby. She was going to be a Nan. It brought tears to her eyes just thinking about it.

She was still looking at Mickey as he strolled happily over to her, picked her up into his big strong arms and swung her around, 'Merry Christmas, Mum.' He looked at all the happy faces. No one would ever take that away from them again. Mickey would kill anyone who tried. This was a new beginning for the Taylor family.

Seeing all her family together made her feel so happy inside. She had survived years of blood, sweat and tears but had learned that she could no longer live in the past and hang on to her regrets – she had to live for the future and lay the past to rest. They were all gradually trying to accept what had happened and heal their emotional wounds, all of them victims who had spent years hiding from themselves and each other.

'Come 'ere you lot,' said Mickey. The whole family came together, all embraced and held each other for a long time. The quietness between them was heart-wrenching. All their eyes filled with tears and they cried together, wrapped in each other's arms, not this time with pain, sadness, regret, anger or hate but tears of happiness, joy and relief. They were close together again, a tender moment, they were a family once more. Finally they all raised their glasses in the air. 'Merry Christmas, Happy New Year. Here's to 1972.'

Lizzie smiled, more contented than she could remember, but her smile froze as she heard footsteps in the hall.

The door opened and Fat Jack ambled in, snow dusting the shoulders of his massive overcoat. 'Merry Christmas all,' he mumbled. But his eyes told a different story.

'What's up?' Instantly Mickey was all business.

'We've got a bit of a situation with the last shipment.'

Mickey headed for the door. 'I'll get me coat.'

Fat Jack nodded. 'Might want to get your shooter, too. Things could get a bit lairy.'

Mickey grinned. 'Lairy?' He looked around at his family, his eyes sparkling. 'If I'm involved, they won't just be lairy. They'll be fucking dangerous!'

The End

About the Author Sandra Prior

Sandra Prior couldn't be more different than Bobby Taylor, the kingpin whose death set off a firestorm in this first novel Dangerous.

Sandra had a storybook childhood — complete with four sisters and a brother, and parents who lived in the same Dagenham home for more than half a century. She describes her childhood as "sunny and safe", living in a place where you could play for hours and wander the streets with your friends, without any fears.

Today, Sandra lives in Clacton with her partner, her youngest son, and her two dogs — who, she notes, were kind enough to "let" her write Dangerous in between their walks on the beach.

Unlike other writers, Sandra took a different path to get where she is today. Dangerous isn't the result of years of schooling and formal writing training. In fact, while she was raising her young children, Sandra took evening classes to complete her English and math qualifications (as she puts it, "I didn't do what I should have at school."). After that, she studied Sociology through the Open University which led to her heading off to the University of East London — where she earned a degree in Cultural Studies.

By 1998, Sandra was a business owner — the owner of a domiciliary care agency, to be exact. It didn't take long for her to learn the value of hard work, passion, and communication — along with the importance of balancing her business commitments with her family commitments. Years later, she would add one more thing to the mix — by balancing her business responsibilities and her family life with her writing duties.

And speaking of writing…

For years, Sandra dreamed of writing a book. Alas, like so many of us, her dream sat in the back of her mind collecting dust. After all, she had a demanding career and a busy family life. How can you add writing a book to all of that?! For years, she told herself that there wasn't enough time, that she wasn't organized enough to pull it off, and that it was a nice thought — but not something that you actually go out and DO.

But then, one day, Sandra's life completely changed when she flipped through the pages of a magazine and read about a man named Anthony Robbins and something called life coaching. She went to one of Robbins' London seminars and actually managed to walk across a 15-foot bed of burning coals!

From there, she decided that if she was going to make the most of her life, she would have to "keep walking"…

That's when she decided to make her writing real, instead of just a fantasy that lived deep in her mind. Sandra sat down and began working on Dangerous – with just Stevie Wonder, Bob Marley, Barry White, Rod Stewart, and the like to keep her company.

Through the laughter, the tears, the shouting, and the frustration, Sandra was able to realize her dream and finish Dangerous. Oh sure, there were times when she didn't think she was going to make it. On more than one occasion, she considered tossing the half-finished manuscript right in the bin and calling the whole thing off. So, when she finally got to write the words "The End" on her novel, it was a huge accomplishment and, in a way, almost an even bigger relief!

However, Dangerous' ending was really just the beginning…

Today, Sandra still spends time running her business. However, those long hours have been replaced with just a couple of trips to the office every month. Most of the time, she handles everything over the phone or through email. That way, she has plenty of time to write!

So, what's next in the writing department?

Sandra plans on devoting an entire series to the Taylor family. She is brimming with ideas as to where future generations of Taylors wind up. One day, she dreams of seeing her name on the New York Times bestseller list! In the meantime, she wants to write one new novel every year. And, of course, Sandra has her own family to keep her company as she comes up with new stories for the Taylor family. She's madly in love with her four children and her three grandchildren.

When she's not writing, Sandra loves spending time at the beach (with and without the dogs!). She enjoys everything from walking along the rocks to enjoying a beach snowfall in the winter. She's also a big fan of the theatre and, of course, reading! In fact, Sandra credits fellow British author Martina Cole as her "inspiration" for getting into the crime-writing business.

www.SandraPrior.co.uk

http://www.facebook.com/sandrapriorauthor

http://twitter.com/Sandra_Prior

Lightning Source UK Ltd.
Milton Keynes UK
UKOW06f1802050216

267846UK00004B/238/P